SEDUCING A ROGUE

Before Gareth could leap from the bed to verify his suspicions, something came across his eyes, shutting him in complete darkness.

He reacted instinctively, pulling at the material that had now been drawn tight across his eyes, effectively blinding him. Then he felt the caress of warm breath against his ear.

"I had thought to surprise you, my lord," a sultry female voice whispered. "Unless you object to my little game?"

A warm, lush female body climbed boldly into his lap. The viscount reached again to remove the covering from his eyes, but the woman's hands closed over his wrists.

"I had hoped you would want to play, my lord. Will you not reconsider? I promise to make the night well worth it."

When she spoke this time her voice was muffled against his throat. She pressed a soft kiss against the starched linen of his cravat, then ran her fingers lightly across his chest.

"If it pleases you, I will leave my blindfold intact." He set his hands firmly on her waist and drew her close to him. "For the moment."

"I salute your daring," came the breathy reply. . . .

—from "The Ultimate Lover" by Adrienne Basso

BOOK YOUR PLACE ON OUR WEBSITE AND MAKE THE READING CONNECTION!

We've created a customized website just for our very special readers, where you can get the inside scoop on everything that's going on with Zebra, Pinnacle and Kensington books.

When you come online, you'll have the exciting opportunity to:

- View covers of upcoming books
- Read sample chapters
- Learn about our future publishing schedule (listed by publication month *and author*)
- Find out when your favorite authors will be visiting a city near you
- Search for and order backlist books from our online catalog
- Check out author bios and background information
- Send e-mail to your favorite authors
- Meet the Kensington staff online
- Join us in weekly chats with authors, readers and other guests
- Get writing guidelines
- AND MUCH MORE!

Visit our website at
http://www.kensingtonbooks.com

ONLY WITH A ROGUE

ADRIENNE BASSO
COLLEEN FAULKNER
DEBBIE RALEIGH

ZEBRA BOOKS
KENSINGTON PUBLISHING CORP.

http://www.kensingtonbooks.com

CONTENTS

THE ULTIMATE LOVER

ADRIENNE BASSO

*To charming rogues everywhere,
and the women who dare to love them.*

CHAPTER ONE

Hampshire, England
Summer 1807

"Is there any news?" the woman asked the moment the servant entered her room.

Her maid nodded and moved closer quickly, displaying surprising agility considering her advanced years.

"The earl called for a second bottle of wine and then he requested quills, an inkpot, and parchment be brought to him in the drawing room. The drawing room!" The elderly female servant rolled her eyes, leaned forward, and continued.

"Hugh said he and Mr. Bascomb were laughing their fool heads off when he left them, not ten minutes ago."

"So Mr. Bascomb is still in the house?"

"Hugh will bring us word when Mr. Bascomb is gone."

Lady Amelia Wheatley, Dowager Countess of Monford, bit her bottom lip and nodded her thanks to her maid, Mildred. If quill and paper had been required by the earl it could mean but one thing. In all likelihood a marriage contract was being written and signed at this very moment.

Amelia blinked back her tears. 'Twas her worst fear come to life.

The earl was her brother-in-law and her only male relative. He had courted the favor of Mr. Bascomb, a rich, social-climbing merchant, for several months hoping the man would be interested in becoming a member of the family. By marrying her. Apparently all that hard work and effort was about to come to fruition.

Amelia had been a widow for three years and would be celebrating her thirty-fifth birthday in a few months. One would think at this stage in her life she no longer had to worry about things like forced marriages and unwanted husbands, but it seemed that fate would not allow her to spend the rest of her days as she wished, living a quiet, peaceful life, blissfully free of the rule of any one man.

"Shall I ring for tea to be brought up, my lady? A good strong cup might settle your nerves."

"How well you know me, dear Mildred." Amelia smiled faintly at the maid, distressed at the adverse effect this was having on the older servant. Mildred's voice was anxious, slightly breathless, her face lined with concern. "However, I insist you have two cups sent up with the tray so you may join me," Amelia declared.

"My lady! 'Tis scandalous to be drinking tea with your maid."

"Then I shall be scandalous." Amelia's smile widened at the very idea. The most daring, outrageous thing she had ever done was put aside her widow's weeds three weeks earlier than what was considered proper and respectful. This one great act of defiance had been met with little reaction, for neither the family nor her neighbors seemed to notice.

Hoping to distract Mildred from the current problem as they waited for the tea tray, Amelia restricted her conversation to innocuous mundane topics. When those subjects quickly ran their course, the pair fell into a comfortable silence.

In the quiet of the early afternoon Amelia could hear the faint patter of raindrops against the window glass. It surprised her, for the day had begun with such bright sunshine.

Hugh arrived with a ladened tea tray. Amelia wanted to scold him for carrying such a heavy burden up so many stairs, but years of firsthand experience with the old footman's stubborn pride kept her quiet.

"Mr. Bascomb is still with the earl," the footman announced. "It's been over two hours and not a peep from them."

Amelia kept her expression carefully blank. "Have they requested anything else? Tea, perhaps?"

"Tea?" The footman snorted. "After polishing off two bottles of the finest claret in the wine cellar? Not likely."

"Mildred mentioned that you brought the earl

quill, inkpot, and parchment. How would you judge his mood?''

"Smiling like a jackal, he was.''

"And Mr. Bascomb?''

"I won't lie to you, your ladyship. They were thick as thieves and up to no good, if you ask me.''

Mildred stared at Hugh. "Oh, stop your blabbering, you old fool. You're scaring my lady half to death.''

"No, Hugh's right to tell me the truth. At least now I'll know what to expect.''

Amelia sensed the footman's remorse. Though he had difficulty showing it, she knew his loyalty toward her ran deep and strong.

"I'll bring you word myself the moment Mr. Bascomb is gone,'' the footman promised.

"I am grateful for your kindness,'' Amelia replied.

The footman left and the room once again fell silent. While Amelia poured the tea, Mildred hovered at her elbow. Though appreciative of her maid's concern, it took great concentration not to spill any of the hot brew.

"This was the perfect suggestion, Mildred. The tea is precisely what I needed to settle my nerves.'' Amelia kept her voice deliberately low and calm, showing none of her inner fear.

Mildred nodded her head encouragingly. "Have a cake, too. They are one of Cook's best efforts.''

Amelia dutifully placed a cake she had no intention of eating on her plate and encouraged the maid to take several for herself.

Feeling frustrated and restless, Amelia put her nearly full teacup aside and walked to the window.

The storm had increased intensity, for the rain now drummed fiercely. She unhooked the latch and pushed open the window, breathing deeply the tang of musky dampness. It smelled of wet earth. She envied the ease with which nature could wash clean its sins and start anew.

"You'll catch your death standing by that damp window," Mildred admonished. Amelia turned absently, unaware that she had been shivering.

"Well, that is one solution to my current dilemma. Though I fully believe he would try, even the earl would have difficulty convincing Mr. Bascomb it would be in his best interest to marry a corpse."

"My lady! 'Tis bad luck to speak of your own passing with such a glib tongue."

Amelia refrained from commenting that death would be preferable to a second marriage, knowing it would sound overly dramatic. The problem was that the sentiment was uncomfortably close to the truth.

Remembering the years of her marriage brought forth a rush of hot and cold chills. Thanks to her indulgent parents, Amelia had been granted more freedom than most young women of her age and class when it came to selecting a husband. George Wheatley had recently inherited his title and the earl had fully captured her impressionable imagination with his striking features, charming manners, and noble bearing.

She believed herself to be irresistibly and wildly in love with George, just as the poems and stories and songs described. So at twenty she had married a man of her own choice, with her parents' blessing.

Naively blinded by love, she had stepped willingly into what eventually became a waking nightmare.

Resolutely, Amelia thrust the memories deep inside her, locking them away once again. She had buried her unhappiness and pain the day George died. That was part of her past—it did no good to look back and remember with regret her many mistakes.

She needed to focus on the future. She looked again out the window, her eyes squinting to see through the steady rain. In the faint distance she could make out the five chimneys of the Dower House. The brick climbed toward the clouds, tall and straight, seeming to mock her by its deceptively strong appearance.

The Dower House was to have been her haven, her reward for enduring twelve years of marriage to an oftentimes harsh and brutal man. For years she had dreamed of setting up her own small household at the edge of the estate, a home that was completely her own, where she was answerable to no one. With Mildred and Hugh as her servants, a small reward to them for their continued loyalty, along with a competent cook and several day maids to handle the heavier chores.

There had even a small provision in George's will for a monthly allowance to maintain that household. Yet, after three years, Amelia had still not taken up residence because the Dower House had fallen into a state of such disrepair it was uninhabitable. The roof leaked in several places, all the fireplaces on the second floor smoked badly, the foundation on the south facade was rotten through, and many panes of glass were broken.

It would take far more than the small allowance she was given to properly repair the house. She needed the help and permission of the current earl, her brother-in-law. Yet he had been steadily refusing her pleas for funds for nearly three years. Amelia finally understood why. Apparently he had decided it would best suit his purposes to marry her off to a rich local merchant.

It seemed the most bitter of irony that George's death had not set her free, but placed her in an even more tenuous position.

"The earl has sent for you, my lady."

For an instant her tongue felt frozen and she could find no words to respond to the message Hugh brought. Her gaze shifted from Mildred to Hugh, then back to Mildred. "Has Mr. Bascomb departed?"

"Yes, he left the moment the rain let up a little."

Slowly, with a despairing sense of the inevitable, Amelia turned around. She nodded reassuringly at Mildred, hoping her show of confidence would help relieve the worry that engulfed the maid's eyes.

Amelia paused when she reached the drawing room, signaling the footman to wait before opening the door. She nervously wiped a damp palm on her skirts, then entered the room cautiously, her eyes alert to the inhabitants of the room.

Though Hugh declared Mr. Bascomb gone, Amelia knew the servant could be mistaken. Both his memory and eyesight were failing and he was known to give incorrect information on more than one occasion. Thankfully he was correct now—Mr. Bascomb was nowhere in sight.

"Ah, there you are, Amelia. Come in, come in. I have some wonderful news to share."

The deep voice of her brother-in-law startled her and she felt her shoulders jump. He strode forward purposefully, lifting her hand to his mouth. Roger's smile was tight and false. Amelia suppressed a shiver. With his square jaw, straight nose, and light blue eyes there were many who labeled Roger Wheatley, Earl of Monford, a handsome man.

But Amelia knew better. That attractive exterior hid a soul that was dark and brooding. Oh, Roger could be charming, even gallant if the mood were upon him. Yet more and more that charm had been strained, especially when anyone tried to thwart his will.

Living in the house that was once her domain and now belonged to him, she had learned one very important lesson that she took pains never to forget. Under almost all circumstances Roger could not be trusted.

Without waiting to be asked, Amelia took a seat on the green silk-covered settee. She folded her hands primly in her lap. "You sent for me, Roger?"

The earl nodded. He selected a chair across from her, casually crossed one leg over the other, and regarded her shrewdly. Amelia glanced uneasily at the hearth, then forced herself to stare directly at her nemesis.

"I am delighted to inform you that Mr. Bascomb and I have reached an agreement this afternoon. A most favorable marriage agreement. You shall be married at the end of next month." He gave her a slick, indulgent smile. "Are you not pleased by this happy turn of events?"

Amelia could feel the pressure of her heart beating rapidly against her chest. Her pride hoped that he could not hear the thunderous pounding.

"Why would you assume that I am pleased by this news, Roger? I have never given any indication that I would look favorably upon Mr. Bascomb's suit. In fact, precisely the opposite is true, and I have told him that on more than one occasion."

The smile on Roger's face became noticeably cooler. "Do you object because he has no title?"

How ridiculous. Leave it to Roger to find the most unimportant detail and magnify it. "Mr. Bascomb's lack of a noble title is hardly an issue. Since I was born the daughter of an earl I shall always retain my rank." She paused. "Honestly, I cannot imagine why he would be interested in a woman of my years when there are so many other younger, prettier, more suitable brides in the area."

Roger laughed. It was a deep, unpleasant sound. "You make it sound as though you have one foot in the grave, Amelia. Mr. Bascomb confided in me several months ago that he prefers an older, more mature woman closer to his own age of forty for his bride."

Amelia did not believe that for an instant. Feeling a bit more desperate, she pressed on. "A man in Mr. Bascomb's position must think of the future. True, he has no title to pass on, but his thriving business would be a wonderful inheritance for any child. As his friend, I would think you would want to encourage him to find a younger woman capable of bearing him children. Most importantly, a son and heir."

"We discussed this at length. Thanks to my intervention, Mr. Bascomb has decided to generously overlook your barren state. Something, I must point out, that not all men would do so graciously." Roger leaned forward slowly, his hard blue gaze piercing her fragile composure. "Fortunately, Mr. Bascomb has a nephew of whom he is very fond. The eldest son of his only sister. He is a smart lad who has exhibited great promise in all areas of the business.

"He has also shown the proper respect and gratitude towards his very generous uncle, and expressed his delight at the many benefits and privileges that have been offered to him. Mr. Bascomb is pleased that this fine young man will one day carry on."

If he thought to hurt her with his talk of barrenness, the earl was sadly disappointed. Amelia had accepted long ago that she would never be mother to any children. In moments such as this she was grateful for her lack of prodigy, for a child would be but another weapon that Roger could use against her.

Amelia shook her head. "I am an unsuitable bride for Mr. Bascomb. He must choose another."

"Don't be so modest, Amelia. Though not in the first bloom of youth, you do have a few feminine charms that a man can admire."

The gall of the man! Amelia pressed her lips tightly together and muttered, "You are too kind, Roger."

"Oh, do smile, Amelia. This is a joyous, joyful occasion. Who knows, your marriage might entice me to consider entering the parson's mousetrap myself." The earl strolled to the sideboard, uncorked a nearly empty decanter, and poured out two goblets. He thrust one at Amelia. She accepted it without thinking. "I insist you join me in a glass of claret to celebrate."

The earl raised his glass. "To Lady Amelia, the future Mrs. Bascomb."

She made no immediate reply, watching with mounting disgust as Roger drained his glass, refilled it, and drank the second as quickly as the first. Agitated, Amelia rose, slamming her goblet down on the table, and walked in the opposite direction.

She stood with her back to Roger for several long moments, gazing out at the green summer lawn below. "You have not been listening to a word that I've said, Roger. I have no wish to remarry anyone, and I am especially averse to a match with Mr. Bascomb."

"Why?"

Amelia's hands clutched the sill. "He is a mean-spirited, humorless tyrant. His relations barely speak to him, his tenants are terrified of him, and his servants are constantly running off because he has a tendency to strike them on a whim."

"Malicious lies and kitchen gossip," Roger retorted with a careless wave of his hand. "I thought you were above believing such drivel. Mr. Bascomb has always behaved like a gentleman in my presence. Yes, he can be forceful with others at times, but that is the mark of a successful man. I find your objections petty and insufficient."

Angered, she spun around to face him. "If those and all the other reasons are of such little consequence, then you marry him, Roger."

The earl's face contorted in rage. For an instant he looked so much like his brother that fingers of fear scraped at Amelia's stomach.

"Do not forget to whom you are speaking, madame."

She swallowed, then moistened her dry lips. "I know in my heart that I can never be happy tied to a man like Mr. Bascomb no matter how hard I try. The marriage is an impossibility for me. I understand that you are concerned for my future and I am grateful for your efforts on my behalf.

"More than anything I fear being a burden to you. Please, Roger, just let me have the funds I need to complete the renovations on the Dower House. Mr. Walsh, the architect, assures me the estimates for repairs are very reasonable and can be completed within the year. Once I move in I can live comfortably on my allowance and promise never to ask you for anything else."

"No."

Amelia nearly screamed with frustration. "How can you be so heartless? Will you bear no guilt for my future unhappiness? Will you condemn me again to a marriage void of love. Void of respect. Void of decency. After George died I vowed I would never again experience such degradation, such boundless unhappiness."

"Be quiet!" The earl slammed his fist on the table. Amelia's full wine goblet tumbled to the floor, spreading a dark red stain on the rug. "There will be no words of slander spoken against my brother in my presence, nor in my home."

" 'Tis the truth," she whispered. "I was so blinded by my own feelings of love that I never realized what George's true feelings were for me until we were wed. And then it was too late. You were not here, you do not know what I endured, what I suffered. Never again shall I willingly give another man such power over my person."

Roger advanced so quickly she did not realize his intent until he grasped her face between his fingers and turned her chin so that she was forced to look directly at him. The expression in his eyes made her blood run cold. "I give you this one and only warning. If you say another word to darken the memory of my brother, I shall order the Dower House burned to the ground."

A choking despair settled in Amelia's heart. She knew Roger's threat was not an idle one. He was certainly capable of such a malicious, vindictive act.

"Let go of me, Roger," she said, surprised at how calm she sounded.

The earl pulled his hand away and turned abruptly from her. Her face felt bruised and raw where he had grabbed her. Roger stalked impatiently to the other side of the room, obviously trying to gather his composure.

"We shall travel to Kent at the end of the week," he said. "The duke and duchess of Hartwell are hosting a house party and we are invited to be their guests."

"I am not acquainted with the duke and duchess and therefore have no interest in attending their party," she said tonelessly.

"I have already accepted on your behalf." Roger clenched his fists tightly at his sides. "We leave in two days. Mr. Bascomb will also be attending. It will be the perfect setting for him to ask you formally to be his wife. Naturally you will accept.''

Amelia lifted her bruised chin and forced herself to meet his gaze. If she lived to be a hundred, she would never understand why Roger was doing this. Deep inside he must have some perverse, twisted reason for forcing this marriage upon her. If only she understood his motivation, perhaps she could change his mind, could save herself from this horrible fate.

''I know you have never held me in great affection, yet surely it will pain you to know that you are responsible for the unhappiness and misery visited upon your brother's widow.''

The earl rubbed his palm over the back of his neck several times, as if it itched. For an instant Amelia thought she might have convinced him to reconsider.

''The settlement that Mr. Bascomb has agreed upon is very generous. I would be greatly remiss in my duties as head of the family if I did not accept this fine offer from him on your behalf.''

Ah, so it was the money. Amelia had suspected that was a large part of the reason Roger was so eager to make this alliance. She had noticed small, subtle changes in the household that were clear indications of attempts to economize. Fewer servants, less imported, expensive items, even fewer new clothes from the earl's exclusive London tailor.

There was also the conspicuous absence of certain valuable items that had once graced the mansion. Paintings, antique vases, and silver plate, even a prized horse was no longer in the stables. Apparently the rumors of the unhealthy state of the family finances were not exaggerated.

Though he had been a dismal husband in almost all other areas, George had managed to provide her with material comforts. He had a talent for business and making money that he had kept well hidden from society, fearing ridicule. After all, a true gentleman did not soil his hands with work, like a common man.

Unfortunately for all of them it appeared as though Roger did not share this financial acumen with his brother.

"I am certain there are many heiresses among the beau monde who would be honored to become your countess," Amelia said, forcing back the twinge of guilt she felt at the suggestion. "All you need to do is make your choice."

"You are strikingly naive," Roger replied, staring at her broodingly. "The young women of society, and their fathers, are not so easily duped."

Amelia's clasped hands turned cold and clammy. Roger must have chased after a bride this Season, yet for some reason had been unsuccessful in arranging the marriage. It made Amelia's situation all the more desperate.

"Must it be Mr. Bascomb? Is there no other solution, Roger?" she asked with quiet dignity.

"Devil take it, Amelia. I am not a complete ogre." He narrowed his eyes. "If you can find an acceptable gentleman who will match the settlement that Mr. Bascomb is offering then I will seriously consider allowing you to dismiss Mr. Bascomb's proposal."

It was a hollow promise and they both knew it.

She was not acquainted with any suitable men and most definitely did not know any male who was desperate enough to offer a large marriage settlement to a widow of her years.

Knowing there was nothing left to say, Amelia walked toward the door. Though feeling utterly defeated and disheartened, she left the room with her head held high, waiting until she reached the privacy of her own chambers before collapsing into sobs.

CHAPTER TWO

The trip to Winchester Manor in Kent was long, arduous, and depressing. Fortunately the rain held off and Amelia was spared Roger's company inside the coach. The earl preferred keeping his own pace by riding his spirited stallion ahead of the carriage.

In the late morning of the third day of travel the earl pulled his horse beside Amelia's open window, bent low, and shouted, "We should arrive within the hour. The house rests on the high ridge just beyond these trees."

" 'Tis a very large home, my lord. I assure you I have no difficulty seeing it," Amelia retorted. She turned her head aside and deliberately pulled down the carriage window shade. Far better to endure the heat than to have to suffer the earl's company.

Amelia had taken some small petty comfort in responding to the earl with thinly veiled disdain every time he addressed any questions or comments to her. Since she had decided it would be futile to make any additional protests, knowing there were no words that could make Roger reconsider this course of action, this somewhat childish behavior was her only form of retaliation.

All too soon they reached the end of the mile-long drive leading to the house. They were ushered into the elaborate foyer by a fastidious butler who summoned an army of servants to attend to the luggage and then informed them that tea would be served at four-thirty in the crimson drawing room. There was no sign of either of their hosts.

"Be sure to inform the duke and duchess that the Earl of Monford and his sister-in-law the dowager countess have arrived," Roger said. He flicked a cool gaze down the length of the butler's body. "At once."

The butler bowed respectfully, but made no promise to convey the message. More than anything, Roger detested being slighted. Amelia's bottom lip twitched with amusement.

"I am sure our hosts are busy attending to other more *important* guests," she said clearly, delighted when a look of pique appeared in Roger's face.

The smile remained on Amelia's face as she followed a footman up the great sweeping main staircase. Thankfully, the earl's rooms were in a different wing of the house, so she was spared his company.

Though having spent all her life among the finer things, Amelia could not help but be impressed by the painted ceiling moldings, gilded door, and window fixtures, exquisite artwork, priceless antique vases, and thick luxurious rugs she passed.

It appeared that the duke and his duchess were not averse to flaunting their enormous wealth and refined tastes.

"Amelia? Is that really you?"

Startled by the familiar female voice, Amelia jerked her head toward it.

"Charlotte!"

Amelia nearly burst into tears when she saw one of her dearest friends, Miss Charlotte Sanford, rush forward to greet her. The women hugged warmly.

"What a delightful surprise," Charlotte exclaimed. "I thought you loathed house parties. Why did you not write and let me know you were planning to attend?"

"It all came up rather suddenly," Amelia said evasively. "There was hardly time to pack my wardrobe."

"I suspect you managed." Laughter sparkled in the depths of Charlotte's warm brown eyes. "Belinda is here, too. Have you seen her?"

"No. We've only just arrived." Amelia gestured toward the footman who was trying to remain as unobtrusive as possible.

Charlotte consulted the delicate gold watch that hung from a chain around her neck. "I have but a few minutes to spare. I promised my brother James I would meet him on the south lawn by three o'clock so I could help chaperon his twin daughters. Can you believe my nieces are already seventeen years old? It makes me feel positively ancient each time I say it aloud."

Amelia smiled briefly. "You hardly look older than seventeen yourself, Charlotte."

"You sound like a randy buck trying to turn my head with such foolish flattery," Charlotte exclaimed.

"I'm being truthful," Amelia insisted. She had known Charlotte, and Belinda, since they were young girls attending Miss Webster's Academy for Young Ladies together. Always considered the prettiest of the three, Charlotte's angular face, smooth complexion, and rich dark hair had indeed become lovelier over the years.

Amelia sighed softly. "If only we could go back to that simpler, happier time in our lives when we were most concerned about completing our lessons and pronouncing our French verbs with an authentic Gaelic accent."

Charlotte tilted her head and frowned. "You seem troubled, Amelia. Is there anything I can do to help?"

Amelia blinked back the sudden onslaught of tears. "Oh, Charlotte, 'tis beyond your help or anyone else's, I fear."

"What is wrong?"

"It's my brother-in-law, Roger. He is being positively horrid." Amelia shot a quick, discreet glance at the footman, who appeared far too innocent not to be eavesdropping on every word. "The situation is much too complicated to explain now. Besides, you promised to meet your brother by three and I do remember how James hates tardiness."

Charlotte's pretty face assumed a forceful, take-charge expression. "I cannot abide seeing you so unhappy. Belinda and I shall come to your room later this evening, so we may speak in private." She grasped Amelia's hand and squeezed it reassuringly. "Remember, dear friend, you are not alone."

" 'Tis settled. We shall all three assess the qualifications of each unattached man in attendance and by the conclusion of the house party elicit a proposal of marriage for Amelia from the most suitable candidate," Lady Belinda Gooding declared solemnly. "She will then inform the earl of her choice and he will be forced to send Mr. Bascomb packing."

Amelia shifted uncomfortably in her chair. It had brought her a great sense of relief to confide the horrendous situation with Mr. Bascomb to her two oldest and dearest friends. They had been indignant on her behalf and quick to offer advice and support. Yet despite their best efforts, Amelia feared a solution could not be found.

"I appreciate your efforts to aid me in my time of need," Amelia said. "Knowing you agree that Roger's actions are despicable is a great comfort and your ideas and plans to thwart him are welcomed. But the simple truth is that I have no desire to be a wife again to any man, no matter how suitable he may appear."

"Are you very sure? Though he was considerably older than I, my years of marriage to Lord Gooding were very happy. It was not a passionate whirlwind of emotions, but we shared companionship, laughter, and a great affection." A shadow of concern crossed Belinda's face. "Not all men are like George."

"I know." Amelia lowered her chin as she felt a blush creep into her cheeks. Charlotte and Belinda knew her marriage had been an unhappy one, yet she could never bring herself to tell them the entire truth. There were some humiliations Amelia could share with no other living soul.

"If you are certain you cannot have another husband, there is only one other solution," Charlotte declared. "You must take a lover and cause a great scandal, so that Mr. Bascomb will withdraw his offer of marriage."

Amelia looked at Charlotte with a pained expression and tried hard not to focus on how the very idea of taking a lover mortified her on so many levels. The physical aspects aside—though that was a rather large portion of the difficulty—it nearly made her skin crawl to imagine the emotional trust she would be giving to a total stranger.

After being free of male attention for three years of widowhood it was in some ways impossible, unimaginable, incomprehensible for Amelia to envision inviting that degree of intimacy from a man.

"I agree a scandal might discourage Mr. Bascomb from pressing his suit," Amelia said slowly. "But must it be a lover?"

"A woman's options in this area are rather limited," Belinda answered. "Though I suppose you could act disgracefully rude and boorish."

Amelia nodded her head thoughtfully. "Lady Morgan became rather tipsy at last year's holiday celebration. She knocked over the punch bowl and a pile of fresh oranges that Roger had purchased especially to flaunt his seemingly boundless wealth. The talk of her disgraceful behavior is only now starting to lessen."

"Men like Mr. Bascomb are used to dealing with drunken sots." Charlotte gave an amused snort. "If you are serious about ridding yourself of his odious suit, then you must take a lover. No man will tolerate a wanton hussy for a wife. Besides, if you are going to be embroiled in a scandal you might as well have a bit of fun!"

"Fun?" Amelia and Belinda queried simultaneously.

Charlotte, who had been reclining beneath an array of plump red and gold tapestry pillows on the four-poster bed, sat up abruptly. "Oh pray, do not tell me that only I, the spinster of our group, finds bedsport a delight?"

"A delight?" Amelia sat back against her chair, her mouth open. Charlotte's bluntness did not offend Amelia. Though unmarried, Charlotte had conducted a passionate and scandalous affair with a handsome and totally unsuitable naval officer the first year the girls had made their debut into society.

Though raised in a narrow world that expected purity from the unmarried females of its ranks, Charlotte had somehow found the courage to give her heart and body to her young man without a pang of conscience or regret. At the time, Amelia had feared her friend's reckless behavior would bring her heartache and had advised caution.

That advice was considered, for Charlotte and her young man had been discreet. Naturally, there had been speculation and gossip, but thankfully no great scandal. When her lover was killed in battle, Charlotte had been distraught for over a year. Through the passing years there had been offers of marriage, but Charlotte never showed any interest in other men.

For a moment Amelia envied her friend. Though of short duration, her love affair had possessed everything Amelia's much longer marriage seemed to lack. Love, intensity, passion.

"If I may be so bold to inquire, what exactly about *uhm,* bedsport do you find so delightful?" Amelia asked.

"Why, everything," Charlotte replied simply. "I can sense however, that you are of a different opinion. No matter. I shall be the one that takes a lover and creates a scandal."

"What?" Belinda, who had her head down, apparently absorbed in reflective thought, lifted her chin. "How will that possibly help Amelia?"

"If I create a scandal and Amelia defends me the scandal will touch her. No man wants a wife who would refuse to shun a disgraced woman. This will force Mr. Bascomb to cry off."

"Oh, I could never—" Amelia began.

"Why do you get to be the one who creates the scandal?" Belinda interrupted in a challenging tone. "Perhaps I would like to be the one Amelia needs to defend."

"I really don't—" Amelia tried again.

"Taking a lover is a drastic measure," Charlotte interjected. "I never thought you would so easily abandon your scruples, Belinda."

"Well, I would. For a friend," Belinda added hastily.

"Belinda, Charlotte, please." Amelia held up her hand, palm out, hoping to prevent another interruption. "I could never allow either of you to do such a thing for me. What of your nieces, Charlotte? This scandal could hurt their chances for a good match next Season."

Charlotte rolled her shoulders nonchalantly. "Do not be concerned about them. By next Season there will be other far more intriguing scandals for the *ton* to relish. Besides, my brother will most likely be the first to condemn my behavior. His outrage will protect his daughters."

Amelia shook her head. "You have too much to lose. I cannot let you make this sacrifice for me."

"Who said it was going to be a sacrifice?" Charlotte said with a throaty laugh. She pulled insistently at a red thread on the pillow she held in her lap. "It has been many years since I lost Douglas. I miss having a man in my bed."

"Truly?" Amelia's mind whirled at the very thought.

"I am the better choice." Belinda's cheeks flushed. "After all, I am a widow with no family that would share in my disgrace."

Amelia turned toward her other friend. "There has never been so much as a hint of scandal in your past," she said with amazement.

"Precisely. It will be all the more shocking behavior coming from me." Belinda's eyes flickered. "Lest you think I am acting purely out of regard for you, I will confess that though I dearly loved Richard, we never shared the passion that Charlotte speaks about so freely. Perhaps this is my chance to experience that mystery."

"My, what decadent little secrets we keep buried within our hearts," Amelia said softly.

There was a heartbeat of pure silence as the three friends regarded each other warily. Then all three women burst out laughing.

"Dear friends, your loyalty humbles and shames me. How can I ask you to do something that I am unwilling to consider?" Amelia took a deep breath. "I believe a scandal just might save me from Mr. Bascomb. Therefore, I shall follow your advice and somehow lure a rogue into my bed."

"Now we will have three scandals!" Charlotte exclaimed with a squeal as she threw her pillow at Amelia. It hit her square in the chest and she started giggling.

"There is certainly no need to have three scandals when one is all that is needed," Belinda said. "I propose we settle this in a fair and random manner."

She walked across the room and opened the large wardrobe containing Amelia's garments. Charlotte and Amelia watched in curious silence as Belinda rummaged amongst the various items. A few minutes later, a short shout of triumph let them know Belinda had located what she sought.

"What are you doing?" Charlotte inquired.

"Devising a way to fairly determine the winner," Belinda replied. She turned and held out her fisted palm. Three bright red feathers of equal height stood at jaunty attention in the center of her closed hand. "We shall each select a feather. The one who draws the shortest plume will seduce a rogue sometime during the house party and create the scandal that will free Amelia from this unwanted marriage."

Charlotte shrugged. "It seems as fair a method as any other." She bounded gracefully off the bed and came forward. Amelia followed at a more cautious pace.

The silence was thick with anticipation as each woman made her selection. Amelia's heart beat in double rhythm as she held her wispy length of red plume aloft. It was clearly the shortest of the three.

"Congratulations," Charlotte said with an amused half smile.

"You are the winner," Belinda added.

"Thank you," Amelia replied. She took a deep breath and attempted to clear her chest of the strange mix of relief and terror that shuttered through her. This idea was desperate, but if executed correctly might very well save her from the unhappy fate Roger seemed so determined to force upon her.

Yet hard as she tried, Amelia could not completely dispel the persistent feeling that she was about to make the biggest mistake of her life.

Gareth Travers, Viscount of Longley, was a man on a mission. He had spent the better part of the Season deliberately waging a carefully crafted campaign to seduce the lovely Mrs. Emma Fairweather into his bed and at long last it seemed those efforts would succeed.

Though it was hardly necessary for the young handsome viscount to pursue women, he had enjoyed himself nonetheless. To Gareth's way of thinking it could hardly be considered sporting to chase a woman if she did not at least make an attempt to run.

Unfortunately, Mrs. Fairweather had done too good a job of eluding his advances and to the amazement of all, including the viscount, he had yet to sample her womanly charms. For the man known to society as the ultimate lover, it was a lowering state of affairs.

"You are certain Mrs. Fairweather will be at the house party?" the viscount asked. He slowed his mount and raised his voice so as to be heard by the elegant nobleman riding beside him.

"The answer to that particular question has not changed since you posed it to me two weeks ago when we visited that London brothel, last week while we gambled at White's, and last night when we barely slept more than an hour at that appalling provincial inn," Lucien St. Simon, the Earl of Danbury replied.

"I just wanted to be certain," Gareth said.

The earl grimaced. "Devil take it, Longley. I believe the ache between your legs has traveled up your body and lodged itself firmly in your brain. You are possessed."

Though loath to admit it, Gareth was honest enough to concede that his friend had a point. During most of his twenty-eight years his body had indeed ruled his mind, especially in matters of erotic pleasures.

He could not have changed that if he wanted to, for it was as much a part of his heritage as his striking black hair and brilliant blue eyes. Gareth was the second son of a duke, descendant of a noble family known for its service to the Crown and for producing at least one scandalous black sheep in every generation.

Gareth had fulfilled that role with relish, indulging his natural devilish, reckless streak at every turn. He was content to live a life of wealth and privilege, a life devoid of responsibility. 'Twas said among the beau monde that if Viscount Longley applied half the diligence to a worthwhile endeavor that he did to chasing women and indulging in every conceivable form of decadence, he would be the most powerful man in the land.

As with all his women, his current obsession, Mrs. Emma Fairweather, was a beautiful creature who possessed that air of sophisticated mischief and mystery the viscount found so irresistible in a female.

She was not especially clever, nor especially witty in her conversation, and Gareth's mind often drifted when she spoke with him for any length of time. And still, he could not for the life of him leave her alone.

"What of Mr. Fairweather?" Gareth asked. "Will he be accompanying his wife?"

The earl shrugged. "It seems unlikely, since he has not been in town once the entire Season. Or last Season, either. I know it would make it more difficult for your seduction plans, but I for one hope the old boy does show up."

Gareth smothered the unaccustomed twinge of hurt that emerged. Though surrounded constantly by men and women who enjoyed his company,

there were a select number the viscount considered
to be his friends. Lucien was one of those few.

"Mrs. Fairweather has proved to be a challenging
enough conquest without her husband in tow,"
Gareth said as he adjusted the speed of his horse
so he could bring the animal even closer to his
friend. "The chance of failure increases tenfold if
he joins the party."

"You are being far too modest," the earl replied
with a sly smile. "If necessary you could have Mrs.
Fairweather on her back with you mounted atop
and her husband snoring contentedly in the bed
beside you both."

"Hell and damnation, now that's a pretty picture!"

The men laughed, then urged their mounts
around a narrow bend. "If Mr. Fairweather does
appear, it will be a boon for me," Lucien explained.
"He has never once been seen in society and since
Mrs. Fairweather hails from such a remote section
of Cornwall there are none to dispute her claim
of a husband. The rumors persist that he is merely
a figment of her vivid imagination."

"I've heard that too," Gareth agreed. "I've also
heard some lackwits have placed wagers in the bet-
ting book at White's concerning the matter."

"Precisely." The earl assumed a haughty stare.
"I have accepted each and every one of them. If
Mr. Fairweather follows his pretty young wife to
Kent there will be no disputing the fact that he
does indeed exist. I may then happily claim my
substantial winnings."

Gareth relaxed, then smiled. "You engage in the most foolhardy wagers, my friend. Mrs. Fairweather is an accomplished flirt and her kisses suggest she is far from an innocent. Yet given the circumstances even I would not play those long odds."

The earl turned about with a flourish. "We cannot all be great lovers. Some of us must exploit our other talents in order to hold our reputations as rogues. You know I've always had an affinity for gambling. For me, the more impossible the odds, the more attractive the wager, hence the sweeter the victory."

Gareth frowned as a sudden thought emerged. "Do not say that you have wagered Mrs. Fairweather will escape me?"

The earl nearly pulled his horse to a dead stop at the notion. "I enjoy taking risks but I'm not a complete idiot. Besides, I was unable to find anyone who would bet against you, Longley."

This time it was Gareth who was almost unseated, as he threw back his head and burst into laughter. "Such a display of male confidence in my prowess warms my heart. And challenges my blood. Come on, Lucien. If we hurry, we shall arrive at Winchester Manor in time to partake of the evening meal."

"And enjoy the delectable Mrs. Fairweather for dessert?"

The viscount raised his hand and motioned toward the empty stretch of road that lay ahead. "A sound plan. However, I must refute your claim of being a modest lover. You have all the necessary qualifications to become a top-notch seducer of females."

"Thank you." The earl inclined his head. "Your superior skill and reputation makes that high praise indeed."

"Oh, stuff it!" Gareth exclaimed, breaking into a good-natured smile.

With a final laugh the two men cantered away.

CHAPTER THREE

"Have you at last made a decision, Amelia?" a female voice whispered in her ear. "Who will it be? Which of these many handsome, dashing men shall you choose for your lover?"

Amelia sprang away from that voice so fast she almost tumbled to the carpet. By only a small miracle was she able to right herself and prevent plunging headlong into the Dowager Countess of Hamlin and her escort, who were each carrying plates of food piled high with supper offerings. In panting breaths, Amelia turned to face her tormentor.

"Charlotte! You must stop sneaking up on me. These days have been trying to the extreme. My poor heart cannot take so much shock."

Amelia felt a gentle hand on her shoulder.

"I'm sorry. I had not realized you were so engrossed in thought that you had gone deaf."

Amelia frowned. Charlotte's voice was sincere, but her friend hardly looked sorry. She actually looked amused.

"My nerves are overset," Amelia said. She snapped open the fan that dangled from her wrist and waved it vigorously. "Roger has informed me that Mr. Bascomb will be arriving by this evening. Above all else, I must avoid his company."

"Of course." This time there was no mistaking the concern shining in Charlotte's eyes. "Stay close by my side. If necessary, I can distract Mr. Bascomb."

"Thank you." The wispy ends of Amelia's stylishly coiffed hair fluttered wildly in the breeze created by her fan. "It is a great comfort knowing I have you and Belinda close at hand to offer support."

"We shall do all that we are able." Suddenly, Charlotte's hand shot forward and grasped Amelia's wrist. "You are waving that so fiercely it is making me dizzy. 'Tis so unlike you to be so fidgety. Even the odious Mr. Bascomb cannot account for this attack of nerves."

"I have been trying to make a decision," Amelia said slowly.

"Concerning your lover?" Charlotte asked brightly. "Thank heavens. It has been three days since you plotted your course, Amelia. You need to choose your partner and start your seduction. Soon!"

Amelia felt the blush of crimson rise in her cheeks. She angled her head so Charlotte could not see the embarrassment framed in her eyes.

"This is proving far more difficult than I imagined."

"If you are lacking courage, all you need do is imagine yourself married to Mr. Bascomb," Charlotte advised grimly.

Amelia shuddered visibly at the thought. Charlotte was right. She must somehow find the courage to act.

"I am starting to feel conspicuous standing here," Amelia said. "Let's at least get a plate of food so we may sit at one of the tables."

She took Charlotte's arm and they strolled over to the dining room sideboard with the same casual aplomb one would assume when promenading in Hyde Park. Since a late supper was planned after tonight's dancing, a lavish respite had been laid out for the guests to casually enjoy, so as to ensure that no one went hungry.

Amelia and Charlotte joined the line of guests. They waved off the assistance of the able footmen who stood ready to help. What was needed most was privacy.

"I noticed you danced with Lord Avery the other evening," Charlotte whispered. "Twice."

"He is very kind," Amelia answered. She speared a thick slice of cured ham she had no intention of eating and placed it on her plate. "We discussed his children, who are nearly grown and the gardens at his country home. It was a very pleasant conversation."

"Well, he has certainly mellowed with age. I thought he might have already made some overtures towards you. The tales of his exploits with women are legendary." Charlotte paused, her hands clenched tightly around a dripping spoon of pickled beets. "Perhaps it might be easier for you to select an older, more experienced gentleman like Lord Avery. Why do you not pursue him?"

"He reminds me of my father."

"Oh dear, that won't do." Charlotte put down the spoon without taking any beets and held out her plate. Amelia dropped a healthy serving of roasted potatoes onto it. "What about Mr. Matthews? I noticed he partnered you for supper after the dancing last night."

Amelia sighed. "His conversation was so dull it nearly put me to sleep."

"His wit is not of primary importance in this instance," Charlotte rebuked.

"I know that," Amelia exclaimed. Her rigid expression softened. "But will it not be easier to accept him into my bed if I like him just a little?"

Charlotte's warm eyes filled with understanding. "Shall we alter the plan? This is obviously a torture for you. I cannot speak for Belinda, but I for one am willing to step in for you."

Amelia shook her head adamantly. "No, I won the bet. I shall take the lover." She pressed her palm against her hot cheek and tried to calm her nerves.

Just saying the words aloud had brought on a flush of emotion. How was she ever going to complete the deed if she could barely even speak of it?

The conversation halted as the women found an unoccupied table. Amelia struggled to swallow a slight portion of green beans while Charlotte silently observed her for a long moment. After a second bite Amelia placed her silver fork on the table and abandoned all pretense of eating.

"Spreading your attention amongst too many men is confusing and daunting and distracting you from moving ahead," Charlotte said earnestly. "If you are going to succeed in finding a lover, you need to concentrate your efforts on one gentleman."

"How can I select one?"

"The same way we chose which one of us would take a lover. It must be a completely random selection."

Amelia let out a nervous giggle. "Won't all the gentlemen be curious when I walk about the room handing out red feathers?"

"You are not taking this seriously," Charlotte lectured.

Amelia curled her lip. Charlotte was right again. Thus far she had given the plan only a halfhearted effort. Yet it was difficult to embrace the notion full-out when a part of Amelia's conscience nagged that this was an impulsive, idiotic idea.

"What do you suggest?" Amelia asked cautiously

"You must make it a random twist of fate." Charlotte's eyes darted sharply about the room. "There are only a few unattached males in the dining room at present. I am certain more will be joining us shortly. The next one who walks into the room is the man you shall seduce into your bed. Agreed?"

Amelia nodded her head, surprised she could do it so calmly. As unobtrusively as possible she adjusted the angle of her chair so that she had an unobstructed view of the doorway.

Nervously she picked up her wineglass, took a

healthy swig, and with her heart lodged firmly in her throat, waited.

There was a brief commotion at the entrance as two gentlemen approached. They stood side by side underneath the double archway, observing the gathering with practiced, cynical eyes.

Garbed in elegantly tailored coats, sporting complex white cravats and tight-fitting breeches, they were a sight to behold. Though dressed similarly to many other gentlemen in the room, this pair seemed more exciting, more dangerous than the usual *ton* rakes. They stood proud, arrogant, and so assured, their very presence was a blatant masculine challenge to all the other males in attendance.

Though it had been four years since she had been in London, Amelia recognized both men immediately. The Earl of Danbury and Viscount of Longley, two men who inspired mysterious, forbidden feelings in nearly every female they encountered, no matter her age or marital status.

Feeling like a character in an overly dramatic play, Amelia stared openly at the two men. Her concentration was so intense that she was unable to contain her gasp of shock when the earl bowed elegantly to the viscount and motioned that he precede him into the dining room.

It could not possibly be happening! Amelia's heart skipped a beat and she shut her eyes tight, yet she could not bear to keep them closed. She opened them wide, then wider still as Gareth Travers, Viscount of Longley, sauntered into the room.

"There, 'tis settled," Charlotte said with an authoritative nod of her head. "Before the house party ends, the viscount will become your lover and aid you in creating the scandal of the year."

Viscount Longley as her lover! The dreamlike quality of the moment persisted. Feeling her fragile self-control beginning to tumble, Amelia pinched her thigh to gather her wits.

"I cannot be his lover," Amelia squeaked.

"Do you find him unappealing?" Charlotte questioned. "Personally I prefer the earl's blond countenance, but you must admit the viscount's combination of blue eyes and dark hair is strikingly handsome."

Amelia ripped her gaze away from the viscount. "He is handsome as an Adonis with the physical attributes of a Greek god and the charm of the devil."

Charlotte smiled deliciously. "What is the problem?"

"Are you joking?" Amelia picked up her fan and waved it vigorously in front of her face. Perhaps a cool breeze would help moderate this light-headed feeling. "For one thing, the viscount is younger than I am."

"Oh, posh." Charlotte clucked her tongue. "What possible difference does a few years make?"

"A few years! 'Tis more like seven!"

"Ah, so that makes you old enough to be what . . . his mother?"

"Charlotte!" Amelia cried desperately.

"I apologize for teasing," Charlotte said in a conciliatory tone. "However, if the viscount will not do, then take the earl. They nearly entered the room at the same time. It hardly matters if you prefer one over the other."

"God save us all, Charlotte," Amelia hissed. "You speak of it as though we are discussing which cakes to eat with our tea."

"We have been friends forever," Charlotte chided. "I would think by this time you had become accustomed to my frank, no-nonsense approach to life."

"It still has the power to shock me on occasion," Amelia admitted. "Especially when we are speaking of such delicate, intimate matters."

It was equally difficult to admit that as much as the notion nearly terrified Amelia out of her shoes and stockings there was also a small, rebellious part of her spirit that embraced the idea of the viscount as her scandalous lover. The erotic notion that she, Amelia Wheatley, could somehow be this handsome, wicked man's woman brought Amelia's sensual imagination to life.

She lifted her head and watched the viscount closely.

He was bowing and smiling as he strolled into the room. Amelia noticed he smiled often, but gave only a select few a greeting of unaffected enthusiasm. Within minutes he was surrounded by guests of both genders who appeared eager to converse with him.

The laughter from this ever-widening circle grew steadily and though he was no longer visible Amelia had little doubt the viscount remained at the center of everyone's attention. Including her own.

Amelia sat up a little straighter. "There is no need for me to search any further. The viscount will serve my purpose most adequately." She turned her head and looked right into Charlotte's eyes. "What do I do next?"

Feeling decidedly peeved, Gareth nonetheless managed to respond to the many greetings with a civil tongue and a smile pasted on his face. He noticed that Lucien was grinning like a fool. Not because he wasn't receiving his equal share of fawning attention, but rather because Mrs. Fairweather was nowhere to be found.

When they arrived, Gareth had refrained from asking outright if she was among the guests, hoping instead to surprise her. For the last few miles of the journey his mind had been consumed by thoughts of her—the sensual mouth made for teasing kisses, high delicate breasts that ached to be suckled, the long, shapely legs that would wind tightly about his waist as he joined his body with hers.

Gareth had strolled through a good portion of the large house on the pretext of admiring the estate, half expecting her to appear around the next corner, with her shy smiles and coy glances. Yet room after room had revealed only opulent riches and other guests the viscount had no interest in meeting. It was a rare form of torture that brought on maudlin thoughts.

"Glad you could make it, Longley. These parties can be a deadly bore without some young blood around to liven things up."

Gareth pulled himself together and shook hands with his host, the Duke of Hartwell. He declined an offer of food, but managed to feign polite interest in meeting several of the duke's cronies, men of an older generation who delighted in telling raucous and clearly exaggerated tales of the viscount's ancestors.

Then, out of the corner of his eye, Gareth saw a flash of lavender coming toward him. At last! A Season of stalking his prey had taught the viscount that delicate hue was a favored shade, for it matched the ring of color around Mrs. Fairweather's extraordinary eyes.

With effort, Gareth resisted the urge to rake his fingers through his hair, knowing it would muss it completely. He almost laughed aloud at his vanity.

"Please excuse my intrusion, my lord," a lilting female voice said. "I did not at first recognize you, but now that I have, I wanted to say hello and extend my regards to your family. Are they here also?"

The woman before him dropped an elegant curtsy and he bowed automatically in response. There was a second of disorientation as the viscount realized it was not Mrs. Fairweather who had spoken those charming words, but rather a stranger.

She was an attractive woman with pleasant features, glossy dark hair and a lush figure. Gareth had no idea who she was, yet by her greeting it was obvious she knew him. Then again, didn't everyone?

Gareth barely restrained his disappointment. "My parents have not made the journey north. They prefer to summer with the Regent in Brighton."

"How delightful for them."

"Yes." He drew out the single-syllable word for as long as he dared, then retreated behind a formal perfunctory smile and a slightly cool manner.

"You must offer your parents my best regards the next time you see them," the woman insisted.

"I will not forget."

"Good."

Though she was standing almost rigidly still, her body seemed to dance with impatience. Gareth raised his brow and turned his neck slightly, a sure and subtle hint that their brief, boring conversation was at an end. Yet the damnable woman did not react as she should. Instead of making a graceful departure she lifted her chin and smiled at him.

Gareth was momentarily taken aback. It was not the come-hither broadness of a seductive female he knew so well. He had been weaned on those sultry advances. Yet unless he was very much mistaken there *was* an invitation in her eyes. Of what he could not be certain.

"I do appreciate your politeness, however, I believe it might prove difficult to keep your word," she commented.

"Pardon?"

"You can hardly give my regards to your parents when you do not know who I am," she said in a serious tone. "Can you?"

Gareth laughed. It should have been a mortifying, embarrassing moment, yet there was no malice in her tone. "You have caught me out, neat and tight, madame." He bowed, deep and low. "I stand before you a defeated and humbled man."

"Oh, I highly doubt that, my lord." She joined his laughter and he found that he liked the sound of it. "I am Amelia Wheatley, Dowager Countess of Monford. We have met in London on several different occasions, though not for a few years."

She extended her ungloved hand. He lifted it to his lips and lightly brushed the edge of her knuckles. A pleasant scent of spring roses tickled his nostrils.

"My apologies, fair lady, for committing the unpardonable sin of forgetting your name." He eyed her curiously as his lips lingered on her petal-soft skin.

"You disappoint me, my lord." She cocked her head, her hazel eyes sparkling with mischief. "A momentary lapse in memory is far from a sinful act. Especially for you."

Gareth's distraction began to evaporate. "I see that my inflated reputation has preceded me."

"Oh, yes. I do believe it arrived a full twenty minutes before you set foot in the dining room."

He chuckled again and finally, reluctantly let go of her hand. She was still smiling, apparently in a good humor. Yet when he looked closer, the viscount observed that though she tried to hide it there was a slight reserve to her expression. Perhaps she was worried that they were being watched?

"Let me assure you, my exploits are retold and embellished so often they rarely resemble the truth."

A ghost of a smile touched her lips. "Have they no merit at all?"

"I would not go so far as to say that," he replied.

"It must be tiresome at times to live up to those scandalous acts," she remarked.

"Fairly exhausting," he agreed. "Yet somehow I find the strength."

"How admirable."

For an instant Gareth's famous glib tongue failed him. In his experience women fell into two distinct categories. Those who had a poor opinion of him and steered clear at all costs and those who openly tried to entice him.

He was having great difficulty trying to determine where the countess fit, for he was getting a strange mix of signals from her. She appeared to be examining him with the same intensity women used when they were about to purchase something, yet there was a remote detachment to her perusal.

Then she blinked. Or was it a wink?

"Pardon my interruption, Longley, but there is something I believe you need to see."

Gareth met Lucien's mocking eyes. No further elaboration was necessary. The viscount swung his head around and all thoughts of the countess fled. Standing on the far side of the room was the delectable Mrs. Emma Fairweather. Her rich hair of spun gold and stunning figure was like a beacon of salvation to a storm-wrecked ship.

Gareth watched her hungrily as she leaned forward to shake hands with a seated matron. Plump swells of tempting flesh fell forward, threatening to spill from the bodice of her low-cut gown. That brief glimpse of bosom ignited the lust that had kept the viscount chasing after her for the entire Season.

He breathed deeply, shackling his desire. "You must excuse me, my lady. I see an old friend." He smiled at the countess with feigned interest, his thoughts now inflamed with the notion of filling his hands with the delicious breasts he had just glimpsed, of flattening his body against Mrs. Fairweather's, pressing his hips into hers.

The countess stiffened noticeably. Her mouth compressed into a thin line, yet remarkably she was able to still keep it curved upward in a smile.

"I shall expect you to dance with me later this evening, my lord," she replied stoically. She eyed him askance and added, "To make amends for forgetting my name."

Words failed him for a few moments. He watched the countess pivot on her heel and turn, leaving behind only a faint scent of fresh roses that he was honest enough to admit intrigued him.

More shocking still was the realization that she had succeeded in making him entirely forget Mrs. Fairweather for several minutes. Remarkable.

CHAPTER FOUR

The evening of dancing was not unlike countless others that Amelia had attended. A small, local quartet of string musicians who played a variety of tunes with competence, if not great skill.

Along with the music, echoes of laughter and conversation could be heard, and even the occasional staccato rhythm of clapping hands as the dancers swirled and pranced to a lively country tune. Standing in the shadows made it easier to observe the gathering, and Amelia was surprised by what she saw.

Perhaps she had always been too busy or too involved before to notice all the flirtations, the lascivious looks, the assessing glances shared between many of the male and female guests. Yet instead of encouraging her with her own plan, this looser, more open attitude only made her feel more inadequate.

With a sigh, she shrank back against the silk patterned paper that covered the walls of the ballroom and searched the room for any sign of the viscount.

She quickly found him on the opposite side of the room, leaning negligently against a wall, one ankle crossed over the other, his hands shoved deep in his pockets. There was a very pointed look of concentration on his handsome face. For an instant she thought he might be daydreaming, then she realized he had something within his sights that seemed to fascinate him.

Curious, Amelia followed the line of his intense gaze. Mrs. Emma Fairweather. Amelia's heart sank. It was difficult enough trying to convince herself that she had the daring, wit, and feminine allure to catch the viscount's eye. If she had to compete with the likes of Emma Fairweather to do so, Amelia feared she did not stand a chance.

"Have you seen him?" Belinda asked as she came to stand beside her friend.

"Yes." Amelia glanced around to be certain no one was near. "He is on the far side of the room. Blatantly ogling Mrs. Fairweather's charms."

Belinda's lips pulled down in confusion. "I just saw him at the card table in the gaming room. How did he get here so quickly?"

Amelia shook her head. "That is not possible. I have been watching him closely for the past twenty minutes. He has not been near the gaming tables."

"You are mistaken," Belinda insisted in a quiet,

yet firm voice. "True, I have met Mr. Bascomb on only two occasions, but I very distinctly—"

"Mr. Bascomb!"

"Yes." Belinda's finely edged brow arched up. "Who did you think I was talking about?"

"Viscount Longley." Amelia felt her cheeks flush with color.

Belinda stared at her with huge eyes. "Charlotte told me you had decided on a . . . uhm . . . companion. So it is to be Viscount Longley?"

"Yes." Amelia glanced away. "However I shall be unsuccessful in my quest for scandal if I cannot manage to separate him from Mrs. Fairweather."

"We shall devise a way to deal with Mrs. Fairweather," Belinda declared. "If you are certain he is the one?"

Amelia let out a nervous flutter of laughter. "I am certain of nothing, except my extreme distaste for Mr. Bascomb."

"Viscount Longley is a rather ambitious choice," Belinda said in a reflective tone. "His skill with women is legendary and he is wickedly handsome. Goodness, my insides flutter and my heart trips a little too fast just looking at him. His mouth is sensuous, yet also ruthless. Can you imagine what it would feel like to be kissed by such a rogue?"

Amelia was about to reply, but Belinda was claimed for the next dance before she had a chance to answer. Yes, Amelia could very well imagine a kiss from the viscount. It would start as just the slightest pressure, the softest caress. But soon he would deepen the kiss, as he parted his lips over hers and pushed his tongue inside to ravish her mouth.

And how would she react? With fluttering sighs and coy protests? Or with honest emotion? Would she allow herself to float on the currents of romantic pleasure or would she feel too inhibited to let her passions run free?

With a start of surprise, Amelia realized she could not remember the last time she had shared a kiss of passion with a man. George had stolen a few kisses during their courtship, but had rarely pressed his lips to hers once they had married. According to Charlotte, a well-executed kiss was among the finer rewards in a woman's life.

Gazing at the lazy smile that played along the viscount's full lips made Amelia want to know more about what she had been missing.

A sudden, unexpected glimpse of Roger's stony countenance among the faces in the crowd effectively squelched that desire. Where Roger stood, Mr. Bascomb was certain to be near. Amelia took a step forward, then looked wildly from side to side, searching for a safe escape. She circled the room cautiously, with a twofold purpose. To avoid Mr. Bascomb and Roger and to somehow attract the notice of the viscount.

The former task required only sharp eyes and swift feet, the latter was a more daunting challenge. Given the viscount's current preoccupation with Mrs. Fairweather, Amelia decided she could strip herself naked and still remain unseen by him.

Yet she was not ready to concede defeat. Amelia approached the viscount, moving with a slow, stealthy steadiness that sparked her nerves with a strange feeling of restless agitation. Oddly it was an almost pleasant sensation.

Perhaps because she felt as if she were finally trying to do something. She was no longer waiting placidly for fate to come along and shape her life. She was trying to take control.

Amelia had nearly gained the viscount's side when she noticed a sudden change overtake him. *Drat, she had waited too long.* With a stark look of purpose on his handsome face, he pushed away from the wall, crossed the room, and joined the circle around Mrs. Fairweather. Within minutes they were paired together on the dance floor, the delicate blond feminine beauty a perfect compliment to his dark, handsome countenance.

There seemed to be little conversation between the couple, but the looks he cast her way spoke volumes. He bent forward to whisper something to Mrs. Fairweather that caused her to toss back her golden head and laugh. Amelia suppressed a sudden feeling of envy.

Then Mrs. Fairweather leaned deliberately forward and brushed herself against his chest. The viscount's eyes burned down at her.

Amelia turned away from the sight, berating herself for feeling such jealousy. She had no right to such feelings, no prior claim to the viscount's affections or interest. She winced, remembering how quickly he had abandoned her in the dining room when the lovely Mrs. Fairweather appeared. No sane person would have reason to believe that would change for the entire two weeks of the house party.

Amelia thought seriously of taking Charlotte's advice and selecting another gentleman. Yet she found she could barely consider the notion. For some odd reason fate had placed the viscount squarely in her path and she was resolved to somehow see this through.

The dance ended. Amelia was trying to decide her next move when she noticed Belinda sailing forward. Amelia watched with delight and admiration as her friend neatly cornered the pair, and with seeming ease and a friendly smile whisked Mrs. Fairweather away.

This time Amelia dared not hesitate. With a smile on her lips and a flirtatious mask firmly in place she glided toward the viscount.

"I shall allow you to claim this dance, my lord, but only if you remember who I am."

He laughed. "My fair countess, I vow I shall never again forget your name. In fact, I feel we are now on such intimate terms that I should call you Amelia."

"I would be honored, Gareth."

Given the tightness in her chest, she was pleased to have delivered the retort so naturally. Amelia moved closer to him. His subtle, masculine scent drifted toward her, causing the back of her neck to tingle excitingly. *Saints preserve us, the man even smelled irresistible.*

He drew her toward him and their bodies collided. Panicked, Amelia wondered if he felt the tremor that shook her as her thigh brushed his. She would have approached him regardless of the next dance, but her heart swelled with delight when she recognized the opening strains of a waltz.

The strong grip he had on her hand sent a hot shiver up her spine. Thankfully her gloves hid her wet palms. With a slight apprehension Amelia went into his arms and felt a mix of emotions rush through her. Suddenly she was once again young and unencumbered, free of worries and cares.

They completed one revolution around the small ballroom before he spoke.

"You waltz beautifully."

The compliment startled her and she nearly lost her footing. Embarrassed by her clumsy move, Amelia searched his face for signs of mockery, but found none.

"Thank you. I would return the compliment, but I imagine you get tired of hearing them."

"Compliments?" He gave her a boyish frown that went straight to her heart. "I believe the last woman to compliment my dancing was my grandmother. Actually you remind me a great deal of her."

His grandmother! What a crushing comparison. Amelia's eyes narrowed. " 'Tis kind of you to partner a woman such as myself, obviously teetering on the edge of the grave. Why I can scarcely believe my good fortune to be dancing with someone who is practically a boy."

"I can assure you, madame, I am very much of a man."

Prove it to me. Oh, how desperately she wished she had the courage to utter that flippant remark.

Instead she followed Mrs. Fairweather's example and let herself stumble against him. Her breasts crushed against his chest and she felt his breathing catch. In the guise of righting herself, she disengaged her hand and splayed her palm across those wide muscles, then artfully trailed her fingertips over the solid contours as she reached out to clasp his outstretched hand.

It happened in an instant, so smoothly that they never missed a step in the dance. The puzzled frown he sent her way let her know he was unsure if it was a deliberate or accidental move.

"My grandmother is my favorite female relative," he said.

Amelia arched a brow, but made no comment.

"I never meant to imply that you were like her, except perhaps for a similar disposition. Beyond that, I doubt you have much in common." An irresistible grin tugged at his mouth. "Unless of course you have seven children, as she did."

"I have no children."

"I'm sorry."

"Don't be. Children are a blessing for many families. In my situation the opposite was true. Considering the temperament and character of my late husband it was a blessing not to have any offspring." *Had she actually blurted that statement out loud?* Amelia had never in her life felt free enough to say such a thing to anyone. Even her closest female friends. "Do you have any children, my lord?"

"I am unmarried, Amelia."

"I am well aware of your marital status. Marriage is hardly a requirement for having children. Do you have any?"

"You have posed a most impertinent question, madame," he said sternly, but she detected the rascally twinkle in his eye. "And asked it not once, but twice."

"One of the privileges of reaching such an advanced age is being able to ask these inappropriate questions." She lifted her chin to a provocative angle. "Besides, you have not answered my question."

"Nor will I." His gaze locked with hers, the scrutiny in those devilish blue eyes causing gooseflesh to rise all over her body. "A man must be very careful where he sows his seed. 'Tis easy to beget children, but far harder to parent them."

It was hardly the statement one would expect from a jaded rogue. Amelia was unsure if this attitude was the result of a pleasant or difficult childhood. "I can well imagine what a handful you were as a boy. It must have taken an army to keep you under control."

"I chased away my fair share of nannies and governesses." Gareth smiled. "My parents are very calm, placid people, especially my father. He was and still is the most affable and patient of men. You know, I shot him once."

"You shot him? With a gun?"

"A dueling pistol." He gave her a stare that was a shade too innocent. "However, that delightful story must wait to be told at another time, for our dance is ending."

As if on cue the music came to an end with a resounding flourish. Amelia swept him a graceful curtsy. Gareth bowed, then held out his hand to help her rise. Once she stood straight, he pulled her hand and placed his lips on the top of her gloved wrist.

The kiss was gentle and fleeting, but Amelia felt it through her entire body. Despite the pounding of her heart, she managed to smile, hoping to encourage the sense of intimacy that blossomed in the air.

He returned her to a secluded corner of the room. She allowed him to seat her on a soft cushioned settee. For a wild moment she thought he might join her on the couch and try to steal a kiss. This time from her lips.

Instead he bowed, bestowed a slow smile upon her that never failed to dazzle the weaker sex, and left. Amelia wisely waited until the quivering in her knees passed before standing.

"What game are you playing at now?"

Roger! She had been too engrossed in her escapade with Gareth to keep tabs on her interfering brother-in-law and now she was caught neatly in his snare.

"Good evening, sir," Amelia said, turning away. Her brother-in-law grasped her wrist tightly, preventing her flight.

"I saw you flirting and carrying on with Longley. You shouldn't waste your time," Roger said, his lips pursed in self-righteous reproach. "He is hardly the type to marry."

"A woman like myself," Amelia added. "Is that not what you really meant to say?"

"I thought to spare your feelings, but yes, that is precisely what I meant." Roger tugged on the black ribbon around his neck and lifted a quizzing glass to his eye.

"Ah, there is Mr. Bascomb. He has been asking about you most of the evening. You should have made a greater effort to be available when he arrived. Well, no matter. He looks rather forlorn standing alone amongst the potted palms. We must go and make him feel at ease."

Amelia dug her heels firmly into the carpet.

"Does he find it difficult to move in such exalted noble company?"

"Hardly." Roger snorted. "These people are not strangers to him. Nearly half the men in this room are indebted to Mr. Bascomb in one way or another."

"Including you?"

Roger smiled slyly. "My position is unique. Mr. Bascomb is soon to become a member of our family."

Not if I can prevent it, Amelia told herself silently. She refused to rise to the taunt, but steadfastly kept her eyes ahead of her as she was marched across the room to greet Mr. Bascomb.

He was a slight man, of average height, with thinning dark hair, a sallow complexion, and an appalling affinity for bright, lavish clothing that suited neither his plain looks nor garish personality. This evening's ensemble was no exception. He sported a scarlet coat embroidered with threads of gold, a patterned yellow waistcoat, and tight-fitting black trousers. None of the garments was in any way flattering to his person.

"Where have you been hiding? I have been waiting most of the evening to see you," Mr. Bascomb said, as he grasped her hand with a proprietary air.

Hard, dark eyes bored into her and Amelia struggled to remain unflinching. "Good evening, Mr. Bascomb. I trust you are enjoying the lovely hospitality of the duke and duchess."

"Hummph." A mottled flush spread across Mr. Bascomb's sunken cheeks. His clumsy fingers had managed to move the edge of her glove away from her wrist and he fastened his limp, wet lips greedily against her bare flesh.

Revulsion washed over her. Amelia dared not insult him outright, but she sniffled deliberately, as if the air surrounding him were mortally offensive. Unfortunately he was too thick-skinned to notice.

Amelia freed her hand and turned her head. Roger had already abandoned her and it was shocking to realize that even the company of her odious brother-in-law was preferable to being alone with Mr. Bascomb.

Desperately hoping to find someone she knew, Amelia's eyes searched the dance floor. She quickly spotted Emma Fairweather. Not surprisingly the viscount was by her side, his attention keenly fixed on the golden-haired beauty. With effort, Amelia suppressed a sigh.

"He's nosing around the wrong bitch this time," Mr. Bascomb said in a lewd voice. "Some might call Longley the ultimate lover, but he won't get to test his prowess in bed with Mrs. Fairweather, that's for certain."

"Whatever do you mean?" The words were so shocking, Amelia did not even pause to consider the inappropriateness of the subject matter.

"Just what I said. All he wants is to get her on her back, but he'll not be able to poke her, no matter how pretty his face or deep his pockets." Mr. Bascomb snorted most unpleasantly. "Poor bastard. I almost pity him."

"*You* pity the viscount?" Amelia asked.

"A bit. It can be lowering to a man to be rejected by a lady he fancies." Mr. Bascomb cleared his throat. "Mind you, not that I have had any personal experience with that sort of thing. Still, it must sting, even for a man as jaded as the viscount. They say he's utterly ruthless with women, but mark my words, Mrs. Fairweather will put him in his place."

Amelia shook her head in puzzlement, not believing she was hearing Mr. Bascomb correctly. "Mrs. Fairweather seems very taken with the viscount."

"It's all an act," Mr. Bascomb declared.

"An act? How could you possibly know such a thing?"

"I know Mr. Fairweather," Mr. Bascomb replied smugly. "He's a smart businessman who works hard for his coin. He doesn't have the time nor the inclination to squire his wife all over London. Besides, he can't stand these aristocrats. She's only carrying on with the viscount, hoping word of this flirtation reaches her husband's ears."

"Why would a married woman wish her husband to learn of her relationship with another man?" Amelia asked.

"She wants to make him jealous and hopes if he knows there are others sniffing after her he'll come to London. 'Tis a stupid idea. The kind of logic that only a woman would devise." Mr. Bascomb's dark eyes hardened. "Make no mistake, if that were my wife carrying on so I'd come and haul her back home so fast her head would spin. 'Course what a woman like that really needs is a few stiff strokes of the birch to keep her under control."

Amelia struggled not to shudder. His implication was clear and she had no doubt in her mind he would carry out such a punishment on his own wife. It hardened her resolve never to be that poor creature.

It also gave her hope that he would cry off from a union between them if he thought she was involved with another man. Especially if that man were Viscount Longley.

Amelia's searching eyes soon found Belinda and Charlotte. The silent plea for rescuing she flashed was hardly necessary. The two women swooped down upon her like a pair of avenging angels. Greetings and pleasantries were exchanged. Amelia marveled at how they managed to be civil to Mr. Bascomb, who was just short of being openly rude.

"The music is so lovely." Belinda sighed softly. "How very disappointing that I have yet to engage in a single country dance this evening."

All three women turned toward the only male in their midst. Even Mr. Bascomb was not lackwitted enough to miss the obvious.

"I would be honored to partner you, Lady Gooding."

"You are too gallant, sir."

He bowed awkwardly, then offered his arm to Belinda. Amelia caught Belinda's eye just before the unlikely couple strolled onto the dance floor. She mouthed a silent, grateful thank you to her friend.

Amelia and Charlotte withdrew to an unoccupied corner of the room where they would not be overheard. "Was it yet another random selection to decide which one of you would be stuck luring Mr. Bascomb away?" Amelia asked.

"Naturally." Charlotte smiled. "This time we drew cards. Belinda lost."

Amelia grimaced. "She is a loyal friend."

"She cares about you, as do I." Charlotte spoke in a guarded tone. "I saw you dancing with Longley. What happened?"

"He was charming and flattering, but that hardly makes me unique among the women that crossed his path. I am very uncertain if I can steal his interest away from Mrs. Fairweather."

"You are being too honest," Charlotte said in a scolding tone.

"Honest?" Amelia rolled her eyes expressively. "I am trying to lure a man I barely know into an intimate encounter so that I may cause a monumental scandal. There is nothing honorable or honest in that action."

"There is nothing dishonorable or shameful either," Charlotte said. "You are both unattached—"

"You are conveniently forgetting about Mrs. Fairweather," Amelia corrected instantly.

"You are foolishly forgetting about *Mr.* Fairweather," Charlotte said pointedly. "Emma Fairweather is the only adulteress in this equation. However, if you find the task of seducing the viscount too daunting, then you must look beyond it. It is not necessary to actually have relations with the man. 'Tis not as if you were planning on having Mr. Bascomb sit on the edge of the bed and watch you fornicate."

"He would probably enjoy it," Amelia said grimly.

Charlotte's eyes widened. She began to speak,

sputtered, then stopped. Amelia smiled. There was a smug sense of satisfaction in finally being able to shock the free-speaking Charlotte.

"Amelia," she said in a crisp voice, "the point I have been trying to make is that even the appearance of an affair with the viscount will suffice. If he is spending his nights in Mrs. Fairweather's chamber, then you should spend part of yours in his vacant bed.

"If you are seen leaving the viscount's bedchamber in the early morning hours the scandal will be born. A servant will do, but if we could arrange for you to be seen by another guest that would be even better."

"What if he were confronted? By Roger or Mr. Bascomb? Would the viscount not deny that we had been together?"

"He is a peer and a gentleman. He will deny the relationship publicly even if you are intimate. But privately?" Charlotte shrugged her shoulders. " 'Tis said that men are even bigger gossips than women. And few men would willingly contradict their virility when bragging with their peers. His reputation as the ultimate lover would only rise by adding you to the total number of his conquests."

Charlotte's argument made sense. Though Mr. Bascomb had claimed otherwise, Amelia doubted the viscount would settle for anything less than Mrs. Fairweather in his bed. Which left Amelia with far fewer options.

"I shall consider your suggestion carefully," Amelia said finally.

She watched intently the remainder of the evening, but there were no further opportunities to be alone, or even dance with the viscount. Feeling weary, Amelia went in search of her bedchamber. Yet as she took to her bed in the early morning hours, Charlotte's suggestion of settling on appearing to be the viscount's lover held firm in the back of her mind.

CHAPTER FIVE

Gareth awoke as the first streaks of morning light began to creep into his room, an unusually early time for him. Sprawled out on his stomach, he opened his eyes and stared absently at the smooth sheet and empty space beside him. Another unusual occurrence. More often than not he woke to the sight of a female companion, warm, soft, and naked, eagerly awaiting his pleasure.

Closing his eyes, Gareth slumped deeper into the mattress, trying to ignore his arousal. What was going wrong? Why was he alone and in such a state of unfulfillment?

The viscount sighed and rolled on his back as confusion consumed him. Though his legendary success with women was somewhat inflated, there was also great truth in the gossip. There had never before been a woman he set in his sights that he did not ultimately win.

Emma Fairweather was the single exception to that fact. Throughout the Season he had misjudged the best way to handle her, had failed to unlock the secret that would bring her into his bed. Was this extended house party going to yield more of the same negative results?

Gareth groaned out loud at the very idea. He had never chased a woman this hard and this long without success. Yet his failure was feeding the drive to continue and win. It was almost as if his need for victory was now almost greater than his specific desire for Mrs. Fairweather. Emma.

She had given him leave to call her by her first name a few weeks ago. A petty, hollow advance. Why, it had only taken a few hours for the Dowager Countess of Monford to afford him that same intimacy.

Amelia. Gareth rolled the name around on his tongue, his thoughts focusing on the woman. He decided he liked her. It was something he rarely even considered feeling for a woman. Initially she seemed rather meek and mild-mannered, but he sensed there must be an inner core of strength inside her. Clearly her marriage had been an unhappy one, yet she had survived and moved beyond it.

If he were not so overpowered by his need for Emma he might even consider a flirtation with the countess. At first he thought her rather plain, but after their dance last evening he realized she had several exceptional features, particularly her expressive hazel eyes and flawless ivory skin.

Realizing that the direction of his thoughts was not aiding his present state of arousal, Gareth threw back the covers and left his empty bed. The viscount rang the servant cord in his room, instructing the footman who answered to rouse his valet.

Forty-five minutes later, freshly shaved and elegantly dressed, Gareth left his bedchamber. Last night the lovely Emma had hinted that she often breakfasted at an unfashionably early hour. Perhaps that was her way of letting him know this was the perfect opportunity for them to be alone?

The viscount met many servants, but no other guests as he navigated the many twists and turns of the large house. He stepped eagerly into the dining room and noted the sideboard had already been laid with silver chaffing dishes. Even covered, the tantalizing aroma of the various foods escaped and drifted about the room.

As he expected, Gareth encountered more servants in the room, eager to assist the duke's guests. He waved them away, for his attention had already been captured by something far more delectable than the food. On the far side of the room, seated at the impossibly long mahogany dining table was another guest. A lady.

There was a familiarity about her that set his blood to pumping. Thanks to the distance and angle of her head, he could not discern the exact set of her features. He started toward her, but as he drew closer the light of expectation in his eyes died.

"Good morning, Gareth. I am surprised to see you up and about. I thought I was the only one who enjoyed the quiet and stillness of the morning."

"Hello, Amelia." Tempering the edge of his disappointment, Gareth seated himself beside the dowager countess. He noticed she was dressed for riding, in a golden hued ensemble that flattered her complexion. "Have you brought along one of your mounts?"

"To breakfast?" She blushed, almost as though she were astonished by her bold quip. "Forgive my jest. The answer to your question, is no, I did not bring along one of my horses. It was a three-day journey here from my home. Only eager young gentlemen ride such great distances on horseback. Creaky dowagers like myself must ride in large, comfortable coaches when traveling."

Amusement lifted the corner of his mouth. "I see you still have not forgotten that passing remark concerning my grandmother."

"Not a single word of it. I might be advanced in years, but I do have an excellent memory." She laughed. "The duke has been kind enough to put his stables at the disposal of all his guests. If you were properly attired I would invite you to join me after you have eaten your breakfast."

The viscount raised his china cup to his lips and sipped his hot coffee. She was allowing him the perfect opportunity to take his leave politely, but for some strange reason Gareth did not seize upon it.

"Unlike a woman, a man can quickly change his garments." He chewed and swallowed a second slice of toasted bread. "I shall meet you at the stables in twenty minutes."

"I will only wait for twenty minutes." Amelia's smile deepened. "In order to force you to live up to your boastful promises."

Gareth leaned over confidently and whispered

in her ear. "Be forewarned, I never boast what I cannot deliver."

He expected her eyes to widen with surprise or perhaps even expectation, but her gaze remained steady and focused. "I sincerely believe you."

He watched her graceful strides carry her from the room. Deciding he might need the sustenance, Gareth quickly ate some cheese and downed a second cup of coffee. The change of garments into suitable riding attire was accomplished in record time. He fortunately located a secondary stair down to the ground floor, so he arrived at the stables with a few minutes to spare. The stable boys were as accommodating as all the other servants of the house and rushed forward to assist him in selecting a horse.

Amelia was a fetching sight, mounted atop a chestnut mare. She waited with a patient expression, though Gareth knew that would have changed had he not arrived on time. He soon joined her, riding a sturdy gray hunter. After confirming the direction with one of the grooms, the viscount led the way out.

In his explorations of the estate yesterday he had learned of a folly. Well hidden and private, it was a solid structure that was not open but had a proper door and windows. He had not yet examined the interior. The views of the ornamental lake and formal gardens were reputed to be glorious from inside, but Gareth was more interested in the seclusion and privacy this spot offered.

It could be the perfect location for a rendezvous with Emma. The quiet of the morning was an excellent time to investigate, and Amelia would provide pleasant, amusing company.

They followed the bridle path at a comfortable pace. As soon as the path widened, Gareth drew alongside the countess. When so moved, Gareth made a comment to which Amelia readily responded. Though limited, the conversation between them flowed easily and naturally.

He was pleased the matching bonnet set at a jaunty angle upon her head did not disrupt his view of her features. Gareth enjoyed watching her face glisten in the sunshine, her expressions varying from thoughtful, to amused, to delighted.

Eventually the path ended, the trees giving way to a narrow field.

"Are you game?" she asked with a questioning smile.

"I make no allowances for the weaker sex," he answered. "And I always race to win."

"I would expect no less." She shot him a challenging glance, then took off.

The unexpected start gave her the initial advantage, but Gareth was soon in hot pursuit. They thundered through the meadow, separated by only a few furlongs, with Amelia in the lead. He admired her skill with the reins, her instinct to win. She kept her head low, her knees tightly hugging the mare's sides as she pushed the horse faster and faster.

The relentless pounding of the horses' hooves set Gareth's blood rushing. He surrendered gleefully to the sensation, completely enjoying the thrill of speed, the excitement of the chase, the challenge of competition.

A forest of mature trees loomed ahead. Gareth knew he only had a few minutes to catch her. He urged his horse on, but the countess still had the advantage. She pulled up at the edge of the trees, and turned her head in his direction. The victorious smile upon her face was unmistakable.

"I would have won if you had not cheated," he declared breathlessly.

"What rot." Her smile widened. The sound of her labored breathing mingled with his and echoed through the air. "You are angered because you lost to a woman and your male sense of self-worth has been compromised. Admit it."

"I admit nothing. Males are larger and stronger and fitter than females. We succeed in *fair* physical challenges because we are better equipped to do so and because we are born with the need to compete at everything. Why else would we relieve ourselves in the snow to see who can shoot the stream the farthest?"

Amelia's eyes widened. For an instant Gareth was not sure which of them was more shocked by his vulgar language. But before he could gather his thoughts to apologize, Amelia spoke.

"Your point is well-made, Gareth. Females are not properly equipped to compete in snow . . . coloring." She steered her mare closer, leaned over, and whispered, "Nor would we ever care to try it."

The trill of a bird broke the moment of silence. Gareth felt the edge of his lips begin to curve upward. This was without question the most bizarre conversation he had ever had with a female, yet there was something so ridiculously appealing about the moment he almost didn't want it to end.

"Have you visited the duke's folly yet?" he inquired.

"No." Something flickered in her eyes. He had a fleeting impression it was anticipation. "I would very much like to see it. I have heard it is rather unique."

Gareth nodded. "I caught a glimpse of it yesterday. Let's see if I can remember where it is located."

Gareth turned his horse onto the path and Amelia meekly followed. They ambled gently through the well-marked path, then came to a narrow turnoff nearly hidden in the underbrush.

They followed it around, with Gareth still in the lead. The quiet stillness of the forest engulfed them, creating a peaceful almost languid mood. The trees gradually thinned to open space and formally laid gardens, which was an amazing sight considering how far they were from the main house.

Gareth halted as they neared the edge of an ornamental lake. Before them stood a stone bridge, arched and narrow, clearly meant only for human traffic. If he remembered correctly the folly stood on the other side of it.

He dismounted, tied the horse's reins to a sturdy tree trunk, then returned to fetch Amelia. She handed him her reins. After securing them to the same tree trunk, Gareth returned.

He reached up, circled his hands about her waist, and assisted her down. He heard a soft gasp and smiled, thinking she felt a heightened sense of awareness, but then her horse shifted and Gareth realized Amelia feared she would fall.

He braced his legs and tightened his grip. She reached the ground safely, but landed against his chest. Heat began to dance beneath his skin, awakening his body. She glanced up and their eyes met briefly. A strange, possessive emotion skittered through him.

"Forgive my clumsiness," she muttered, stepping away.

He extended his arm. She clasped it lightly and they proceeded over the bridge.

"Is that it?" Amelia asked in a surprised tone.

Gareth lifted his chin and gazed ahead. Nestled among the trees was a building, not of classic or traditional design, with a domed center and opened sides, but rather a fully enclosed stone structure that in many ways resembled a country cottage.

"It must be. Though the duke strikes me as the type who would create a Gothic ruin or ancient temple or even the more common tower when creating a folly."

"This is a somewhat eccentric choice."

"A privilege of his age, rank, and wealth." Gareth shrugged. "Of course, as a gift to my mother on her fiftieth birthday, my father had a pyramid folly built."

"Was she pleased?"

"Inordinately." They exchanged amused grins. "My mother has always prided herself on being at the center of the latest trends. These structures are quickly becoming all the rage and are being erected with seeming random abandon about the landscapes of many grand houses. One can hardly visit a country home without eventually tripping over one."

"That should not be a problem in this case," Amelia commented. She tilted her head and gazed about. "I doubt many guests can even find the folly."

The verbalization of that simple truth seemed to charge the atmosphere with an electric current, as it emphasized how completely alone they were. The rising blush of color in Amelia's cheeks let Gareth know she felt it too.

If it were any other woman he would have moved closer, by instinct or habit. But there was something unique and special about the countess that Gareth did not want clouded by a sexual dalliance. Besides, there was Emma to be pursued and presently she required every ounce of his attention.

"At least the cottage is picturesque," the viscount interjected hastily. "The rumor persists that the Earl of Dunmore is constructing a gigantic pineapple building at Dunmore Park."

"A pineapple! Good heavens." She let out a shaky laugh. "Well, that only confirms my original impressions of the earl. Though I have encountered him only intermittently over the years, I never thought him to be a man who possessed an excess of good taste."

"Shall we go inside?" He opened the door before she could answer.

Amelia obediently stepped forward. Gareth had to duck his head to avoid hitting the cross-beam, but once inside he could stand upright without difficulty.

"This is utterly charming," Amelia declared.

The viscount agreed. Though the outside of the building was simple and quaint in design, the inside boasted elaborate, decorative refinements. There were elegant wooden chairs with detailed tapestry cushions, a cozy settee in a pale green velvet that matched the thick carpet covering most of the wooden floor, a bookcase filled with titles, a chess table with ivory carved pieces arranged and ready to play.

The windows were simply adorned with dark green silk curtains, pulled back to emphasize the tranquil view of the lake and artfully arranged gardens surrounding it.

"The flowers in the vases are fresh. This folly must be well used," Gareth commented.

"It seems almost like a place from a fairy tale," Amelia said. She trailed her finger along the edge of a polished table as she walked to the windows. " 'Tis very much like I imagine the French queen's hamlet near Trianon. I read that Marie-Antoinette selected the site of the lakeside village at Versaille herself and often enjoyed playing at being a shepherdess."

"And they say the English aristocracy is odd." Gareth moved to stand behind her. "Trianon is pretty, but I think the duke's cottage has more appeal, more ambiance."

Her head whirled around. "You have seen it? The one in France?"

Gareth nodded. "My grand tour included not only Italy and Greece, but France. Have you ever traveled abroad?"

She pulled a face. "No, though I always longed

to make the journey. My late husband saw no merit in anyone or anything that was not English. Except for fine French brandy."

He looked at her, deeply thoughtful. "Will you marry again?"

"God no!" Her face paled. "My brother-in-law, Roger, has other ideas, but I shall not heed them. I am entitled to live at Dower House on the family estate and once the repairs are completed will happily take up residence. It will provide me with the peace and independence I have earned."

He sensed there was more to the story than she was reluctant to reveal, but would not press her.

"What of you, Gareth. Will you marry soon?"

His jaw dropped. "Marry?" he repeated in a bemused tone. "I had not thought . . . what I mean to say, is that there is no expectation—" He paused, took a deep breath, and marshaled his thoughts. "I am a second son. There is no need for my prodigy."

"Children are not the only reason to wed," she said airily.

Gareth sighed and tried to put his objections into words that would not make him appear like a total bounder. "Marriage is not a state I find myself eager to embrace. Perhaps when I am older, more settled, the notion of home and hearth and one woman will have greater appeal."

"Your tone might be sincere, but I am not convinced, sir." She raised her head to look at him and he saw the sparkle of laughter in her eyes. "Just speaking of marrying makes you look as though you have swallowed a lemon."

"It feels more like a horse," he confided.

"I understand, even applaud your attitude. Marriage is not necessary to make all right in the world."

"Exactly." He was pleasantly surprised by her reaction, unusual in his experience for a woman. "My older brother will soon select a bride, as is his duty, yet I firmly believe if he chooses wisely he will be content to live within the rules and conventions of the institution."

"You are very different from your brother?"

The viscount nodded vigorously. "Nearly exact opposites. John is everything I am not. Levelheaded, steadfast, responsible. He visits all the minor and major properties each year, which is no small feat, while I have not stepped foot on my own inheritance in years. The ducal title would be in dire straits if circumstances were to somehow make me the heir."

She looked at him with a slight frown. "You exaggerate the differences by saying that your older brother is everything you are not. Yet, I think you are wrong. He is everything you choose not to be. There is a vast difference."

He paused for a moment to consider her words. "I cannot ever imagine myself making a success of heading the family."

"Your reputation suggests you are a master of all vices, but in our short acquaintance I have learned that you are neither spineless nor a dullard. If you set your mind to doing something competently, then it would be accomplished."

Gareth froze to stare at her. For almost all of his life the expectation had been for him to be a wastrel, a rogue, a man who indulged his every whim.

He had embraced that role with wholehearted enthusiasm, yet there were rare instances when he pondered if he was even fit or capable of another kind of life.

"Only one other person has ever expressed such confidence in my abilities to succeed," he admitted.

"Who?"

"I hesitate to say." Gareth flashed a wicked grin.

Her hazel eyes darkened first with understanding, then with merriment. "Your grandmother?"

"The very same."

She burst into laughter, her head falling forward. It landed squarely against his chest, sending a warm shiver of delight shooting up his spine. Without thinking, Gareth encircled her in his arms. When she tilted her head, no doubt in surprise, he kissed her, full on the lips.

It was a quick joining, with no overt sexual intent, but the sudden pressure of her cool, firm lips shook him. For an instant Gareth wanted to let the wave of passion he felt flow through them, but he resisted.

This was possibly the most interesting situation he had ever found himself in when alone with a lovely woman. Every rakish instinct within him screamed for him to begin an all-out seductive assault, yet a part of him demanded that he hold back.

He broke the contact and stepped back, staring at her in disbelief. Their eyes held for what seemed far too long. With effort, he conquered the urge to reach for her again. Amelia made no move toward him, indeed she made no movement at all, though he sensed she wanted to say or do something. Unfortunately the viscount was too rattled by his own reaction to try and determine what that might be.

They left the folly in silence. Gareth studied her openly as they rode back to the house, regretting, yet not regretting the kiss. At this juncture he felt it would have been unwise to change the tenor of their relationship. It was blossoming into a rare friendship, something Gareth thought far more valuable and lasting than a few weeks of spirited bedsport.

An ironic smile flickered over the viscount's mouth. He had no idea that being noble could be so damn difficult.

Amelia drew the reins and paused at the divide in the well-worn path, biting her lower lip as she considered which road to take. The woods were hushed and silent this afternoon, a reminder that she was very much alone. She had successfully broken away from the party of guests that had set out for a spirited ride about the property as soon as she realized that Roger was among the group, but there was a purpose to her solo journey other than just avoiding her odious brother-in-law.

The viscount was also a member of that riding party. He, too, had disappeared, just before she made her escape, and Amelia had a suspicion he had come this way, for it was in the general direction of the folly. Besides, on their previous visit he had as much as told her he would be returning.

On one level she was well pleased with the subtle, fundamental way that things had changed between them over the past few days. She knew she did not possess the sexual attraction to peak his interest, so instead had concentrated on becoming his friend.

It had been a successful strategy. While he still openly pursued Mrs. Fairweather, with limited success, Gareth now also made a point of spending time with Amelia. It pleased her no end, while at the same time infuriating both Roger and Mr. Bascomb.

To Amelia's way of thinking, that was real progress. Initially she had been tongue-tied and nervous when near the rakish viscount, especially when considering that the underlying motivation for advancing the relationship was to become his lover. She had solved that problem in a rather clever fashion by using dear Charlotte as her inspiration.

Whenever she was stuck searching for the appropriate attitude or phrase, Amelia tried to imagine how Charlotte would react. That notion had carried her through the first few encounters with the viscount, but the technique was needed less and less as time progressed, for it had somehow freed the spirited part of Amelia's own nature that had been systematically crushed for years as George's wife.

It was a warm and slightly breezy afternoon and Amelia knew she could not let her horse stand too long in the warm sunshine. Selecting the path she thought would lead to the folly, she steered the mount down the road, paying careful attention to the hanging branches and menacing tree roots that appeared on the path. This was hardly the place to have her horse come up lame, since it was so secluded and far away from the main house.

Soon the sound of lapping water let Amelia know she had chosen the right direction. She sighed with delight when the ornamental lake and formal gardens came into view, but somehow took a wrong turn and was unable to find the narrow bridge that led to the folly.

After several failed attempts Amelia found herself approaching the sturdy cottage from the opposite side. This vantage point afforded her a clear view of the inside of the building through the large windows. As best she could tell it was empty.

Good. It would appear more coincidental if she was alone when Gareth arrived. Amelia imagined herself settled casually on that lovely settee, perhaps with a volume of Shakespeare in her hand. Hopefully the intimate, familiar scene would give her the courage to push things between them beyond a mere kiss.

Fraught with nerves and a tingling excitement, Amelia approached the cottage. The moment she opened the door she realized her initial assessment was incorrect. The cottage was not empty.

Two individuals were seated on the settee. *Her* settee. One male, one female. Actually only the male was seated, the female was perched upon his lap. Though their backs were toward her it was clear from their entwined positions that they were kissing and caressing each other. Rather heatedly.

Amelia hesitated as a dreamlike feeling of unreality settled over her. There were moans and muttering as the couple shifted. The female's pelisse was open down to her waist, the man's hand was inside the garment, resting on her breasts, his fingers thumbing the bare nipples.

Though Amelia swore she stood as still as a statue she must have made a movement or a noise, for the gentleman suddenly raised his head, startled by the interruption.

Amelia's eyes met Gareth's. Her breath caught in her throat as she realized she had never understood the meaning of embarrassment until that very moment. It hit her full force, like someone slamming a fist into her stomach.

Panic engulfed her and Amelia's first instinct was to turn and run, to hide from the reality of truth. But she did not. Instead she stared boldly at the couple, almost as though she were daring them to continue.

Emma Fairweather's eyes widened in shock. She looked, Amelia thought, like a frightened rabbit facing a hunter's snare. With one hand held to her gaping bodice, Mrs. Fairweather jumped off the viscount's lap. She hastily adjusted her clothing, then moved forward.

It took a few seconds for Amelia to realize she was blocking the only exit. Wordlessly she stepped aside. After a final desperate glance in her direction, Emma Fairweather bolted out the door.

The silent stillness of the room surrounded the two remaining inhabitants. Though it took more courage than she feared she possessed, Amelia raised her chin and met Gareth's eyes.

Half lidded and smirking, the blue orbs revealed only amusement. "Mrs. Fairweather's sudden departure leaves me in quite a predicament," he announced in a deep, calm voice.

Amelia's eyes shifted downward. Gareth flexed his shoulders, and leaned back against the settee, doing nothing to hide the telltale bulge of his aroused sex.

Her eyes narrowed. "I believe your current state of excitement is merely a reflection of your usual, natural condition."

He gave her a sultry grin. "If I tried walking around with this between my legs I would never move more than ten paces." The light of expectation in his eyes sent a shiver coursing through her. "Since you have so inconsiderately deprived me of my afternoon's sport, perhaps you should take Mrs. Fairweather's place?"

"Perhaps I should." Her senses leapt. But then doubts struck her, serious and prideful, too strong to be ignored. "However, you will have to ask me with far more charm and enthusiasm than you are exhibiting at the moment."

Tension built slowly in her chest, making her knees feel weak, but Amelia somehow found the strength to turn on her heel and walk away.

CHAPTER SIX

As the guests gathered to await the start of the evening's musical interlude, the sultry sound of feminine laughter echoed through the high-domed conservatory. That tingling noise drew several interested gazes toward the source, some shifting completely in their seats to catch a glimpse. Amelia, however, did not bother to turn her head. She knew well the owner of that laugh and the individual who had brought it forth.

Mrs. Fairweather and the Viscount of Longley.

Three days had passed since Amelia had interrupted their illicit meeting at the folly. Nothing further had been spoken about the incident by any of them. In many ways it was as though it had never occurred. Yet the nature of Amelia's relationship with the viscount had changed dramatically.

He no longer arrived early at the breakfast table, no longer sought her out for a few moments of private, amusing conversation, no longer teased or flirted or made her feel they had a special, unique bond. All the progress she had made had vanished in an instant, for such was the fickle heart and temperament of a rogue.

Time was running short. Eight days were already gone, in another six the house party would end and the guests would go their separate ways. Mr. Bascomb was pressing her, Roger was pressing her. They expected an announcement of an upcoming marriage before the week ended. Amelia was growing desperate.

So, it appeared, was the viscount. His pursuit of Mrs. Fairweather was the talk of the house party, his open regard for the pretty blonde a source of gossip and amusement and speculation. Time and again Amelia told herself she was being foolish for feeling such jealousy, such disappointment.

Another twinkling laugh had Amelia lifting her chin to gaze at the pair. She saw Mrs. Fairweather shift in her chair, tilt her head playfully, and smile broadly up at the viscount. A light blush had risen to her cheeks and her breathing was no longer steady.

The viscount's eyes flared, turning stormy. He lifted his gloved hand and delicately traced the side of her neck. Amelia sighed as she caught the look that passed between them. There was little doubt as to where Gareth would be spending his night. In Emma Fairweather's bed.

Though she was far from happy with the unfortunate turn of events, Amelia knew she had no one to blame but herself. Her chance had come and gone that fateful afternoon at the folly and she had not had the courage to grasp it.

Yet she would not admit defeat. Over and over, Amelia's thoughts returned to Charlotte's words—she need only appear to be his lover, his conquest, to create the scandal that would make Mr. Bascomb cry off from the idea of marriage.

Amelia had been mulling the notion over for days. It had taken some time to accustom her mind to the idea, but in the end Amelia knew she must be practical. If the viscount was not going to be using his bedchamber this evening, she might as well spend her time there. And then be seen by at least one other member of the house party leaving that same bedchamber in the morning.

"You seem very pensive this evening, Amelia." Charlotte, looking very handsome in a daring gown of red watered silk took the empty chair beside her. "Is there anything I can do to help?"

"Yes." Amelia snapped her fan shut and placed it in her lap. "Would you have your maid slip a note, along with a coin to the viscount's valet tonight?"

Charlotte's lips tightened. "I need not ask which viscount, do I?"

" 'Tis Longley, of course." Amelia schooled her face into blankness. "I have lost any chance I might have had with him, so I must be sensible. Time grows short. I shall take your advice and create the illusion of being intimate with him."

"I would pay good money for someone to explain precisely what he sees in Mrs. Fairweather," Charlotte said. "Her conversation is not particularly interesting, she can barely sit a horse without sliding off, and her looks are passable, but hardly unique. Despite his reputation for chasing skirts, I had thought better of the viscount. He is a charming young man. I cannot for the life of me understand why he must think with his—"

"Charlotte!" Amelia hissed.

The militant gleam in Charlotte's eyes softened. "I'm sorry. I know you are not the type to make decisions lightly. Are you very sure this is what you want to do?"

Amelia gritted her teeth as another of Mrs. Fairweather's giggles filled the room. "Yes, I am very certain this is the right course of action."

Amelia had little awareness of the events of the rest of the evening after that moment. At one point, between the violin solo and the harp melody, Charlotte leaned over and whispered simply, "It is all arranged."

"Were there any difficulties?" Amelia asked.

"None." Charlotte crossed her arms tightly. "The note, written in my hand, requesting that his lordship's valet vacate the viscount's bedchamber until morning, has just been delivered, along with appropriate compensation. I can only surmise from the ease with which the exchange took place that this was hardly the first time it had occurred."

Amelia snorted. "I shall leave the moment the performance concludes. If Roger or Mr. Bascomb asks, tell them I have retired for the night. With a headache."

"Gladly."

Once in her room, Amelia's maid, Mildred, helped her undress, then don an ivory silk nightgown. It was simple in design, with a low-cut neckline that exposed the tops of her breasts, and delicate lace trimming on the sleeves and hem. Its purpose was clearly meant to tempt a man.

Amelia had never worn the garment before, but decided it was the perfect apparel for an illicit rendezvous. At least she hoped that would be the impression she gave when seen leaving the viscount's bedchamber in the morning.

She dismissed Mildred, who was obviously curious about her choice of evening clothes, but made no remark. Once alone, Amelia sat in front of her dressing table rhythmically brushing her hair. When she finished, she picked up a matching silk ribbon to tie it back, then caught a glimpse of her reflection in the mirror.

She looked almost wanton, with her hair spilling about her face and the lovely silk of the nightgown clinging to her womanly curves. Though there would be no man to admire her lush sensuality she decided to leave her hair unbound, the curling strands hanging down her back to her waist.

Now all that was left to do was wait. Feeling the nerves of a virgin bride on her wedding night, Amelia listened to the tick of the clock on the mantelpiece for a full half hour. Then she began the long walk to the opposite wing of the house. She encountered no one, not even a servant, for it was barely ten and they were all still below stairs attending to the needs of the other guests.

Amelia knew well which bedchamber Gareth had been given, for she had casually and deliberately walked past it many times these last few days. Her hand hesitated for an instant as it hovered above the door handle. What if the valet had not yet left?

Amelia's nerves flared as she considered the possible mishaps, the potential for embarrassing misunderstandings. Taking a fortifying breath, she wiped her damp palms against the cool silk of her nightgown, then with a firm, resolute grasp turned the latch and entered.

The room felt warm. It was lit by several candles, each casting a warm, yellow glow about the chamber. The shadows danced about the room in mock warning, seeming to know she was an intruder. Amelia ignored her fanciful imaginings, crossed to the windows, drew back the heavy curtains, and opened the window. She lifted her face to the incoming breeze, savoring the sweet, clean smell of the night.

Amelia stood there for several long minutes, calming her beating pulse and wryly reflecting on the circumstances that had brought her to this room at this point in time.

'Tis only for a few hours. Surely I can endure that in order to gain my independence. She turned from the window and examined the chamber, trying to decide how best to be comfortable while she waited. She gave the large four-poster bed only a cursory glance, ruling that out instantly as a place to rest.

There were too many candles lit also. She picked up the one nearest and held it aloft as she extinguished the others. As she crossed back toward the windows to settle herself on the upholstered chair, she noticed a linen band laid carelessly on a small table.

Gareth's cravat. His valet must not have achieved perfection the first time when dressing the viscount this evening, so a second cloth had been used.

Unable to resist, her fingers reached out and snatched the garment. She crushed the fabric to her chest and inhaled the scent that was so uniquely his.

It brought on a shudder she could not control. If only things had worked out differently she might be here with Gareth. In that lovely bed.

Still clutching the cravat to her chest, Amelia assumed her seat, curled her feet beneath her, and lolled her head against the cushion.

It was going to be a long, lonely night.

Mrs. Fairweather was indisposed. She had sighed most prettily and lamented this dreadful state of affairs with an attitude that seemed genuine. Yet Gareth was uncertain. Her apologies and excuses were always sincere, but he still spent his nights alone. Truth be told he had missed his chance to have her thrashing beneath him three days ago.

Or rather his perfect opportunity had been interrupted by the cavalier countess, Amelia. He was surprised at the time of the interruption that he had felt only mild anger and very little regret. True, it had been disappointing to see Emma run off like a scared fawn, but it had been even more interesting to see Amelia's reactions to the unfolding events.

With wicked thoughts filling his mind he had flashed her a devilish, seductive grin, had issued a blatantly sexual invitation. For a moment, just a moment, Gareth thought he had seen real temptation in Amelia's eyes. But she had not taken the bait. Pity.

The clock struck midnight, reminding the viscount he had yet to solve his current problem. Gareth stood on the third-floor landing, riddled with indecision. He glanced down the hall to where his room was located some distance away. It was far too early to go to bed, especially if one was alone.

In Gareth's mind there was nothing worse than lying in bed, weary and frustrated and unable to sleep. He turned to walk down the staircase, intending to join the gentlemen at the billiards table, then paused. It was no secret he had been pursuing Mrs. Fairweather. And no secret that he had been less than successful.

If he entered the billiard or card room at this hour of the evening he would be announcing his failure to all. Again. Not a pleasant thought.

A board in the hallway creaked as he made his way down the deserted corridor. Gareth turned the knob and walked into his bedchamber.

A pool of flickering candlelight illuminated a section of the chamber, but that glow was extinguished the moment he shut the door behind him.

"Richards? Richards?"

The valet did not answer. Odd, the servant always waited up for him, no matter how late, or early the hour. Moonlight slanted through the open window, casting enough light so Gareth could move about the room without knocking into the furniture. With only minor difficulty he located the bell cord and tugged it impatiently to summon his valet.

His hands searched the table near his bed blindly, but he could not locate a flint to relight a candle. Due to the warmth of the night, no fire burned in the grate.

Brimming with impatience, the viscount sat in a chair to wait. A strange sound drew his attention to the floor-length drapes. For a second he thought he saw something move, a female figure, shrouded in the shadows.

"Hello? Is anyone there?"

Gareth's call received no answer. He blinked, then started forward to investigate, but his toe caught on the edge of the heavy wooden bed frame.

"Hell and damnation!" The pain shot up his calf, sharp and stinging. Gareth hobbled onto the bed, cursing loudly with each step. He removed his shoe, which had offered little protection, and rubbed the injured toe gingerly, hoping to alleviate some of the sting.

Though his attention was centered wholly on the pain in his foot, Gareth's neck suddenly began to prickle with awareness. Someone else *was* in the room with him. Before he could leap from the bed to verify his suspicions, something came across his eyes, shutting him in complete darkness.

He reacted instinctively, grabbing at his face, pulling at the material that had now been drawn tight across his eyes, effectively blinding him. Gareth tried to stand, but the softness of the mattress and his aching foot made him clumsy, awkward. He listed to the right, with arms flaying wildly as he tried desperately to regain his balance.

Then he felt the caress of warm breath against his ear.

"I had thought to surprise you, my lord," a sultry

female voice whispered. "Unless you object to my little game?"

Gareth stilled, then lifted his chin. "Emma? What are you doing? I left you not ten minutes ago. How did you get here so quickly without my seeing you?"

There was no immediate answer. Instead a warm, lush female body climbed boldly into his lap. The viscount reached again to remove the covering from his eyes, but the woman's hands closed over his wrists.

"I had hoped you would want to play, my lord. Will you not reconsider? I promise to make the night well worth it."

When she spoke this time her voice was muffled against his throat. She pressed a soft kiss against the starched linen of his cravat, then ran her fingers lightly across his chest. Gareth's mind froze. There was something not quite right about this situation, but he had no time to dwell on his doubts.

"If it pleases you, I will leave my blindfold intact. He set his hands firmly on her waist and drew her close to him. "For the moment."

"I salute your daring," came the breathy reply.

Gareth lifted his face and waited expectantly, filled with an intense craving to feel her lips against his own. Being deprived of his sight heightened Gareth's other senses. He could hear her breath become short and rapid, could feel the rise and fall of her chest. In anticipation?

He sensed her face moving closer to his. Their breath mingled and then her lips fused with his. He welcomed her with his lips and tongue, teasing and tempting her desire.

She moved her body, wriggling excitedly in his

lap. Gareth smiled and deepened the contact. Of their own accord, his hands began to explore the unknown territory of her body. Time slowed as his questing fingers roamed.

He soon discovered she was wearing a nightgown. A silky, sensual garment that hid none of her charms, for she was deliciously naked beneath it. As his fingers stroked, he almost could not tell where the garment ended and her flesh began, for it was the softest skin he had ever touched, smooth and fine as the material.

It was only when he felt the warm heat beneath his fingers did he realize he was brushing her bare skin. Excitedly he ran his hands along her collarbone, then lower, lower, until he found what he sought. A plump, round breast. He cupped it lovingly, fingers caressing the sweet roundness. Her nipples puckered tightly as her gasp shivered through the room.

"Stop."

She reached out and held his arm. He frowned in puzzlement. "Do you not enjoy my touch, fair lady?"

" 'Tis I who wish to pleasure you, my lord," she declared huskily. "Lie back and allow me my fun."

She shoved him, none too gently, and he fell against the mattress. She sidled up beside him, pressing herself wantonly against his chest, stomach, and upper thighs. The tip of her tongue laved a sensitive spot behind his earlobe as her questing fingers worked steadily on loosening his garments.

She managed to untie the cravat and pull it free. "Arch your back," she whispered throatily.

He obeyed her command and she easily stripped

off his coat, waistcoat, and shirt. Her fingers next busied themselves with the buttons of his trousers. This time he did not wait to be instructed, but lifted his hips off the bed so she could peel the breeches from him.

Gareth gave an audible sigh of relief as his aroused cock sprang free. He imagined her staring at him, enjoying the sight of his erection. It made him feel wickedly powerful. He reached down and stroked himself, smiling when he heard her sharp intake of breath.

The mattress shifted and he realized she now knelt beside him. She caught his hand, as he intended, and moved it to her shoulder. Her head lowered and she wetly kissed his chest, his throat, his chin.

Gareth's nose detected the faint scent of roses. He opened his lips and slipped his tongue out, capturing his partner's mouth in an ardent kiss. She responded willingly, returning the pressure with equal measure, arching her body as his hand caressed the length of her spine.

He touched her gently, tracing the contours of her form with deft precision, feeling each curve, creating the picture in his mind that his hand revealed. A brief smile lit the viscount's face and a flash of immense satisfaction invaded. The mystery had been solved. It was not Emma Fairweather he held in his arms, but Amelia.

Amelia swung her leg across Gareth's body, straddling his middle. Her heart was beating so fast and so loudly it almost hurt her ears, but she ignored her feelings of fright and concentrated instead on the desire and passion coursing through her entire being.

She had panicked utterly when the door to the viscount's room had opened and he walked inside. Fumbling, she had blown out the lone lit candle and hid behind the window curtains, uncertain of what she would do. Initially she had hoped he had returned to his bedchamber because he needed or had forgotten something. He would find whatever it was he sought and then leave.

But the viscount had bellowed for his servant, stumbled, cursed, and fallen to the bed. It was at that moment that a rush of pure madness seized Amelia and she acted upon it. The blindfold was an inspired choice. Though she desired him greatly, she felt too shy, too uncertain to play the wanton a man of his experience would crave.

But the anonymity of the blindfold gave her a sensual advantage. It let her take control, be in charge. Something that had rarely happened in her life and had never occurred in the bedchamber with a man. It freed her spirit, freed her soul.

She tilted her head and brought their faces together. The scrap of linen that surrounded his eyes did not in any way diminish the handsomeness of his face, the raw male beauty that was him. She blew softly against his cheek, then favored him with a deep kiss, her tongue playing intimately, eagerly with his.

The entire surface of Amelia's skin felt flush and damp. She was aware of the ache that was building in her loins, intensifying each time Gareth's fingers and lips caressed her. Her body strained toward him as her senses were kindled to a new awareness of physical pleasure. She wanted to lure and possess this man who had come to mean so much to her.

Her hand slipped between his thighs. She ran her fingers up and down the shaft of his sex, brushing the silken skin that was stretched so taut. His hips bucked upward.

"Temptress," he growled.

She laughed with powerful delight. He made her feel as no other man had ever done. Powerful, strong, desirable. Amelia squinted in the darkness. The streak of moonlight that invaded the chamber illuminated the subtle details of his form. She took her time admiring him. The strong muscles of his chest and forearms were shaded by dark hair that felt wonderfully crisp beneath her searching palms.

His shoulders were broad, his chest wide, his waist and hips narrow. His legs were long. Both his thighs and calves had swells of muscles. The trail of dark hair that began at his navel ended in a nest of curls where his fully aroused penis jutted forward. That gloriously aroused body sent her senses spinning.

She returned her hand to his sex, running her fingers around and over the head, sensually rubbing the glistening drop of moisture that appeared back into his hot flesh. Tempted beyond bearing, she moved her head lower. He was beautiful. She had never seen her husband naked, a circumstance for which she was profoundly grateful.

But the sight of Gareth's bare flesh brought forth the notion of pleasure that was too tempting to resist. Perfection such as this should be worshiped, revered. Amelia's lips descended.

"Mother of God!"

His growl startled her. Amelia's head jerked up. "Did I hurt you? Have I done it wrong?"

"Not hurt. Surprised. Delighted." Gareth licked his lips and fought for self-control as he felt her face rest once again against his lower belly. "Use your teeth gently, love. Ahh, like that. Now the tip of your tongue." He groaned louder, the pleasure searing through every inch of his body as she eagerly followed his instructions.

Beneath the blindfold Gareth's eyes closed tightly. He knew this was her fantasy, respected this was her unique way to express her feelings and desire for him. But his self-control was being pushed beyond its endurance.

He sunk his hips low into the mattress as her hands continued to stroke and knead between his thighs, as the wet warmth of her mouth fully engulfed him.

Suddenly his self-control snapped. He reached for her shoulders, grasping the top of her nightgown. With a single pull he ripped it from her body. The action startled her, moving her mouth away from him. Taking advantage of her momentary disorientation Gareth flipped her over onto her back and flung her into the middle of the bed.

He heaved himself forward, landing precisely where he wished. Her naked breast rose and fell against his chest, her body lay trembling beneath him. "Hush," he whispered. "I will allow you control again soon. But if I do not taste you, love, I shall go mad."

The blindfold, still intact, did not heed his mission. He caught her wrists, then stretched them tautly above her head, anchoring them securely with one hand. She moved her legs restlessly and he realized she felt his erection rigid against her thigh. He released her wrists and shifted his weight, then felt her fingers caress his shoulders, digging tightly into the muscles of his forearms.

"No," he rasped. "Keep your hands high above your head. As if you were tied to the bedpost."

Gareth sensed her hesitation. Then felt her compliance as her body arched forward, awaiting his pleasure. Instinct, desire, and an irresistible primal urge led him to his goal.

His lips trailed slowly down her throat to her breast. He circled, then suckled the nipple. Her body tensed. He waited, then tormented her again with his lips and tongue until she began to squirm and writhe with eager anticipation.

Gareth ran his fingers along the length of her body. Her skin felt hot and dry to the touch. He found her knee, then pushed it gently, parting her thighs. His exploring hand soon found her other leg, and pushed that also.

The musky scent of her arousal enchanted him. With a sensual growl of impatience, Gareth buried his mouth between her legs. He kissed her softly at first, then lightly suckled her swollen flesh. She whimpered as he licked and traced and stroked. Her hips thrashed and surged forward, her cries growing louder, more urgent.

He pressed her knees, keeping her thighs wide, wetting the aching need that he could feel building inside her. A moan escaped her, then she shivered and arched herself against him. He continued to tease the lush opening of her body with the tip of his tongue as she strained and shuddered in ecstasy.

Exhausted, dazed, satiated, Amelia slumped against the pillows. It took several deep breaths to overcome the lethargic state that had overtaken her body. She turned to her side, to study the man who lay beside her.

"Thank you," she whispered in a thick and husky voice. She hugged him tightly, kissing his cheek, the corner of his mouth, the top of his shoulder.

She rubbed her leg against his thigh and realized his body was still in a state of full arousal, strung tight with tension and unreleased desire. Her emotions were engaged, her curiosity was at its zenith, and the opportunity was too perfect to reject.

Amelia rose to her knees. Balancing her hands on his naked chest she moved her legs until she was sitting astride him.

"Ahh, now this is a far better demonstration of your thanks, love," he purred.

"I should like to please you, my lord."

Amelia raised herself higher, moved forward, then slowly, carefully, erotically lowered her body onto his hard, thrusting penis. She sank down, pushing in and out with long easy strokes and felt the tension gripping him increase.

The need to see her face, to look deep into her eyes now bordered on obsession. Hastily Gareth tore the linen from his eyes, but once free of the restraint saw only darkness. The little minx! She had pulled the heavy bed curtains closed, surrounding them in a cocoon of darkness. He could barely see his hand pressed in front of his face, let alone his beautiful, sensual bed partner.

The distraction of darkness however was quickly forgotten as she exhaled slowly, pressing her flanks tighter against his thighs. Gareth gritted his teeth as the slick, sweet heat of her welcoming body surrounded him.

He grasped her hips and stretched his legs out. Experimentally she began pushing in and out with long easy strokes. He soon found her rhythm and matched it, rising to meet her. Each thrust fanned the flame of desire. She was so hot and tight around him.

Her breasts swayed invitingly before him and he took one within his mouth, sucking the nipples savagely. She screamed then and clung to him. He felt her begin to spasm and knew her next climax would soon be reached.

He hoped to last longer, to pleasure her a third time, but it was impossible to hold back. As the wave of tension broke, her body began to contract around him. She shivered and arched her back. Gareth's own body tightened, the heat burning bright, the sensation climbing to an excruciating height.

He plunged deeper. The depth of pleasure that washed through him was unparalleled. With a shout of pure male triumph he drove in the final thrust of release, straining and shuddering in ecstasy.

The sound of their labored breathing slowly began to ease. He stroked her shoulders, the small of her back, then moved his hands down to her hips. Though completely sated, Gareth found it nearly impossible to stop touching her. This possessive act was an unusual occurrence, but was not everything about this magical evening not unusual?

"I have died." Her voice was a breathy proclamation.

Gareth smiled. He knew her legs must be cramping from the awkward position she still held, but he was reluctant to disengage himself from the warmth of her body.

Still, it was bad form to make a lady suffer. He gently eased her forward, then withdrew. Lifting her hips, Gareth slid from beneath her.

His hand snaked across her chest, laying a possessive palm across her left breast. "I still feel the beat of your heart, love, so I must insist that you are very much alive."

She giggled and rolled to face him. Although she could not see his expression in the darkness, she felt that he was smiling back. "I do feel alive, my lord. More than I ever have before. Thanks to you."

"Modesty prevents me from taking all the credit." He reached out and pulled her against him. "You have fulfilled some of my wildest and most erotic fantasies this night, my lady."

"Only some?" Her voice was an erotic whisper that sent a chill racing up his spine. "Then you must fantasize some more and show me your desires."

Gareth heard her sensual laugh echo through the room just before his mouth closed over hers.

CHAPTER SEVEN

The scent of sated lust hung heavily about them. The window remained open, the humid air trapping the aftermath of their lovemaking within the bedchamber. Amelia slowly opened her eyes. Through the window she could see the gray streaks of early morning sky beginning to disappear. Dawn was fast approaching.

Of their own accord her eyelids closed and she snuggled deeper into the soft bedding. She was so tired. Her muscles ached, though in a pleasant fashion, and the place between her thighs contained an abundant amount of wetness. How strange that—

My God! Amelia's eyes flew open. She stared for a moment blank-faced at the man whose head rested on the pillow beside hers. There was a faint line of stubble edging his jaw, his dark hair was rumpled, and his brilliant blue eyes were wide open. Staring directly back at her.

If she was not so mortified and embarrassed, Amelia would have admired how remarkably handsome the viscount looked at this ungodly hour of the morning.

"Is something wrong?" A frown formed on his brow. Amelia squelched the most bizarre impulse to press her lips against his forehead and sooth it away.

"I must leave."

She tried to rise from the bed, but soon discovered his right arm was slung possessively over her lower back. Effectively trapping her.

" 'Tis early." The arm tightened, drawing her closer to him. "We have plenty of time, Amelia. No need to make such a frantic rush as we indulge our pleasures. Unless you prefer it that way?"

Though Gareth asked the question, he gave her no time to answer. He adjusted her position, then kissed her lips softly. His hands began a swooping caress of her throat, shoulder, and breast.

Amelia felt the stirring of desire begin, that sensation of need and want that would soon have her mindless with excitement. She fought it.

"Why are you behaving so calmly? Are you not surprised to find me in your bed?" she asked, lowering her face to avoid his gaze.

The hand cupping her breast stilled. He moved it to her face and tipped her chin so he could gaze into her eyes. "I am honored that you chose to sleep here with me." A twinkling gleam appeared in the depths of his blue eyes. "And proud to say we achieved little sleep last night."

Amelia felt the color burst into her cheeks. She could not indulge in the memories of last night while he gazed so intently at her. It was mortifying. "That is not what I meant. The blindfold, the darkness—"

Gareth placed two fingers over her lips to silence her. "I knew it was you in my bed last night, Amelia. Almost from the first. And the knowledge thrilled me."

Her breath caught in surprise. "How? How did you know?"

He leaned forward and kissed her forehead. "Your intoxicating scent." Kissed her eyelids. "Your sultry voice." Kissed the corner of her mouth. "The splendid curve of your hip."

The languid comfort in his tone and in his kisses began to melt away some of her doubts. "I had not thought you so observant of my person."

"I was always very aware of you, dear countess, especially when you least suspected." He cast her a mysterious grin. "After last night, I would venture to say I know far more about you than any other man alive."

Oh, not everything, my lord. Guilt for the true reason she had come to his bed washed over Amelia. She tried to pull away, but Gareth's arms locked around her, drawing her closer. "I think I need to remind you of my intimate knowledge of your loveliness. And my deep regard for you."

He kissed her soundly, then rolled her expertly on her back. Amelia forced herself to hold his gaze. She could feel his erection pressing into her upper thigh.

She knew he desired her. The proof of that was

rather obviously poking at her. And while it might be considered foolish to trust and believe such a handsome rogue, Amelia admitted his words touched her heart, allowing her to face the fact that she, too, cared for him, perhaps even loved him a little.

Her conscience however demanded that she make some attempt at honesty. "I should return to my bedchamber before anyone sees me."

"The duke's servants are well trained and discreet. They will turn a blind eye to anything they see."

He nuzzled her neck, kissed her jaw, then raised his head to stare into her eyes. There was a trace of boyish delight in his handsome face as he spread her legs with his knees, then slid inside her body.

Amelia caught her breath and he stopped. "Have I hurt you?"

"No." The warm strength of him filled her completely, making a shiver of pure pleasure rush through her blood. " 'Tis a perfect fit."

"For the perfect lady." He raised her hand and kissed it tenderly in a gallant, courtly gesture.

Amelia felt her heart turn over. Emotions swirled and swelled inside her as she twisted and adjusted her hips. She surrendered then completely to the moment, arching her back, pressing herself closer to his heat, his strength, his power.

She understood and accepted that this moment of passion would be their last. It was a bittersweet joining, filled with all the emotions and feelings she knew she could never express in words. It lasted a long time, yet seemed so quick.

As his large body began to shudder with the

power of his release, she tightened her arms around his broad back and held him close. Amazingly her own climax broke at the same instant, creating a rare experience of shared pleasure.

It was a fitting end.

When their ragged breathing finally slowed, Gareth's mouth moved gently over hers. Amelia kissed him back. He eased away and stretched beside her, opening his arms in invitation. Amelia accepted, allowing herself one final moment of bliss.

He caressed her hair, stroked her back and buttocks with slow, lazy circles. Sleep threatened, but Amelia fought it. Gradually the caresses slowed, then ceased. Amelia placed her palm lightly on Gareth's chest. She could feel the muscles expand as he breathed in a steady rhythm. He was asleep.

She dared not linger any longer. Taking great care to make as little movement as possible, Amelia slipped away from the warm protection of his embrace and slid off the bed. She found her nightgown flung in a corner of the bedchamber. It was cleanly torn down the middle and completely useless.

Amelia tossed it aside and searched for something else to wear. She hastily picked up Gareth's discarded shirt and pushed her arms through the sleeves. The white linen enveloped her body, but came only to the top of her knees. The few buttons at the top of the garment were missing and it gaped open in a provocative manner.

She removed it and tried his evening coat. That fell below her knees, but there was a wide rent in the sleeve where it attached to the shoulder. Amelia surmised that damage had occurred when she was eagerly yanking the coat off Gareth last night.

She sighed in frustration. Was there not one garment that had not been ripped, torn, or destroyed? She padded barefoot over to the armoire that stood on the far side of the room and opened it gingerly, trying not to make a sound. Inside she discovered a silk robe in a shade of midnight blue. It was far too large, but she wrapped the belt twice around her waist and pulled tightly.

Satisfied it would stay in place, Amelia moved quietly toward the door. On her way she noticed a rumpled strip of white linen thrown on the rug. It was Gareth's cravat, the one she had used so naughtily as a blindfold.

Without a second thought she scooped it up and shoved it in the pocket of the robe. Then she carefully threw the door latch and eased out of the room. Swift feet carried her to the opposite wing of the large house.

Breathless, Amelia entered her empty bedchamber. She walked soundlessly to the window and threw back the draperies, flooding the room with sunlight.

It was later than she thought. The other guests would soon be stirring and another day of mindless activities would begin. If only—

Amelia gasped as a shocking realization suddenly entered her mind. She had remained unseen by any guest or servant leaving the viscount's bedchamber and on her long walk back to her own room. She covered her face with her hands and groaned loudly.

It appeared that her quest for scandal had gone unanswered.

Gareth awoke to an empty bed. The sight gave him a momentary pang of regret, but then the practical side of his nature asserted itself. Amelia was the type of woman who would not want to flaunt this relationship. It was therefore logical that she would leave before any of the duke's servants or guests saw her.

After careful attention from his valet, the viscount felt ready to face the day. The first person he met upon entering the grand salon was his friend, the Earl of Danbury.

"Lucien, good morning. I have not seen much of you these past few days. I trust you had a good night's sleep?"

"It was most peaceful. And you?"

"Splendid. But I do confess to being famished. Will you join me for some breakfast?"

"It is after noon," the earl replied in a wry voice.

"Ahh, so it is. But surely I am not the only one who slept in today? I imagine the duke's servants have left fresh, hot food in the dining room. Will you take coffee with me?"

"Certainly." The earl's lips twitched. He clasped his hands behind his back and followed Gareth into the dining room. It was empty of other guests. "You seem to be taking everything rather well, Longley. I must confess, I am proud of you."

Gareth, who was in the process of filling a dish with kippers and eggs, glanced up at his friend with a puzzled frown. "For what?"

The earl's brow's lifted in amusement. "Showing your face today. Pretending that all is right and well in the world."

"I have no idea to what you are referring, Lucien."

"Gossip, Longley. The like of which even my jaded ears has never heard."

"About me?"

"Most definitely."

The two men seated themselves at the table. "You know I never listen to gossip, especially when I am the main topic of conversation."

The earl sipped his coffee. "I know that has been your attitude in the past. Yet when a lady is involved, a lady you appear to care for a great deal, I assumed your feelings would be altered."

Gareth slowly lowered his fork. His gut twisted and his raging appetite rapidly disappeared. Through the years all sorts of shameful gossip had made the rounds concerning him and his various women. He always emerged unscathed, but occasionally a female partner's reputation had been brutalized, ripped to shreds by gossiping tongues.

He usually felt a pang of regret, a bit of distress for these hapless females, but had never been moved to do anything about the situation.

Yet the very notion of anyone speaking against Amelia had him ready to draw pistols.

"Exactly what sort of tales are being spread about the countess?" Gareth asked, taking care to keep his face free of expression.

"The countess? Which countess?" The earl speared him with a piercing, perplexed glance. "The lady I am referring to is Mrs. Fairweather."

"Emma? What mischief has befallen her?"

"You really don't know?"

The viscount sighed. "Apparently not."

Lucien grinned widely and the viscount felt a prickle of unease skitter down his spine. "I had honestly felt a twinge of guilt over the matter since it was such good news for me and such devastating news for you. Or so I believed."

"Are you going to tell what has occurred, Lucien, or will you just continue to torture me?"

"Sorry." The earl grinned again. "I have won a tidy sum of money, thanks to you. *Mr.* Fairweather arrived late last night and hauled away his errant wife, who apparently left sobbing pitifully while denying all his adulterous accusations."

Gareth blinked. "So Mr. Fairweather really does exist?"

"Indeed." The earl cocked his head. "Given your dogged pursuit of Mrs. Fairweather the entire Season, I thought this news would distress you."

Gareth leaned back in his chair and considered his emotions carefully. "No, Lucien. It does not bother me in the least." Appetite restored, the viscount picked up his fork and resumed eating his breakfast.

When his meal ended, the two men parted company. Gareth, to search for Amelia, and the earl to search for some of the gentlemen attending the house party who had foolishly wagered against the existence of a husband for Emma Fairweather.

The viscount's quest brought him out-of-doors to the east side of the manor house. He knew Amelia admired the formal gardens in this section of the estate. Perhaps he would be fortunate enough to find her here alone. If memory served him, Gareth recalled a particularly challenging boxwood maze that could provide some tantalizing privacy, a place to steal a kiss or two or even engage in more sensual delights if Amelia was so inclined.

He followed the path beyond the circular fountain, admiring the flowering plants and roses. For the first time in many years he thought about his estate, the property from which he collected a handsome annual profit, yet never visited. He wondered what sort of gardens were planted on the grounds. And if they were properly maintained.

Turning the corner of a waist-high stone wall, Gareth spotted Amelia in the distance. She stood in the center of what appeared to be a miniature meadow, ablaze with summer blooms. It was an enchanting sight to behold. However the countess was not alone. There was a man with her. A gentleman, by the look of his fashionable clothes.

They appeared to be engaged in earnest conversation yet even at this distance Gareth could see that they were arguing. He quickened his pace.

Amelia turned her head and walked deliberately away from her male companion. He stomped behind her, grasped her arm, and whirled her around to face him. The expression on Amelia's face revealed her own anger, but she seemed in control of her emotions.

The same could not be said for the man who held her in his grasp. His mouth opened wider with each word he spoke, his face was twisted with rage. The words were still indistinguishable, but the intent was clear.

Gareth broke into a run.

Suddenly he saw the man raise his arm as if to strike Amelia. Blinding rage consumed the viscount. He ignored the pathways and roared through the flowering bushes at a frantic speed, descending on the pair like an avenging angel.

They turned simultaneously to gape at him. It was at that moment that Gareth noticed Amelia's hand clasped to the man's forearm.

"Did he strike you?" Gareth demanded to know.

"No."

"Then I will allow him to live."

"Such gallantry, my lord," the man exclaimed in mocking tones. "One would hardly expect a nobleman to defend his whore so vigorously. She must be quite a tasty morsel between the sheets."

Gareth lunged toward him, fists raised, but Amelia stepped between them. "Stop it, please." She pressed herself forward, then pitched her voice low, so only he could hear. "I know this is difficult, but if you have any compassion for me at all you will cease this barbaric behavior at once."

The viscount hesitated for a moment. This rude, arrogant man was dangerously close to having his head bashed against the nearest tree trunk, but the distressed look in Amelia's eyes helped Gareth master his rage.

The viscount stepped back, but he took Amelia with him. Together they faced her adversary.

"I am Viscount Longley. Who are you?" The question was uttered in a harsh tone.

"I am the Earl of Monford, the dowager countess's brother-in-law." His expression was severe. "You have interrupted an important discussion of a family matter that does not concern you. Please leave at once."

"No." Gareth set himself back on his heels and folded his arms across his chest.

"Amelia?" The earl appealed to his sister-in-law.

Gareth felt her tremble slightly, but her voice was strong and steady when she spoke. "There is nothing left for us to say, Roger. Mr. Bascomb has recanted his offer of marriage. Even if I wanted to, I am powerless to change his mind."

The earl laughed. It was not a pleasant sound. "You think you have won, Amelia. But we both know that this is just the beginning." He turned to Gareth. "You are welcome to her, Longley. For now. I am a patient man. I shall be waiting to take her back when you have cast her off."

Gareth's fist itched to bury itself in the earl's smug face, but the gentle pressure of Amelia's fingers on his wrist kept his clenched hand by his side.

He waited until the earl faded from the distance, then turned to face Amelia. "Who the hell is Mr. Bascomb?"

Her brow rose fractionally, from either his tone or language, but Gareth was too distraught to care.

"Mr. Bascomb is a wealthy merchant Roger had hoped I would marry. Those hopes have now been dashed."

"How?"

"You just heard me explain it to Roger. Mr. Bascomb withdrew his offer of marriage."

"Why? Why did he decide not to marry you?" Gareth hated the edge of despair in his voice, but was unable to completely hide the distress he felt.

"And why have you never spoken of Mr. Bascomb before?"

"I did not mention Mr. Bascomb because he was unimportant." Amelia cleared her throat uncomfortably. "I never intended to marry him. That was Roger's desire, not mine."

Gareth struggled to maintain an impassive facade. There was more to the story than she was revealing. He realized then how little he really knew of this woman who had suddenly come to mean so much to him.

"Why has Mr. Bascomb changed his mind?"

The smile she was trying to force disappeared. "He now knows where, and with whom, I spent last night."

"What?" Gareth shouted. "How is that possible?"

"I told him. Actually I told a room filled with people, including our hosts. The duke and duchess were quite shocked, but far too well bred to make a scene. Still, I feel I should probably take my leave this afternoon, so as to make it less uncomfortable for everyone else."

"Have you lost your senses?" Gareth scowled. In confusion, in anger, in shock. "What could have possibly possessed you to make such a rash, irresponsible declaration?"

"It was the truth. And it was the only scheme I could devise to force Mr. Bascomb to back away. I knew Roger would insist upon the match and I knew I could never sanction it." The defensive glint in her eye softened. "I am sorry to have brought you into this scandal, but I feel my revealing our night of passion aided you in some small way.

"There was wild speculation that Mr. Fairweather had found you naked in bed with his wife last night and had challenged you to a duel, but you refused. I could not let anyone believe you capable of such a deed. You are many things, my lord, but you are not a coward."

Bitterness spread through him. "Is that why you surprised me in my bedchamber last night? To create a scandal?"

"Yes." She hesitated. "I am very sorry if I have angered or offended you in any way. That was never my intention."

Angered? Offended? Gareth nearly laughed out loud at the absurdity of those remarks. She had done far more than that. She had hurt him in ways he had never imagined he could be hurt. She had deceived him. She had pretended to be his friend, pretended an interest in his person, in his life and future. She had looked beyond his reputation and claimed he was meant for better things, for a higher purpose. And then she had used him.

If he was not filled with such pain he would admire her skill. She was as clever and heartless as any rogue. Certainly more clever than he.

"You said you are leaving this afternoon. With your brother-in-law?" Despite telling himself her welfare was none of his concern, the notion of her under that brute's power rankled.

The color in her face deepened. "I will be traveling to the home of my dear friend Lady Gooding. She has kindly offered me her hospitality. My maid and I plan to stay with her until the repairs on the Dower House are completed."

He jerked his head down in a curt nod. "I wish you a safe journey, Countess."

The viscount turned to leave, but her soft voice beckoned him back. "Gareth."

He halted, twisted his head, and looked back at her over his shoulder. Her brow wrinkled in a deep frown and she appeared to be struggling to find the right words. She closed her eyes briefly, then shook her head. "I shall miss you."

He suspected that there was more she was trying to say. Their gazes locked, but no other words were spoken. This time when he turned away Gareth did not cease walking until he located a decanter of the duke's finest brandy and drained most of it.

CHAPTER EIGHT

Amelia had not expected that it would hurt this much. As the days turned into weeks she thought the deep, wrenching pain she felt would begin to lessen and eventually fade. Yet as hard as she tried, Amelia discovered she could not find a way to easily or quickly remove the viscount from her heart and mind.

Then one day he appeared. She was relaxing in Belinda's pretty garden, heard a noise, looked up from the embroidery she was stitching, and found him standing before her. Dressed in a blue coat that exactly matched the color of his eyes, tan breeches molding his muscular thighs, black Hessian boots polished to a mirror shine. Looking every inch the devilish rogue she knew him to be. Her heart turned over.

"How did you find me?" she asked.

He cocked his head and smiled boldly. "You gave

me your direction that afternoon in the garden before you left the house party. Do you not remember?"

"It must have slipped my mind." The breath that escaped her was nearly a sigh. Though she was ridiculously glad to see him, she wished he had not come. Seeing his handsome face, his endearing smile, brought back the memories of the reckless passion they had shared and reminded her too sharply of the things that could never be. "Your visit is rather a surprise."

"A pleasant one, I hope?"

Amelia bit her lip to hide her nervous giggle. "Is there a lady in all of England who does not find it a pleasant experience to be in the company of the Viscount of Longley?"

"Only those with bloodthirsty husbands object," he decided.

This time she did allow her laugh to escape. "How is Mrs. Fairweather managing these days?"

"I have no idea." He sat beside her on the garden bench. "Nor do I care."

His words pleased her. She always felt he deserved better than the crumbs Mrs. Fairweather was willing to throw his way.

"Why have you come here, my lord?"

"Must a gentleman always have an ulterior motive for visiting a beautiful lady?"

"If the gentleman is you, then the answer to that question is yes."

He laughed low in his throat. The sensual sound caused a shiver of chills to race up Amelia's spine.

She lifted her head and it seemed to her that their eyes remained fixed upon each other for a long time.

"Perhaps I have come today because I wanted to see you," he said quietly. "Perhaps I have been unable to sleep, unable to concentrate, unable to function as the carefree, fun-loving rogue that I am. Perhaps I find myself too frustrated and restless to attend to even the simplest matters. Perhaps the thought of spending my days and nights, without you has filled me with a gloom and despair that I can no longer tolerate."

She could not answer him. Her eyes filled with tears that threatened to spill over at any moment. "You were so angry when you left. And I knew in my heart I could not blame you. I had duped and humiliated you and felt only a twinge of remorse for my actions. I deserved your scorn."

"No, you did not." He reached into his breast coat pocket, pulled out a white linen handkerchief, and gently wiped her eyes. "Dearest Amelia, you can be so very naive at times. True you were less than honest with me and that stung my pride. As for our night together, well, my dear, you hardly had to tie me to the bed."

"Gareth!"

"That would have come later. On our second night together." He flashed her a wicked grin. "But there was no second night. You ran away, Amelia."

"I had no other choice," she whispered.

"I understand that now. Words cannot express

how sorry I am that it took me so long to make that realization. Will you forgive me?"

She searched his eyes, trying to judge his sincerity. "It would please me greatly if we could part as friends, Gareth."

"Friends?" His eyebrow arched. "I had hoped to be far more than your friend, Amelia. I want to be your husband."

"My God! You cannot be serious?"

The viscount compressed his lips. " 'Tis fortunate that I am a man possessed of a healthy dose of self-confidence, madame. It has taken me weeks to accept the notion of being a husband, yet when I ask the woman I love to share my life and make a new beginning for us both, I am soundly humiliated."

Amelia pressed her hand to her heart. "Goodness, this certainly is a day filled with surprises." She licked her dry lips. "You love me?"

The viscount grimaced, then nodded his head. "I am miserable without you, pining away for just a glimpse of your lovely face. Remembering all that we shared leaves a peculiar tightness in my chest. Lucien declared it sounded suspiciously like a bad case of indigestion, but wisely recanted that statement when I threatened to punch him in the nose."

Amelia's heart began to pound so hard it made her light-headed. Surely she had misheard, had misunderstood. "I am having difficulty believing this, my lord."

"I know precisely what you mean." The viscount reached out and stroked her cheek. His touch was gentle, loving. "This realization has been quite a shock for me, I can assure you. Yet that does not make it any less truthful. I love you, Amelia.''

She began to tremble. She stared at him with round, unblinking eyes and tried to formulate some sort of response. "I believe the usual answer to such a declaration is I love you too.''

"Thank heavens!''

He gathered her in the circle of his arms and bent down his head.

"Wait,'' Amelia cried, pushing against the unyielding muscles of his chest. "Before you kiss me I must tell you that I cannot marry you.''

He paused in the act of lowering his head, then tightened his hold on her. "Are you scared?''

"Terrified,'' she whispered.

He nodded his head in agreement. "So am I, but I believe that is a good sign. It shows we are being practical and realistic. Marriage is no easy road. It is a lifetime commitment, filled with both joys and sorrows. Only those couples who are truly dedicated to making a success of it are happy.''

She sighed. "There is so much for us to overcome. The scandal that I created, not to mention the difference in our ages will keep the gossiping tongues wagging for years. We are not at all like other couples, Gareth.''

"No. That will be our salvation. We shall be outrageously unfashionable and demand respect and fidelity from each other. The *ton* will not know what to make of our union.''

Her eyebrows lifted. "If we married *you* would be faithful?''

"Yes, because I know you will only agree if I promise that I will.'' He bowed his head sheepishly.

"Yet it will not be a hardship, for I have discovered that I want no other woman but you, Amelia."

The sincerity in his voice told her he was being truthful. Riddled with indecision, Amelia gazed at him. "You speak as if I have already agreed."

"I am hopeful." He lifted her hand and pressed it to his lips. "Yet I want this to be your choice, made with your free will and your full heart." He lowered her hand and placed it gently on his knee, shifted his position and withdrew a paper from his coat pocket.

"This is the deed to the Dower House and fifty surrounding acres on the Monford estate."

Amelia's eyes narrowed in confusion. "Why would you want to purchase that particular property? And how on earth did you ever get Roger to agree?"

The viscount grinned triumphantly. "I didn't. I feared I would be unable to keep my tongue or my fists under control around your obnoxious brother-in-law so I sent my friend, Lucien St. Simon, the Earl of Danbury, to negotiate the sale.

"Apparently Roger was so badly in need of funds he did not bother to ask many questions. I think he probably believed he was thwarting any future attempts you might have to gain your freedom from him. But if you look closely at the name on the deed you will see that we have defeated Roger soundly."

The hand holding the parchment shook slightly. She accepted it, gazed down, gasped, squinted, then pressed the document so close to her face it touched her nose. Yet the name of the new owner remained clear and legible. Amelia Wheatley, Dowager Countess of Monford. "You have bought the house for me? Why?"

"I suspected you might not leap at the chance to marry me, even though I am considered by many in society to be the catch of the Season." He gave her a self-deprecating grin. "I understand your need for independence is strong. My one hope remains that if we do not marry at once I can at least be a frequent overnight guest in your home and in your bed."

"Gareth." Amelia dipped her chin and blushed.

He ran his fingers gently across her bowed head. "When the weather begins to warm we shall travel. You said once how you long to see the sights of Europe. Let me show them to you. There are still many beautiful places where the Corsican monster has not invaded. I have told you that I prefer we marry, but I won't insist upon it. I want you to be happy, Amelia."

She gripped his knee tightly, still feeling shock. He was giving her everything she had always wanted, had ever dreamed about. Her freedom. And his love. What could be more perfect?

"I was able to bring my maid with me when I came to stay with Belinda, but there is an elderly servant, a footman named Hugh, employed by Roger whom I wish moved to the Dower House. Can you arrange that for me?"

"It will be done as quickly as possible. Now give me a real challenge."

She shook her head, hardly daring to believe in his confidence, his enthusiasm. "Our future is so uncertain, so unsettled. How will we manage it?"

His mouth tightened with amusement. "A

woman I respect and admire once told me that if I set my mind to it, I could accomplish any task."

"She sounds demented."

"No, she is very wise and very beautiful. She has captured my heart and holds it firmly in the palm of her hand. I am hers to command."

The emotional upheaval in Amelia's heart began to settle. "I do want to be with you," she admitted. "Yet I insist we delay any marriage plans until we have been together for at least several months. Perhaps even a year."

"Done!" Clasping his hand around her head, Gareth brought Amelia's mouth to his. He kissed her deeply, his mouth warm and inviting. When it ended, she felt him smile and pull away. "I do however have one condition upon which I will not bend," he whispered. "If you become pregnant with our child during that time you will marry me immediately. I cannot sanction the idea of my son or daughter growing up without my name, without a real father to love and protect them."

"I agree." She blew out her breath quickly before the image of their child had her crying with longing. "After all, how can I refuse the man who once told me he shot his father with a dueling pistol when he was just a lad?"

"How indeed?" The viscount's broad grin was infectious. " 'Tis a fine, entertaining tale, my lady. I promise I shall tell it to you in great detail on our wedding night."

"Gareth! You just said that you would not pressure me to—"

The viscount growled softly, bent his head down

swiftly, and captured her lips firmly before Amelia could sputter any additional protests. Yet it was not necessary. She returned the kiss with equal measure, for they were in truth a well-matched pair.

THE PLEASURES
OF A WAGER

COLLEEN FAULKNER

CHAPTER ONE

"What an excellent morning for an outing," Anne Thompson remarked, gazing out across the fine lawns of Hyde Park. "And such fine sights to be seen."

Alison May forced herself to smile her companion's way and pressed her gloved hand to her stomach as it growled. She was hungry and ready for breakfast, not another turn in this blasted park. "It's true, the grounds are pretty," she managed without sounding too bored.

Ally despised these expeditions in which she and other companions from Mrs. Trumbell's School for Ladies climbed into an open carriage and rode round and round in circles in the park. The point was to see and be seen, it had been explained. She thought the whole concept rubbish. Where she came from, on the Tidewater in America, a lady didn't get into a carriage unless she actually had somewhere to go. Better yet, she took a horse.

Anne nudged Ally's side with her elbow. "I did not mean the greenery," she whispered, her tone conspiratorial. "It is the gentlemen I was referring to. Everyone who is anyone seems to be here this morning."

The other two young ladies sitting across from them in the carriage giggled.

Ally let loose a sigh of boredom, not caring what anyone thought, as she fiddled with the sleeve of her pale green crepe traveling gown. "I'll lay odds that by the time we return to Mrs. Trumbell's, the poached eggs will be chilled, and Grace will have eaten all of the sausages. Have I any takers?"

"Alison, really dear," Lucy Granger, Ally's nemesis, plied sweetly. "You should enjoy the morning outing and not think so of your appetite . . . nor of gambling." She turned her head to nod politely at a plump young man passing in a shiny black gig.

"Good morning," he called as he tipped his hat. "Fine day."

All the women in the carriage but Ally nodded politely. "Good day," they echoed one after the other like a flock of cooing doves.

"It is not becoming of a young woman," Lucy continued, turning her attention back to Alison, "to speak of such matters."

At the sound of pounding hoofbeats, the ladies looked to their left just in time to see two curricles careen by on a path just beyond them.

"Really," Elspeth Morris, Ally's third companion, murmured, "these poor men will not be satisfied with their foolish racing until someone is injured."

Ally grinned at the sight of the two men as they flew by. She couldn't help but envy them. Before her father had sent her to London to be educated as a lady at Mrs. Trumbell's, she had raced with her brothers, both on horseback and in two-wheeled carts. She always won. Her brothers insisted that she beat them because she felt no fear. Her father always chided that it was because she had no sense.

A phaeton pulled up beside Mrs. Trumbell's carriage. "Good morning to you, Miss Morris, Miss Granger, Miss Thompson." Sir Jonathan Bark tipped his hat, his gaze upon Ally. "Miss May," he said, emphasizing her name.

Alison was not attracted to Mr. Bark in the way that she knew for a fact that Elspeth was, but she could never be unkind to him. Only last week at a ball he had trailed after her as faithfully as a pup, fetching her punch and worrying over whether or not she was overly warm from dancing. "Good morning, Mr. Bark. Fine rig you have there."

He squirmed in his gray flannel coat. "New. A gift from my papa."

She eyed the dappled pair pulling the small, sleek vehicle. "And a superior pair of geldings you've got. Muscular for their compact size."

Anne gave a little gasp of shock. Ally supposed that young women weren't supposed to notice the sex of animals.

"Is it fast, your rig?" Ally questioned, sliding forward to the edge of the leather bench seat. A thought had popped into her head. An utterly unladylike thought . . . and utterly tempting.

Elspeth laid a gloved hand on Ally's arm, unable to even look at Mr. Bark. "Please, Ally . . ." she murmured, seeming to sense what Ally was up to.

"I . . . well, I suppose it is," Mr. Bark mumbled into his starched white cravat. He glanced in the direction the racing vehicles had gone. "But it is new, as I said, and I . . . I've not had time to try her out properly."

"Of course." Ally smiled sweetly as she rose to her feet in the moving carriage. "Albert, halt the carriage."

Her companions gasped in unison. While it was perfectly all right to speak with a gentleman while taking a turn in the park, one certainly did not stop to speak.

"Yes, Miss May," the elderly gray-haired gentleman on the driver's seat called.

"Ally, what are you doing?" Anne begged, grasping for her hand. "Sit down. You are making a scene."

"I am not making a scene." Ally climbed over Lucy to the side of the carriage. "Mr. Bark has just said that he has not been able to measure the speed of his new phaeton. I've a mind to give him aid. After all, what are friends for?"

"You can't drive that carriage," Lucy scoffed "You'll both be killed. There will be nothing left of that curricle but a pile of timber."

Ally tossed her damask reticule on the carriage seat and put out one gloved hand to the frightened-looking young man. "If you'll be so kind, Mr. Bark, as to help me transfer from this vehicle to yours, Albert will not have to climb down from his perch."

"I—well, certainly, M—miss May," Mr. Bark stammered, rising to his feet.

"Lay me odds, ladies. Your breakfast sausage, Lucy, for the win against yonder gentlemen." Ally grasped Mr. Bark's hand and began to maneuver down into his curricle, which was lower to the ground than Mrs. Trumbell's carriage. "And if I lose—"

"If you lose," Lucy muttered, "we will sweep you up in a dustpan."

"If I lose, you may have my new pearl earbobs. The ones you so admired."

"Alison." Elspeth gasped. "They were a gift from your father."

Ally turned to her friends as she stepped into Mr. Bark's vehicle and tucked her morning cape behind her. "Then I had best not lose the race, had I?"

With a grin of satisfaction, Ally slid onto the seat beside the shocked Mr. Bark. She took the reins from him, weighing the heavy, dark leather in her hands. It had been too long since she had driven her own carriage. "So, shall we see how she fares, Mr. Bark?"

"Y—yes, well yes, I suppose. By all means," he muttered.

Ally lifted the reins, gave a very unladylike cry of "Get up!" and the vehicle lurched forward.

It didn't take Ally long to find the two men who had been racing. One was a distant cousin of Grace Addison's, a student at Mrs. Trumbell's. He had been to tea only last week. "Mr. Carlton, would you care to take another turn?"

Mr. Carlton stood up in his curricle, obviously bemused. "Why, Miss May, I thought that was you I saw. Mr. Bark." He nodded.

Mr. Bark made some reply beneath his breath.

"Mr. Bark here has just procured this fine new vehicle, and we thought to take a run in her. To try out her wheels, you might say." Ally flashed a grin that Mrs. Trumbell would have declared utterly inappropriate.

Mr. Carlton eased into his carriage seat to lift his reins and roll forward. "I would never deny a request from you, Miss May. Lead on and we shall mark the start and finish."

The course Mr. Carlton set out was impossibly easy. Just a straight path along Park Lane that lined one side of Hyde Park. Ally thought to increase the difficulty by adding a turn or two but Mr. Bark was already so pale she feared he might faint if she suggested such an alteration in the course.

"I'll say *go*," Mr. Carlton's previous racing companion called from the side of the starting line. "May the best man, *or lady*,"—he tipped his hat to Ally—"win. Now, on the mark . . ."

Ally gripped the thick reins tightly, wishing she wore leather gloves rather than useless cotton ones. The horses seemed to sense what was about and snorted and pawed at the ground, anxious to be off.

"Set . . ."

Mr. Bark took a strangled breath.

"It will be all right," Ally assured him with a light pat on his knee. "Just hang on."

Mr. Bark seemed incapable of any response beyond a horrified stare at his knee.

"Go!"

"Ha!" Ally slapped the reins. The dappled pair bolted forward, and Mr. Bark cried out as he gripped the side of the phaeton.

Ally pulled up beside Mr. Carlton, the ribbons of her bonnet flapping at her cheeks. The road was narrow here, barely wide enough for two carriages traveling at such a speed, but she wouldn't give her opponent the advantage by dropping back until the path widened. She forced herself to look forward, keeping her eye on the road. The phaeton was lighter than she had expected, and though it was nimble, it careened from side to side.

Ally saw a flash of her companions' faces, and she streaked by them. The coachman's mouth shriveled to a pickle. Poor Elspeth appeared more frightened than Mr. Bark.

Ally glanced sideways at her competitor. The wind blew in her face, caught her bonnet, and slid it back over her head, setting her hair free. She shoved a hank of honey-colored hair behind her ear, fearing it would impede her vision.

Mr. Carlton was gaining on her and that would not do. "Ha! Ha!" Ally grabbed up the buggy whip and snapped it over the horses' heads, then turned to look triumphantly behind her as she passed Mr. Carlton. She gave a wave of one gloved hand. She was almost at the finish line.

Suddenly, a man in a black coat appeared before her from out of nowhere, his head all but buried in a newspaper as he crossed the road into the park. She cried out in warning, and yanked hard on the reins to pull left, but she feared she was too close. What if she couldn't veer off in time?

At the last possible moment, the man glanced up, his startled gaze registering the situation. In the nick of time, he leaped out of the way.

Ally careened by in the phaeton, passing the finish line and beating Mr. Carlton by more than two carriage lengths. He must have reined in when he saw the pedestrian.

"Sweet Mary, Mother of God," Mr. Bark murmured, his hands clasped in prayer, his eyes squeezed shut.

Ally pulled up the horses, breathing almost as heavily as they were. She put on the brake and climbed down on her own. She patted one dapple and then the other. "Good boys," she murmured. "Good boys."

"Fine ride," Mr. Carlton called as he rolled by at a walk and tipped his hat. "See you another morning, Miss May?"

Ally grinned and waved. Knowing she must look a fright, she grasped her straw and silk bonnet and attempted to yank it back on her head, stuffing her hair beneath it.

"Fine driving," a deep voice said from behind.

Ally whirled around to see a man in a black coat, carrying a paper. It was the man she had nearly run over.

"Thank you," she said, still fighting her bonnet, her vision obscured by a wayward ribbon. "I . . . I apologize. I didn't see you and suddenly you were before me." She gestured with one hand to the place where she had nearly run over the tall gentleman with the most intriguing eyes. They were so pale blue that they appeared gray in the morning light. "You were reading your paper and must not have seen us," she said.

He smiled handsomely, taking his time to respond, his reply bemused. "Well, I will be more careful from now on," he said as he walked away. "I had forgotten how dangerous a morning walk in the park in London could be. Good morning to you."

"Miss May, are you all right?"

Ally turned to see Mrs. Trumbell's carriage approach. Her companions stared over the side of the carriage at her.

"I won," she said victoriously. She turned back to Mr. Bark, who had recovered enough from his frightened stupor to take his reins again. "Thank you, Mr. Bark," she called. "Do come by Mrs. Trumbell's and call on Miss Morris and me."

Elspeth gave a little gasp of fright.

"I—Yes, of course, thank you, Miss May—thank you for your company." He tipped his hat. "Ladies." He drove off at a sedate pace, as if he had not been frightened out of his wits only moments before.

With an arch of her brows at the aplomb with which Mr. Bark had recovered, she elevated the man a notch in her esteem.

Albert climbed down from his seat to open the door to help Ally back into the carriage. "Fine driving," he whispered as she passed him.

She gave him a smile of thanks and took her seat beside Lucy again.

"Heavens, look at your hair. Your bonnet. You're a mess." Anne gasped.

"Do you know who that was whom you nearly ran down?" Lucy hissed, gazing behind them at the gentleman making his way through the park, his nose in his paper again.

Ally tugged off her gloves, which were stained from the oil of Mr. Bark's reins. "He should have been looking where he was going."

"That was the Viscount William Bridle, just come back from a year in Africa."

"*The* Lord Bridle?" Anne gasped.

Ally glanced at Lucy. "*The* Lord Bridle. What does that mean?"

"They say he left London in scandal. They say he got Elizabeth Monroe *in circumstance,*" Anne whispered. "That's why she was whisked off to the country in the midst of *the Season.*"

Elspeth gasped and covered her mouth with her hand.

Ally rolled her eyes. "A week does not go by that some gentleman of the *ton* is not said to have gotten someone pregnant."

Elspeth, shocked by her bluntness, began to fan herself with a gloved hand.

"Miss Monroe's family is of Parliament. He would not wed her, they say."

"They say, they say," Ally muttered. "You ladies would do well to mind your gossip. Albert," she called forward. "I think we are ready to return home."

"Yes, Miss May." The coachman turned the carriage back the way they had come.

"I've an assignation with not only my sausages," Ally said impishly, as she finally tied her bonnet beneath her chin, "but with Lucy's as well."

CHAPTER TWO

Viscount William Bridle entered his mother's bedchamber and crossed the room to take her hand. "Mama."

She sat up in bed, surrounded by pillows and what seemed like acres of linen and lace. She wore a ridiculous little ruffled cap on her head that nearly made him laugh.

"Oh, William, I am so glad you came to me before you set out for your evening." While she allowed him to kiss her hand, she rested her head back on the pile of pillows, making what he was sure she believed to be a dramatic sight. "I'm seeing spots again. Black and floating. I fear I may be near the end."

He grabbed a chair from beside the bed, turned it around, and straddled it so that he could lean forward on the back. His mother despised it when he sat in such an ungentlemanly fashion, but at past thirty years of age, Will thought he had a right to sit the way he pleased and fashion be damned.

"You are not near the end. You are barely sixty, Mama. You have another good twenty years of complaints left in you."

She lifted her head off the pillow rather quickly for a woman in the throes of death. "Jest now! When I am dead and gone you will miss your mother."

He sighed. This talk quickly became old with him. "Why don't you get up, call Missy to dress you, and accompany me to Mrs. Davenport's ball?"

A small dog sleeping beside her lifted its ears as she threw her head back on the pillow again. William hated his mother's little lapdogs. They did nothing but bark and leave puddles on the floor. In Africa, they would have been eaten for a Sunday meal.

"Ball? I cannot go to a ball. I told you I'm seeing black spots before my eyes." She waved pudgy fingers before her face. "I've already asked Missy to call for the vicar."

"Mama, you cannot call the vicar each time a black spot floats by. He's already come three times in the last week to see you off to heaven. He'll not come when you truly need him if you keep this up."

"You ridicule your mother." She rested back on the pillows and stroked the dog's head. Another tiny head popped up from the sea of bed linens and that dog whined to be petted, too.

"If you're seeing black spots, it's because you haven't been up out of bed in nearly a week." He rose from the chair and walked to the window, yanking open the heavy velvet drapes. "It's hot in here and there's no air."

"Don't do that." She waggled a finger at her son. "You'll let ill spirits in."

He grabbed the window and lifted it up. A breath of fresh night air blew in. "What I'll let in is a little unsullied evening air." He turned back to his mother. "Now, you may lay abed until morning if you like, but come tomorrow, you and I are going for a ride. I'll even take you shopping on the Strand, if you like."

"You're going to Mrs. Davenport's ball?"

He nodded. "I told her I would. She has some foolish notion that my appearance at her ball will make it the social triumph of the week." He frowned. "So I will go for a short time and then be on my way to White's for cards."

"Do stay long enough to dance a few dances. Meet a proper young woman." The dowager sat up with enthusiasm.

He sighed. In the last six weeks since he had returned from Africa this had been his mother's primary subject of conversation. She had it in her head that she was dying and she was anxious to see him wed before she departed her earthly coil.

"I don't care to meet your proper young ladies. They have no more substance than the cakes they serve with tea." He turned his back to her, gazing out at Park Avenue below them. The sun was just beginning to set and the street in front of their town house was alive with activity as ladies and gentlemen bustled off to various affairs.

"Nonsense. You must meet proper young ladies so that you can obtain a proper wife."

"Mother, as I have said. I am not opposed to wedding. I would like a family one day, but these matters take time."

She crossed her arms over her ample chest. "William, let me say again, you cannot find a proper wife if you do not meet proper young women."

"What would you have me do?" He spun around. He did not usually lose his temper with his mother. She was who she was and he loved her anyway. But this subject had stretched his patience thin.

"What would you have me do?" he repeated. "Marry the first proper young woman I come upon on the street?"

"If that will get me a grandchild," she harrumphed, "that would be fine with me." She threw up one hand. "Any chit will do, so long as she is accepted in polite society."

William dragged his chair back to where he had gotten it. "I must go. Matthew waits with the carriage." He leaned over, this time kissing her on the cheek. "I mean it, Mama. Tomorrow you and I are going on an outing."

One of her dogs leaped up and barked at him.

"And you," he said, pointing at the little hound, "will not be going to the market 'else I will be selling you for a stew pot."

William strode out of his mother's room without another word.

"I'll bet you one shilling Mrs. Trumbell will lean over Mr. Thompson and show off her cleavage before the minuet," Ally said as she allowed her cloak to be taken by a footman. They had just arrived, under Mrs. Trumbell's chaperonage, at a ball given by one of their neighbors, Mrs. Davenport. Only a few minutes after eight and the town house was already pushed to capacity with ladies and gentlemen vying for each other's attention.

Anne lowered her lashes as she, too, allowed her wrap to be taken. "Really, Ally, you mustn't speak that way. You will get into trouble one of these days with your wagers."

"Look, she is with him already." Ally nodded, knowing that if she dared point, Anne would reprimand her for rudeness.

Lucy fluttered her lashes as she joined the line to be received by their hostess. "You think you're so clever, Miss Alison May. You speak thusly now, but wait until the night is over and you've not a name on your dance card."

"There she goes," Ally commentated. "First Mrs. Trumbell taps his arm with her fan."

Anne giggled behind a gloved hand.

"And then when she has his attention," Ally continued, "she purposely speaks softly so that he can't quite hear."

"The old goat is deaf," Lucy said with irritation.

"And now she leans closer so that he might hear." Ally clapped her hands together with delight as Mrs. Trumbell leaned just as she predicted, showing off her ample bosom. "And at last, ladies, we have *the display*."

"I think you're clever," Elspeth said softly. "Even if others do not."

Ally smiled and squeezed Elspeth's hand. The poor girl was painfully shy, terribly plain, and so in love with Mr. Bark that she could barely stand to be in the same ballroom with him. It was a wonder their encounter in the park with him that day had not sent her to her bed with a fit of the vapors.

Ally looked to Lucy, who was just ahead of her in line. "What do you prattle on about, Lucy dear? Who says no one will dance with me?"

Lucy turned to face Ally, smoothing her new white Grecian-style gown. She would have been beautiful in it with her cascade of blond curls had it not been for the sour look on her face. "By now the word has spread all about town," Lucy hissed.

"What word?" Ally frowned. She was normally the kind of person who could get along with anyone, but lately, Lucy was sorely trying her patience.

"About your scandalous behavior in Hyde Park, of course." Her blue eyes seemed to spark with animosity. "No gentleman in this town will dare dance with you. It's a wonder Mrs. Trumbell even allowed you to show your face. I'm greatly surprised that she didn't send you packing right back to your father." She turned her head, her lips puckered in a mew. "And considering the circumstances *there*, that truly would be a travesty."

In truth, Mrs. Trumbell had been exceptionally angry with Ally. She had vowed that Ally would not be allowed in public without her chaperonage if she couldn't better conduct herself. But in the end, all had blown over as it always did. Ally guessed that it was her father's money that always smoothed Mrs. Trumbell's feathers.

As for Lucy's insinuation concerning the circumstances at home, she was referring to Ally's family's sordid past. In America, Ally's father was a respected businessman, an importer and exporter of goods. But his father before him had not been quite so reputable and word of her grandfather's reputation had somehow reached Mrs. Trumbell's within a fortnight of Ally's arrival. Mostly, Ally just ignored comments such as Lucy's. After all, how could she be responsible for the things her grandfather had done? She had never even known the man.

Elspeth slipped her hand into Ally's to comfort her. "She's jealous," she whispered, keeping her gaze downcast. "Don't let her ruin your evening. I know your dance card will be filled up in no time."

Ally looked up at Lucy. "So you think no one will dance with me?" she challenged. They had nearly reached their hostess in the receiving line; Mrs. Davenport was sporting a feathered headdress that looked to Ally as if some sort of bird were resting on her head.

"I think not," Lucy said, gazing down her long nose. "Even pitiful Elspeth is more likely to have a dance partner than you tonight."

Ally tightened her mouth. Lucy could pick on her all she wanted, but to say such a thing about Elspeth—and right in front of her—made Ally so angry that she wanted to pop Lucy in the nose. Elspeth was notorious for spending the hours of a ball beside the punch bowl and never on the dance floor, and Ally knew this fact hurt the girl deeply.

"My card will be full before yours," Ally spat out.

Lucy moved forward in the line. "Is that right?"

"I'd bet my virginity on it," Ally challenged from clenched teeth.

Anne gasped.

Elspeth squeezed Ally's hand so tightly that Ally feared the girl might break her bones.

Lucy lifted an eyebrow, not in the least shocked. "Is that a serious wager, Miss Alison May?" She leaned closer.

Ally swallowed hard. She didn't know where that had come from. It had just popped out of her mouth before she'd had a chance to consider the ramifications of such a wager. But now that she'd said it, she certainly wouldn't take it back. Not with Lucy looking the way she did right now. Not when she had said such a terrible thing about Elspeth.

"It is a wager, Miss Lucy Granger. My dance card will be filled before yours—"

"Or?"

"Or I will give up my virtue." Ally took a step closer, her eyes narrowing. "But if I win, you must vow to be Elspeth's personal servant for the next fortnight. You must loan her your prettiest frocks. You must run and fetch for her and you must make appointments for tea for her each day with the gentlemen of her choosing."

Elspeth gasped and swayed.

Ally instinctively extended her arm to steady her. "No fainting, Elspeth," Ally instructed in a low whisper. "We've only just arrived. If you faint, I will have to go home with you and I will surely lose the wager then."

"You're serious?" Lucy said, meeting Ally's stony gaze.

Ally trembled, she was so angry. She'd gotten in this deeply; she might as well take the final leap. She was a woman of her word. "Entirely."

Lucy nodded. "Then you have a wager, my dear."

"Don't do it," Anne begged Ally. "This is foolishness, Alison. Please don't do it."

"Anne will be the judge," Lucy declared. "The first one to reach her with a filled dance card wins." She lifted a haughty chin. "You had best look closely at these gentleman, Ally, because one of them is going to get to know you better than he expected."

Lucy presented her back to Ally.

Elspeth gripped Ally's hand. "Don't do it. Don't do it," she whispered, tears slipping down her pale, hollow cheeks. "Please, Ally."

"She has no right to treat you this way." Ally extricated herself from her friend's grasp. "It's time someone poked a hole in her conceit."

"But what if you lose the bet?" Elspeth begged.

"Then I shall lose more than a bet, won't I?"

"Oh, Miss May, so nice to see you this evening." Their hostess offered both hands.

Alison smiled sweetly and made some appropriate remark as she took Mrs. Davenport's gloved hands and gazed up at the bird looming over her head.

A moment later, free of the receiving line, Ally gave Elspeth a quick peck on the cheek. "Don't worry. I won't lose." She lifted her gaze to a gentleman she recognized from the park who was trying to catch her eye. "Now if you'll excuse me, I see a prime spot there along the wall. I want to get it before Lucy does." She raised the small folded card in her hand. "I have a dance card to fill, you know."

Half an hour later, Ally's cheeks were warm and her pulse was racing. As she walked up to the punch table, she traced her dance card with a finger. The place she had picked to stand and wait to be approached by gentlemen had been perfect. She had only one more dance and her card would be full. She would win the stupid bet and take Miss Lucy Granger down a notch.

"Oh, Ally," Elspeth breathed as her friend approached, "are you certain you won't reconsider? I fear you have really gone too far this time."

"It's all right, Elspeth. Look, my card is nearly full. And there is Anne standing in yonder doorway waiting. Lucy has not approached her. I'm going to win." She flashed a smile. "Now let me have a sip of punch and then I'll be on my way. One more gentleman and Lucy will be dusting your shoes."

As Elspeth turned to fill a punch cup, Mr. Bark approached them.

Elspeth turned with the punch cup, gasped, and tried to turn away.

Ally grabbed her friend's arm, preventing her from making her escape. Ally knew how much she wanted to talk to Mr. Bark. Elspeth had to learn not to run the other way every time she saw him.

"Miss May." Mr. Bark nodded as he approached.

He was dressed handsomely in white breeches, a starched white cravat, and a cinnamon-colored evening coat. With his receding hairline and hooked nose, Mr. Bark was not a handsome man by any means, but he had kind eyes.

"Miss Morris," he acknowledged.

Ally smiled and dipped a curtsy. Elspeth tried to

balance the punch cup in her hand and maintain decorum as she curtsied.

Mr. Bark came to stand beside Ally, putting her between him and Elspeth. "Fine ball," he commented, fiddling with his cravat.

"That it is," Ally agreed, though in truth, the dancing had not yet begun. Guests were still milling about, taking refreshment and speaking with friends. The music would begin shortly, though, and Ally would be obliged to dance with the men on her card. If she was going to fill the card, she would have to hurry.

"I wondered, Miss May. Have you . . ." He halted, took a deep breath, and started again. "I wondered, is your dance card quite filled up? If it is—"

Elspeth turned sharply away, taking the punch cup with her.

Ally knew that Elspeth had hoped Mr. Bark had approached them to ask *her* to dance.

"I certainly would understand," Mr. Bark continued.

Ally's heart ached for Elspeth. She had more dance partners than she knew what to do with. Elspeth wanted only one.

Of course Ally only needed one more name on her dance card. One more dance and she would win. Out the corner of her eye, Ally spotted Lucy. She was laughing gaily, offering her card to some gentleman to fill in his name. One more partner and Ally would win. This wasn't a wager she could afford to lose.

But Ally took one look at Mr. Bark and lowered her head to speak privately to him. "Unfortunately my card is full, sir. But my friend Elspeth would love to dance.''

Ally heard Elspeth gasp again. If the girl fainted into the punch bowl, Ally wouldn't forgive her.

Mr. Bark gave a polite nod. No gentleman would dare refuse such a suggestion.

"Miss Morris," he said, crossing to Elspeth, who still had her back to them, "will you do me the honor of a dance?"

"Give him your first dance," Ally encouraged. "You might not get a chance to dance with him again if your card fills."

Elspeth turned to Mr. Bark, her face as pale as the white of her gown.

Ally took the punch cup from her hand.

Slowly, Elspeth lifted her gaze to meet Mr. Bark's and then her face filled with the most beautiful smile Ally had ever seen.

In turn, Mr. Bark's face lit up.

Maybe no one had ever smiled at Mr. Bark that way before.

Ally wasn't certain if she believed in love at first sight, but the smiles on their faces made her heart swell.

Turning away from the two of them as they fell into conversation, Ally spotted Lucy hurrying toward Anne, as fast as decorum would allow. She was waving her dance card.

Ally suddenly felt sick in the pit of her stomach as she watched Lucy hand her card over to Anne. Behind them, in the ballroom, the musicians were beginning to tune their instruments. Guests were milling toward the waxed dance floor.

Anne looked up to meet Ally's gaze across the

room and, against her will, her eyes filled with tears.

Lucy glanced up triumphantly.

Ally turned away, letting her dance card fall from her hand.

She had lost the wager.

She would have to go to Lucy and beg forgiveness. She would have to renege on the bet.

Except that *never* in her life had Alison May, daughter of Jeremiah May, granddaughter of Billy May, the pirate, *ever* reneged on a bet.

A lump rose in Ally's throat and she feared she would burst into tears right there in public. Unwilling to give Lucy the satisfaction of having brought her to tears, Ally hurried off in the opposite direction. Her head down, she rushed through the receiving hall not knowing where she was headed. Not caring.

She knew she had done the right thing for Elspeth, but now what?

Ally slipped out an open door onto a small brick patio. She hurried down the steps, the satin of her pale green ball gown crumpled in her fists. Blindly, she rushed down the path into the walled garden.

Her *virginity?* She had just wagered away her virginity? How could she have done such a foolish thing?

Ally pushed farther into the garden, where hedges formed a wall, blocking the view from the house. The music had begun. A minuet. Poor Mr. Jarson, her first dance partner, was probably looking for her, but Ally couldn't let him see her this way. She couldn't let anyone see her this way.

Torches lit the garden, and Ally followed the

brick path. Unable to hold back her tears, she could no longer see. Catching the toe of her slipper on the edge of a brick, she nearly tripped. She caught herself and crumpled onto a stone bench.

Ally dropped her head to her hands. Her father would be so upset with her, so disappointed if he knew. He expected her to be a woman of her word. Because of his father's past, that above all else was what mattered to Jeremiah May. Being an honest, upstanding citizen. He would expect her to stand by her wager.

But then there was the other side of the coin.

Ally's father had given her a free rein when he sent her to England. He gave her all the money she needed, and his permission to come and go as she pleased. He didn't care as much for propriety as he did for his daughter, but he had made one request when he had allowed her to leave the Maryland shore. Knowing his headstrong daughter would do as she pleased and then extricate herself with a skill he could only admire, he had imposed only one rule on her behavior—that she save herself for marriage. And now this.

A sob rose in Ally's throat. She had no hanky so she cried into her hands. She had never felt so lost in all her life.

"May I be of assistance?"

Ally started at the sound of the male voice. Where had he come from? She had never heard him approach.

Looking up, she recognized the man immediately, though she doubted he could identify her with her face swollen and red the way it must be now.

It was the Viscount Bridle, the man she had nearly run down in the park.

She tried to wave him away.

He pulled a handkerchief from his gold waistcoat. "It cannot be that bad."

She accepted the handkerchief.

Without asking her permission, Bridle settled beside her on the bench. "Now tell me, what is this all about? Slighted by a young man? Worse, a woman?"

Ally shook her head as she crumpled the handkerchief to her face. "Worse," she managed.

"Worse?" He crossed his arms over his broad chest, which was accented by a small waist. "Worse than being slighted at a ball?" he teased. "We speak of true tragedy, do we, puss?"

Ally yanked the handkerchief from her eyes, anger bubbling up inside her. Who did this man think he was to judge what was and was not trivial to her? "I have just lost my virginity, sir." She met his gaze, her own steely eyed with anger. "Is that tragedy enough for you?"

CHAPTER THREE

For a moment Will was so stunned that he could not speak. "Pardon me?" he finally managed.

The young woman had taken him quite by surprise and there were not many people who could surprise him. He felt an instant attraction to her, despite what he thought she had just said.

"You heard me." She wiped her eyes and tossed him the handkerchief.

He frowned with sudden alarm, and shot up off the bench. "You haven't been *assaulted* have you?"

She shook her head as she pushed back a lock of hair that had come undone from her elaborate Grecian-style coiffure. She had the prettiest hair, a light, golden brown that was glossy and thick.

She exhaled with exasperation. "No, of course not. I did not mean that in the literal sense. I meant—" She hesitated, gazed down at her hands on her lap, and then back up at him. "You've no desire to hear my sad tale, sir. I'm truly all right. Please return to the dancing."

Will had no intention of going anywhere. The girl had him intrigued now. What kind of young lady would say such a thing to a gentleman she did not know? He almost smiled as he sat beside her again. This fetching woman was obviously of an ilk different from the others he'd met since his return to London, and he intended to know her better.

"All right," he said. "You cannot leave me wondering like this." He met her gaze and resisted the temptation to catch the lock of hair that had fallen again. He watched her push it behind her ear with obvious impatience. "My name is William. Will, to my friends and family."

"The Viscount Bridle," she said.

His brow creased. Were they acquainted? Surely he would have recalled such an exquisite creature. She had the face of an angel and right now, the angry eyes of . . . he didn't care to make the association. Yet there was something familiar about her, or perhaps it was her voice. "We *have* met, haven't we?"

"Only when I almost ran you down in the park the other day."

He grinned, recalling the incident immediately. So that was she. He really hadn't gotten a good look at the young woman in the curricle. Her hair had come unbound and her bonnet had been so askew that he had not been able to see her features. That, and he had been preoccupied with his newspaper.

"My name is Alison May. I am called Ally by my friends."

He nodded. They were so far from decorum sitting here in the darkness on this bench that nothing else seemed necessary. Alison May . . . Alison May. Where had he heard that name before? He was certain it had been mentioned in some gossip his mother had babbled.

"Ally, what a delightful name. I apologize for not remembering you. Now please tell me what you meant by your statement that nearly had me choking on my cravat."

She chuckled, though it seemed against her will, and her face lit up. She was even more beautiful when she smiled. "It's ridiculous, really. You don't want to know. I have gotten myself into this muddle, and I shall get myself out. I always do."

"Something tells me you are more than capable, Miss May. He slid his hand to cover hers on the bench between them. "But I want to hear, just the same."

She exhaled, shaking her head. "I cannot believe I am telling this to a complete stranger," she muttered. But without further hesitation she relayed a story that had Will on the edge of his seat.

A lady who liked to wager. A lady who liked adventure, obviously. And there in the park he had just assumed the horses had gotten away from her. He hadn't realized she was racing.

Will was fascinated, delighted, by her candor and lack of coy affectations. He hadn't realized such young women existed and certainly not in London. Miss Alison May—Ally—was most definitely cut of a different cloth from the other women he knew.

"And so there you have it." She plucked off one white glove and then the other. "And now what am I to do? My father would be devastated if I did not remain chaste." Her unyielding gaze met his. "I may have my wild ways, sir, but I am not *that* kind of woman."

"But you are the kind of woman who sticks by a wager."

She stiffened beside him. "Absolutely."

William's mind began to tick in an utterly shocking direction. He recalled the conversation he'd had with his mother before leaving their residence this evening. He looked at Ally. "Were there stipulations to the bet?"

"Stipulations?"

"A particular gentleman was not named?" he asked, trying to be delicate while making sure she understood what he meant. How refreshing that Miss Alison May had a stronger constitution for such talk than most women.

"No particular gentleman, of course not." She threw up one hand. "I said it on impulse, of course. I did not truly mean to gamble away my virtue. The lady in question just made me so angry."

"So technically, you could fulfill your bet within the confines of, say, marriage?" He gestured. "Given the event took place within a reasonable time frame, of course."

Ally turned to him, the shock plain on her lovely face. She had stopped crying and the swelling around her eyes was receding. She had the deepest jeweled green eyes. "Marriage? Whatever do you mean, Viscount?"

"I mean that if you were to surrender your innocence to a man you were wed to, you would fulfill your obligation to your wager while protecting your reputation. Would you not?"

Ally stared at the Viscount Bridle for a moment as his meaning slowly sank in. "Yes, I suppose I could wed," she said. "I hadn't thought of that." She couldn't believe she was speaking so calmly about this subject with a stranger. But Will had made her comfortable right from the start. He was easy to talk to. He didn't seem to care about all of the proprieties of the day. He treated her as an equal, as a friend.

Ally gave a laugh. "Of course it is not as if I have anyone to wed up my sleeve."

"You may be in luck." He held up one finger. He did not wear gloves as most men did. He had the most beautiful hands—large, well-shaped, masculine hands. "Now hear me out," he warned. "No fainting."

"I do *not* faint," she defended.

"No, I don't suppose you do," he mused, then rushed on before he could think himself out of what seemed to be—at the moment—a splendid idea. "I've need of a wife and you have need of"— his tone changed slightly—"a husband."

His meaning should have shocked Ally. The man was utterly wicked.

And she was utterly fascinated. "A marriage of convenience, you mean?" she questioned.

"Certainly not. If we wed, it would be a true marriage in every sense of the word."

She felt her cheeks grow warm. "That's outlandish. I don't know you."

"Do any man and woman know each other before they are wed?" he asked pointedly. "Certainly not. A man and a woman meet at a ball. They dance a few dances. Her mother invites him to dine and then the next thing you know, a license is being acquired.''

The viscount was right of course. Still, Ally couldn't imagine agreeing to such madness. She studied him carefully. ''You said you've need of a wife. Why is that?''

''My mother is ill, or in all likelihood, just perceives she is ill.'' He rolled his eyes. ''She insists it is time I marry and, honestly, I agree with her. I just haven't met the right woman yet . . . at least not until tonight.''

Ally stared out into the shadowed garden, her emotions in a state of confusion. She was flattered that the viscount would pay her such a compliment. She was frightened by it. By herself. ''I should be shocked by your proposal, my lord.'' She wrinkled her nose. ''At least I think I should be shocked. I should want to jump up and slap you for your insolence.''

''I'd rather you didn't.''

She laughed, liking his droll sense of humor. ''It's madness.''

He rose from the stone bench and offered both of his hands to her. ''Utter insanity.''

She allowed him to pull her to her feet, and dared a saucy smile. She could not believe she was even considering his proposal. ''We'd be the talk of the *ton*.''

He held her gaze, making her feel warm right to her toes.

''The *ton* needs something to gossip about.'' He lifted one shoulder. ''It would be the adventure of a lifetime; you could place a wager on that and be assured of victory.''

"What would we say to others? To my chaperone, Mrs. Trumbell? What explanation would we give?''

"Why give any? I take it you are over twenty-one.''

"You take it correctly.'' She liked the feel of her hands in his. Gloves were worn so extensively here in London that Ally hadn't realized how much she missed the simple touch of a hand.

"Then you may marry without permission from your father. The marriage can take place as soon as the arrangements can be made.'' He paused. "Will your father be angry with you?''

She smiled, thinking of her father. "Papa could never be angry with me. Annoyed, perhaps, but''— she looked up into Will's eyes—"he would want what would make me happy.''

"Do you think I could make you happy?''

Will was so direct and Ally had grown so accustomed to society's dissembling that she found herself struggling to know how to respond. At home in America, a man could have been this direct. If Will had asked her the same question on the bank of the Chesapeake, how would she have responded?

"I think you could make me happy,'' she whispered. "I don't know why. We barely know each other, but . . .''

"But we are alike in many ways, Ally. We both know that instinctively, don't we?'' He smiled down on her. "So. Has the decision been made? Are we to wed?''

She laughed, but just as she was about to answer,

it occurred to her that he knew nothing of her family. Of her family's past. "Wait a minute," she said. "There is one thing I believe I should tell you." She released his hands and went back to sit on the bench.

"Whatever it is, it can wait."

"It cannot wait. Sit." She pointed to the place beside her.

William sat.

"It's about my family." She saw a flicker of recognition in his face. "You've heard?"

"Actually, I do recall hearing your name mentioned before. The young lady from America staying with Mrs. Trumbell."

"What did you hear?"

He waved his hand in dismissal. "That you are the daughter of a Colonial pirate or some other such nonsense."

She exhaled. "The granddaughter, actually."

He gave an incredulous laugh. "You jest?"

She cut her gaze to him. "The fact of the matter is that my father runs a completely legitimate shipping business. His father was not so law-abiding." It was her turn to shrug. "Apparently he was a pirate, and a good one at that until he swung from a yardarm by his neck." She met his gaze. "So I would understand if you wish to withdraw your proposal."

"Withdraw my proposal?" William laughed. "I'm getting a beautiful wife, one with a wicked past to boot. Why would I want to withdraw my proposal?" He stood up. "Now come." He offered his hand.

Ally rose. "You don't care, truly?"

"Not a bit." He smiled, seeming utterly enchanted with her.

Ally slipped on her gloves and tried to smooth her hair. "I'm a mess," she mumbled. "Perhaps I should slip out a side door."

"Nonsense." He pushed aside her hands and lifted the stray lock of hair. "Turn around," he ordered.

Ally did as she was told.

William tucked the hair back into her coiffure and took her by the shoulder to turn her to face him. "Perfect," he said.

Ally could feel his breath on her lips. She couldn't drag her gaze from his. If anyone came into the garden now, she'd not be welcome in anyone's parlor for committing such an impropriety.

"I want to kiss you, Ally," he said, again shocking her with his forthrightness. "What do you think?"

Ally had never been kissed before. But she wanted to be. She wanted to be kissed by this man. This man whom she barely knew. This man whom she had just agreed to marry.

"I should like that," she whispered.

He needed no further invitation. Viscount William Bridle lowered his mouth to hers.

Ally didn't know what she expected, but this was not it. The instant his lips met hers she felt a pulse of shock, of delicious pleasure.

She parted her lips slightly as she lifted her hands to rest on his shoulders. He smelled faintly of shaving soap, leather, and masculinity. The garden had grown cool and Will was so warm.

Ally heard herself sigh and she felt her legs

weaken. She leaned against him for support, hoping his kiss would last forever.

It did not.

She lifted her lashes and smiled as he withdrew.

He smiled back. "I think you and I will get along well, Ally," he said huskily and offered his arm. "Shall we go inside and make our announcement?"

"Here?" Her eyes widened. "Now?"

"Can you imagine the look on the young lady's face when she hears of how her wager has been satisfied? She will leave the ball tonight with a filled dance card. You, my puss, will leave with a future husband."

"Mrs. Trumbell, are you certain you're all right?" Ally waved her chaperone's painted fan in front of her face.

Mrs. Trumbell's eyelids flickered. "I knew you would be the death of me, Alison May. I just knew it."

During a break in the music, the Viscount Bridle had gone to his hostess and asked her to make the announcement of his and Ally's engagement. Mrs. Trumbell had fainted dead away, taking a table linen and a tray of sweets with her. Ally had run to her aid and with the assistance of several footmen had brought her to the lady's retiring room. She was now stretched out on a long couch set here for just this purpose.

Ally sat beside Mrs. Trumbell and began to wave the fan again.

Elspeth burst through the door, a cup in her

hand. "Here, Ally. Punch with spirits added, just as you asked." Her plain face was lined with concern. "Is she all right?"

"She will be fine." Ally took the cup. "Now go back to the dance floor." She smiled slyly. "I saw Mr. Bark talking with you. Don't keep him waiting."

Elspeth's face pinked with a mixture of delight and embarrassment. "He is very kind, as well as a good dancer. I told him it wasn't proper that I dance with him more than two or three times, but he seems unwilling to take no for an answer." Tears welled suddenly in her eyes. "I cannot thank you enough. What you did for me—"

"Nonsense, I'll hear nothing more. Now go. Dance while you can with your Mr. Bark."

Elspeth nodded, but still hesitated.

Mrs. Trumbell seemed to be looking better. Her gaze was focused again, and color was returning to her cheeks.

"Is it true?" Elspeth whispered. "Are you truly engaged to the Viscount Bridle?"

Mrs. Trumbell gave a cry and put her head back on a pillow, closing her eyes.

Ally couldn't resist a grin. "It is true. I'll tell you all about it later," she added in a whisper. "Now go."

As Elspeth left the ladies' retiring room, Lucy burst in. "Have you lost what little wits you possessed, Alison May?"

Ally glanced up. "Whatever do you mean?" she asked innocently.

"You know what I mean," Lucy hissed. She grabbed Ally's arm and pulled her off the couch, so that Mrs. Trumbell could not hear. "I know why you're doing this and it's madness. Admit you were wrong and I will release you from your ridiculous wager."

Ally pulled her arm from Lucy's grasp. "I will do no such thing. I lost the wager." She had no intention of telling Lucy how she had lost. "And now I will pay the price. The viscount and I will wed within a fortnight, depending on when a special license can be acquired, and that night I will surrender my virginity."

Lucy's lower lip trembled. "It is not right, you of all people wedding before any of us," she accused.

"Alison? Alison?" Mrs. Trumbell raised a hand. "Are you there, dear? Have you my refreshment?" She struggled to sit up. "I fear I am feeling dizzy again."

"Here I am, Mrs. Trumbell." Ally left Lucy to return to the couch. "Here is your punch." She sat on the edge of the couch again, holding the cup to her chaperone's lips. "Here you go. I'm sure you'll be recovered in no time."

Ally turned back to Lucy just in time to see her flounce out of the room, slamming the door behind her in a most unladylike way.

Ally couldn't resist a smile. She didn't know quite what she'd gotten herself into yet, but whatever happened, she was certain her life was not going to be dull anytime soon.

CHAPTER FOUR

"Lady Bridle?" A soft tap on the bedchamber door startled Ally. "Lady Bridle, can I come in?"

It took Ally a moment to realize the woman on the other side of the door was addressing her. *She* was Lady Bridle now, wife of the Viscount William Bridle, and had been for nearly six hours.

"Yes, of course," she called. "Come in."

A young girl with a shock of orange-red hair entered William's bedchamber with an armful of towels and a pitcher of water. She kept her gaze downcast, her cheeks pink with the day's excitement. "My Lord Bridle asked me to see if there was anything else you need before he joins you."

Ally couldn't resist a smile. The girl appeared more nervous about the wedding night than Ally did. "I am quite fine, thank you." She smiled reassuringly. "Tell me, what is your name?"

The redhead laid the towels and pitcher on the

washstand on the far side of the room. She tucked her hands behind her back. "Fanny, m'lady."

"Well, it is nice to make your acquaintance, Fanny. Thank you for the towels."

Fanny glanced sideways at the postered bed that dominated the room, then back at Ally. "Shall I turn down the bed, m'lady?"

"That won't be necessary." Ally, dressed in a filmy lavender sleeping gown and robe, walked to the door. "Thank you, dear. That will be all for tonight, but I do like to take tea in my room first thing in the morning."

"Yes, my lady." Fanny curtsied again and hurried out the door. "I'll be up soon as you wake."

Alone, Ally began to pace. The last three weeks had been such confusion that this was the first time she'd actually been able to catch her breath. Since the announcement of her engagement, there had been a blur of parties to congratulate her and her prospective bridegroom. There had been a flurry of shopping for her trousseau, and it seemed that every house in London had wanted her to call so they could get a good look at her. She had seen Will almost every day since the night of Mrs. Davenport's ball, but she didn't feel as if they had really gotten to know each other yet. And now they were married. It was their wedding night, and in the morning Ally would be able to say she had met her wager with Lucy.

Ally glanced at the door. She wasn't so much nervous about tonight as she was eager to get to it. She knew what was involved in coupling, and did not think of it with distaste as many of the young women at Mrs. Trumbell's did. Ally's father had always been forthright in talking with his daughter. He had told her quite plainly that when the time was right, when the man and woman were right for each other, married relations were a pleasure for both.

Ally hoped she and Will were right for each other.

She glanced at the closed door again. As the minutes on the mantel clock ticked by loudly, she became more nervous. Will had said he had a matter to see to in his study and then he would be in for bed. Where was he? He had been gone more than an hour. She knew he was just being polite. Giving her time to get into her bedclothes. But now that she was ready for him, she wanted no further delay.

Ally walked to the door, opened it, and peered into the hall. She knew her mother-in-law slept at the end of the dark hallway. She could hear her snoring. Light spilled from beneath a door just to the left of Will's bedchamber. Ally walked to the door, hesitated, then knocked.

"Come in," Will called, no doubt assuming it was Fanny come to check on him.

He glanced up from the book he was reading, his face registering obvious surprise. "Ally." He rose from the chair, setting aside the book.

Ally stood in the doorway, unsure of herself. The room was small and paneled with dark wood. Very masculine. It smelled slightly of tobacco and the scent of Will, which had become familiar to her in the last weeks.

"I didn't mean to disturb you. I only . . ." She gave a little laugh, letting her sentence fade into silence. She raised her hands. "I have no idea why I'm here, honestly." She met his gaze, uncertain of herself.

Will stood for a moment and studied her. He was dressed for bed as well, in a blue silk dressing robe, his dark hair damp and freshly combed.

"What?" she asked, beginning to squirm under his scrutiny. "Why are you looking at me like that?"

"I was just thinking that I married a very lovely woman today, that's all." He approached her and took her hands in his.

She smiled. He was sweet, her Will. *Her* Will. It seemed such an odd thought. She was married to a man she didn't know, a man her father didn't know.

Ally had sent her father word in America of her impending marriage immediately. She'd not yet heard from him, but only because of the time it took a letter to reach America and a reply to England. Once she received the congratulations she knew he would send, she would feel better. Right now she needed her father's reassurance to boost her confidence.

Will brushed his hand over her shoulder, pushing the heavy curtain of her honey brown hair back. "Would you like some claret?" He indicated a glass decanter on a table.

Ally wanted to keep her wits about her, but she was growing more nervous by the moment. The truth was, she was beginning to look forward to discovering exactly what went on between a woman and her husband and she wasn't sure how she felt about that. She smiled shyly. "I would."

Will poured them each a glass. "Shall we retire, puss?"

Ally nodded. She blew out the oil lamp beside his reading chair and followed him down the hall to the room that had been Will's, but was now her bedchamber, as well. They had briefly discussed separate chambers. Will said ladies often preferred it that way, but Ally would have no part of it. Women on the Chesapeake certainly didn't sleep separately from their husbands.

Will stepped back and let her enter the room first, then followed, and closed the door.

Ally walked to the middle of the bedchamber before she turned to face him. Suddenly the large room seemed smaller. The lovely papered walls appeared to be closing in on her. The bed loomed like a great monster in the darkness.

Will pushed the glass into her hand. "A toast," he murmured in that husky voice of his. "To us."

She clinked his glass. "To us." She took a sip, then another. The warmth of the spirits ran down her throat.

Will drank and then set his glass down. He took her hand and led her toward the bed. "Don't be afraid," he soothed.

She flashed him her bravest smile. "I'm not really."

He took her glass from her hand and set it beside his. He settled his hands on her hips. "Did you see the look on Miss Granger's face when the ceremony was complete? The chit was near green with envy."

Ally chuckled and the sound of her own laugher seemed to break her nervousness. She was dying to be kissed again, kissed by Will.

He took his time, moving slowly. He caressed her cheek with his hand, then slid it down, across the back of her neck.

Ally let her eyes drift shut, enjoying the nearness of her husband, and the newness of feelings she hadn't known existed until she met him a few weeks ago. It was true she didn't know her husband well yet, but she did know that she was attracted to him. Immensely.

Will pulled her close, covering her mouth with his.

She slid her hands over the smooth silk of his dressing gown, over his broad shoulders. His body felt good pressed against hers, his hardness to her softness.

Will teased her lips apart and she moaned softly. He tasted of claret and that same maleness she found intoxicating in his scent.

Will stepped back, taking her in his arms with him. He sat on the edge of the bed and drew her onto his lap. Another shared kiss. Two. Three. Ally felt the room spinning around her. The more he kissed her, the more she wanted to be kissed.

When Will slid his hand into her dressing gown, it seemed so natural. Suddenly, she realized she wanted to feel his touch on her breast. The first brush of his thumb against her nipple sent such an exquisite shock of pleasure through her that she cried out in surprise.

"I didn't hurt you, did I?" he whispered in her ear.

She laughed, feeling oddly on the verge of tears. Her whole body was pulsing. "No," she breathed, hungry for his mouth. "It feels wonderful."

Will cupped her breast in his hand and Ally tightened her arms around his neck. He kissed her mouth, then her chin. She lifted her head, exposing her neck to him, and he planted a row of brief, fleeting kisses, moving downward to the hollow of her throat.

"You're good at this," she whispered, not wanting to know the history of his experience. What mattered was that he was hers now. All hers until death did part them.

It was his turn to chuckle. "I'm glad you approve." He lifted his gaze. "Because I want you to be happy, Ally. Especially considering the circumstances."

She pressed her mouth to his. "I am happy right now," she whispered against his lips. "Happier than I think I've ever been in my life. I didn't know it would be like this."

He turned on the bed, gently laying her back so that her head rested on the pillows. Slowly, he opened her wrap so that only the thin silk lavender gown lay between his hand and her bare skin. "Do you want me to blow out the lamps?" he asked.

She gazed out at the soft flicker of lamplight that illuminated the room. "Are we supposed to?"

He laughed, smoothing her hair, which tumbled over her shoulders. He gazed into her eyes, which were heavy-lidded with desire for him. "Oh, Ally, you're a delight I never for a moment anticipated. I'm a lucky man."

He took her mouth hungrily this time, but Ally was not afraid. She was not afraid of Will, or of her own awakening desire.

He removed her slippers and tossed them to the

floor. Her dressing gown floated off the edge of the bed. Ally closed her eyes as he lifted the hem of her gown, running his hand over her calf . . . and upward.

Will's dressing gown fell open to reveal his bare chest. The feel of the dark, springy curls beneath her hand fascinated Ally. When she inadvertently brushed his nipple with her finger, he groaned with pleasure. The thought that she, too, could give him pleasure made her bold. She explored the muscles of his chest, his shoulders, and even the flat of his stomach.

They rolled in the bed and his dressing gown fell further open. The proof of his desire for her brushed her bare leg and she shivered with a heat that took her by surprise.

Ally didn't know how or when their clothing fell away, but she found herself naked in the bed beneath him. The room spun. She was hot and cold at the same time. Laughing one moment, near to crying the next. Her whole body ached for that which she had never known.

When the time at last came that she thought she would have to embarrass herself and beg, Will took her. He was gentle, sweet, as he covered her face, her neck, her bare, aching breasts with kisses.

Ally felt no pain, only an overwhelming feeling of fullness followed by a sense of relief.

When Will began to move slowly over her to feed his own growing desire, she found herself matching his rhythm. They were bound together by her hair and their bare limbs, moving as one. She felt as if she were floating somewhere above her body and she wondered if this was what heaven was like.

He moved faster, pressing her deeper into the bed. Her breath came faster, her heart pounding in her chest. All she wanted was . . . was . . . She didn't know what she wanted, only that no one but Will could give it.

Relief came in a great tidal wave that took her utterly by surprise. She cried out. Her muscles tightened in glorious release and then relaxed. Will gave a final thrust and moaned and then Ally felt as if she were floating again . . . floating back to earth, to London, to the bed she shared with her new husband.

Will slid off Ally and onto the bed beside her. He drew her against him, wrapping her securely in his arms. "That was incredible, puss," he whispered, his voice still husky.

She turned to look at him, the bed curtains casting shadows across his handsome face. She couldn't resist a smile. "I cannot think of anything to say." She lowered her lashes. "I didn't know it would be like this."

He kissed her again, closing his eyes. "I think, then, that we are very lucky to have found each other. Good night, wife, granddaughter of a pirate."

"Good night, husband," she whispered and let her eyes drift shut. She knew she should blow out the lamps but she didn't have the energy to rise from the bed. Ripples of pleasure still washed over her. She felt as if her bones were jelly. She was anxious to sleep so that the new day would come and she would begin to get to know this man she had fallen in love with in the last hour.

* * *

Ally awoke in the morning to a tapping on the door. She glanced at the empty place beside her on the bed and then at the clock on the mantel. It was after nine!

"Yes?" she called. Then, realizing she was still as naked as the day she had been delivered, she grabbed for her dressing gown. It lay folded neatly on the end of the bed. Will must have picked it up off the floor for her when he rose earlier. She hadn't heard him go. She must have slept better last night than she had ever slept in her life.

Ally slid her bare feet to the floor and pushed her arms into the gown. "Fanny?"

The door opened. "Good morning, daughter." Ally's mother-in-law, the Dowager Viscountess Bridle, hustled her plump self through the door.

Embarrassed, Ally quickly drew her robe tighter, trying to tie the sash and cover herself. She doubted her mother-in-law could help but notice her sleeping gown laid across the bed linens, but she could think of no way to dispose of it. She could do nothing but smile weakly.

Ally had met the dowager on several occasions, but she knew her no better than she knew Will. She had hoped they could get a better start today than this.

Mother Bridle drew open the heavy gold velvet drapes that covered the windows. Sunshine poured through the floor-to-ceiling windows. "Let us hasten, Miss Laze-in-the-Bed. We've an appointment with Mrs. Gaffey at eleven sharp, and you've not even begun to dress." She walked to the large wardrobe Will had purchased just for her and opened the door. "Let me see what you should wear." She pulled out one frock after another.

Ally didn't know what to say. She didn't want her mother-in-law to riffle through her belongings or to choose a gown for her, but she didn't know how to stop her without being rude. She wondered who Mrs. Gaffey was and why they had an appointment with her. "Where is Will?" she asked.

"He's an early riser. We are all early risers here." The dowager looked at Ally down the end of her nose. "So he's off for the day. His gentleman's club for breakfast, then riding, then I don't know." She fluttered a hand covered in jeweled rings. "Whatever it is that men do so that we ladies can be left alone."

"Tea, m'lady." Fanny entered with a tray in her hands.

Ally threw her a look of thanksgiving. A familiar face. One not quite so hostile. "Thank you, dear. On the table would be fine."

Mother Bridle glanced at the tea tray and then back at the wardrobe, her mouth turned down at the corners in a frown. "Ordinarily I take my morning tea downstairs at seven-thirty. Tomorrow you will join me."

Fanny poured Ally a cup of tea and backed toward the door. "You need anything else, m'lady, just give me a ring." She pointed to the bell cord beside the door, curtsied, and made a fast exit.

"Thank you," Ally called after her.

"You need not be so friendly with the help," Mother Bridle said the moment the door shut. "If you become too friendly with the staff, they will take advantage of you."

Ally wanted to ask just how a housemaid could take advantage of her mistress, but she bit her tongue and reached for her teacup. "Did Will say when he would be home?"

"He did not. Late I suppose, unless you two have an engagement. Then before six to change." She pulled out a frothy white gauze frock Ally didn't care for. "This is perfect for me to show you off in, my dear." She dropped the gown onto the bed. "Now hurry and dress. If you have need, Fanny is trained as an abigail as well." She moved toward the door, the gray taffeta of her too-tight gown crackling as she walked. "And do something with that hair, Alison. It's frightful!"

Before Ally could think of a good retort, the door was shut and she was alone on her first full day of marriage.

CHAPTER FIVE

Ally stared at the clock on the bedchamber mantel. It was nearly one in the morning. She rolled over in the big bed and placed her hand on the smooth, cool sheet beside her. She was tired, but she couldn't sleep. Where was Will at this time of night?

She rolled onto her back again and stared at the deep crimson bed hangings. It had been a long day. She had spent most of her waking hours accompanying her mother-in-law from one parlor to the next. The dowager said she wanted to "show off" her new daughter. By suppertime, Ally felt more like one of Lady Bridle's pet dogs than a new member of the family.

She had spent the entire day smiling, forcing polite conversation, and dodging not-so-subtle questions concerning her family's past. All day, Ally had kept thinking that if she could just get through it, she would be rewarded with an evening with Will. She had daydreamed of going to the theater, or out for a light supper, or better yet, taking supper in the privacy of their room, where they could talk. She wanted to know so many things about this new husband of hers. What were his dreams? His ambitions? What kind of foods did he like? What had made him spend an entire year in Africa? What had drawn him there? More importantly, what had kept him there?

Ally brushed her hair off her forehead and sighed. She had returned home from her outing with her mother-in-law, hoping Will would be waiting for her. Instead, she had been the one waiting . . . all evening. Each time she heard a carriage roll by beneath her window she had run to see if it was him. And now it was after one and she had not received so much as a note from him.

Had he changed his mind about wanting to be married to her, she wondered. Last night had been wonderful, a dream from which she hadn't wanted to wake. He had seemed pleased with her. Had she misunderstood? She had known they would be making no wedding trip, but she had still assumed he would spend some time with her. Will had financial matters to deal with because he had been gone so long. But once those matters were wrapped up, he had said he thought they could travel to America so that he could meet her father. He said he had never been to America and she was his perfect excuse to go.

Could he have changed his mind about her this quickly? Did he think he had made a mistake in wedding her? Ally was usually full of confidence, but she was beginning to second-guess herself. What would make a man leave his wife the day after their wedding and not return until after one on the morning?

What if he didn't return at all? What if he just left her with his mother and sailed for Africa again?

Ally heard another coach outside her window, but she made no attempt to get up. When she heard it stop in front of the town house, heard a male voice, and then doors open and close, she still didn't rise. It had to be Will. And now that he was home, she was annoyed with him. What right did he have to treat her this way? Hadn't he agreed they would be man and wife in every sense of the word? This was not what she had in mind when she married him. She wanted them to be partners. Friends. This was not the way to begin a friendship, much less a marriage. They would have to discuss this matter immediately.

The bedchamber door opened. Without having to look, she knew it was him. She could smell the scent of him—tobacco, shaving soap, port, the scent of his skin. He moved about the room, quietly removing his coat and hat. He sat on a chair to pull off his polished shoes.

She watched him by the flickering light of the single lamp that burned on the far side of the room.

He studied her still form in the darkness. "I woke you," he said quietly. "I'm sorry."

She shook her head slowly as she studied him in the dim light. He was so blessedly handsome, even in his state of undress. Perhaps more so. "I'm not asleep yet. I was waiting for you."

He padded in his stocking feet across the room and sat on the edge of the bed. "You shouldn't have, puss. You need your sleep." He caressed her cheek, and against her will, her eyes drifted shut as she let the pleasure of his tender caress wash over her.

She was angry with him for leaving her alone with his mother all day, but the anger seemed to melt away at his touch. Her intention to discuss the matter wavered. "I thought you would come home sooner," she said.

He rose to continue undressing. "Didn't you have a nice day? Mama said she had great plans for the two of you."

Ally wanted to say that that was all well and fine, but she didn't want to spend her first day as a married woman with her new mother-in-law. She wanted to spend the day with him. But now that he was here, the matter seemed trivial. He hadn't sailed to Africa; he had come home to share her bed. She held her tongue, realizing she didn't want to argue. Now that he was here, she wanted nothing more than for Will to climb into bed with her and make love.

"My day was fine. Your mother is a dear woman."

He flashed her an all-knowing grin. "She is not, but it is kind of you to say so."

"She is well-meaning and I do think she likes me."

"How could she not?" He removed his cravat and tossed it on a chair.

She couldn't help smiling back, nor could she help but slide over in the bed as Will removed the last of his clothing. She felt her cheeks color at the sight of his nakedness, but she didn't look away. She liked his body, so fascinating with its hard lines and muscular planes, so different from her own.

He climbed into bed beside her and she lifted the bedcovers to make a place for him. "Do you think we could do something tomorrow?" she asked. "There's a bookstore near the Strand. They have some wonderful travel books there. I thought we could find something on America for you."

He slipped his arm beneath her and drew her close. "I'm sorry, puss, I've meetings all day. Why don't you take the carriage tomorrow and see what you can find for us? Perhaps your lady friends would like to join you."

She bit down on her lower lip, trying not to sound disappointed. "I could do that, I suppose."

"I'll leave money on the mantel."

She gazed into his eyes. "I've my own money, Will. I told you that. My father has provided well for me and there will be a more than adequate dowry."

"My goodness," he teased, "I have never seen you so heated." He tickled her. "I like that fire in those green eyes."

"I am not 'heated.' " She slapped away his hands. "I just do not want you to get the wrong idea. I didn't marry you for your money." She wanted to say that she wasn't sure at all right now why she married him, but she held back her thoughts.

"And I do not want *you* to get the wrong idea," Will said. "What I have is now yours and I have a great deal, Ally. You are my wife and I only wish to share it with you." He kissed her gently on the mouth.

"What about a late supper, then?" she asked, redirecting the conversation. She would not give up easily.

He buried his face in the crook of her neck. "Perhaps," he growled playfully.

Ally wanted to say something more, to make definite plans, but all conscious thought slipped from her mind as he began to kiss her in earnest. Caress her body . . .

Tomorrow, she thought as she kissed him back. Tomorrow they would discuss this matter further. Tomorrow when she again had command of her wits.

"So how is married life?" Lucy purred. She picked up one of the dowager's porcelain trinkets from a table in the morning room and turned it over to read its mark.

"I like it very much," Ally said, smiling. In truth, in the last two weeks she had become rather disenchanted with the whole institution of marriage, but she wouldn't have told Lucy that, not for all the teas in China.

Ally loved Will. She loved being with him. But that was just the trouble. He spent almost no time with her, save at bedtime. He stayed out late at night and left early in the morning. At first Ally had made excuses to herself for him. He had "business" to attend to. Men to call upon. Business associates to confer with. But upon questioning him, she found that much of his day was spent at men's clubs, boxing matches, and the racetrack. He said he wanted to be married. He told her he wanted a wife. She had concluded that he apparently wanted to have a wife and still carry on the life he had led as a bachelor.

Ally indicated the doorway. "Breakfast is served, ladies, do join me in the dining room."

Elspeth and Anne each took Ally's hand as they passed into the dining room. "I'm so glad you invited us," Anne said. "I have been dying to see Lord Bridle's home." She giggled. "Your home, I mean."

"Yes," Elspeth said. "We are so glad to see you. We want to hear all about married life and the dashing Lord Bridle."

Ally linked her arm through Elspeth's and escorted her into the next room. If Lucy wanted to inspect every piece of porcelain in the house, Ally didn't care. "Let's not talk about me. How are things going with Mr. Bark?" She waggled a finger teasingly. "I have heard rumors he is quite smitten with one of Mrs. Trumbell's young ladies."

Elspeth's face flushed. "He has called on me four times in the last fortnight. We see him almost every morning in the park, and he has invited me to the theater next week. We are going with others, friends of his, of course, but I cannot wait for the night to come."

Ally brushed her cheek against her friend's arm. "I truly think he is smitten with you, Elspeth."

Elspeth could not contain herself. "Do you think? I am trying not to be too hopeful, but oh, Ally, he is such a wonderful man. So kind. So gentle. He is a barrister, you know. His family is well respected in Bath, where his parents reside."

"Smitten," Anne remarked, taking one of the

places that had been set at the table. "Our Elspeth is too modest. He's madly in love with her."

Elspeth wiped her eyes with her handkerchief. "Please, Anne. You embarrass me."

"Who is in love with whom?" Lucy asked, joining them in the dining room.

Elspeth took her seat, staring down at the plate.

Ally knew how Elspeth felt. Lucy could ruin a sunny day. "Me," she said, taking her place at the head of the table. "I am madly in love with my husband."

"How romantic," Anne said dreamily.

Lucy only lifted a brow as she sat and unfolded her napkin. "I still cannot believe you have done this, Alison. I cannot fathom what will become of you." She lifted her gaze to meet Ally's. "Once Lord Bridle has tired of you."

"Lucy!" Anne said.

Lucy glared at Anne. "Well someone needs to tell her." She turned back to Ally, pressing her palms to the table. "There are rumors he is all about town in the evenings. *Alone* . . . so they say."

Elspeth made little mewing sounds of distress.

Ally tightened her hold on her napkin, half rising from her chair.

Just then, Fanny entered the room to serve the first breakfast course. Ally took a deep breath and held her tongue. She was so angry that she was trembling. But she would not embarrass herself or Fanny by responding to such a rude comment. She would not be inviting Lucy to her home again either.

Ally reached over and patted Elspeth's hand. "So tell me," she said, settling in her seat again as

Fanny served her. She made a point of turning her attention away from Lucy, toward Anne and Elspeth. "What is about at Mrs. Trumbell's? Has she said when she will have her ball?"

Ally spent most of the day with Anne and Elspeth. After breakfast, Lucy excused herself, saying she had a touch of a headache. She took Mrs. Trumbell's carriage home, and Ally and Anne and Elspeth spent the day shopping. At five, Ally returned the ladies to Mrs. Trumbell's and returned home to dress. She and Will were attending a ball that evening and she was anxious to see him.

Fanny helped her with her hair, and by the time Will arrived home, she was dressed and primped.

"Goodness," Will said, coming into their bedchamber, "you are a sight to behold this evening, my Lady Bridle."

She blushed at the compliment. Curtsied. "I'm glad you like it."

The gown was high-waisted and spun of a silky gold fabric. The hue would complement her complexion and the color of her hair, the modiste had assured her.

While Will dressed, Ally searched for a reticule in her wardrobe. "Your mother says she is not feeling well and won't be attending with us. You should visit her before we go."

"Is she ill?"

Ally shook her head. "Tired, perhaps. She spent the day with her friends. She says she is too old for balls anyway." She flashed him a saucy smile.

"She thinks balls should be left to young romantics like you and me."

As he picked up his coat, he grabbed her by the waist.

Ally squealed.

He pulled her against him and kissed the back of her neck. "I'm sorry," he murmured in her ear. "I am crushing your frock."

"I don't care," she said. She turned his arms. "I've missed you."

He kissed her and let her go. "Missed me, whatever do you mean?"

She hesitated, not sure if this was the time for this conversation. But for the last two weeks she had been trying to figure out just when the best time for this conversation was.

'It's just that you're gone so much and I'm here alone."

"You're not alone." He slipped into his coat. "Mama is here. You have your friends."

She rested her hands on her hips. "It's not the same thing."

"Same thing as what?"

"As being with you."

He looked at her as if he had no idea what she was talking about.

"Will," she said, "you are gone every day, all day."

"My business—"

"It's not just business," she interrupted. "You spend hours at the racetrack. You admit so yourself. You play cards and drink with your friends."

"I haven't come home intoxicated," he replied.

"I didn't say you did." She bristled. "Would you

listen to what I'm saying? You told me you wanted a wife. You don't want a wife. You want a bed partner."

His mouth tightened. She had made him angry. A part of her wished she hadn't, but a part of her felt as if it was time she stood up for herself.

"I have known these men for many years," he said coolly. "They are my friends."

"I am not asking you to give up your friends," she said.

He glanced at the clock. "We're going to be late."

Ally sighed, letting her hands fall to her sides. "I don't want you to be angry with me," she said. "Can't we just talk about this?"

"I have noted your concern." He walked out the bedchamber door. "I'll say good night to Mama and meet you below."

Ally stood alone for a moment, wanting to call him back. She hadn't meant to make such a mess of things. She just wanted to talk to him. To make him understand how she felt.

Tears burned behind her eyelids as she grabbed her reticule. Maybe he would think over what she said. Maybe they could talk about it later.

Or maybe she had made a terrible mistake in marrying him.

CHAPTER SIX

Ally stood in the midst of a group of women in a small hall off the ballroom of a lord and lady she had not known until she was presented to them an hour ago. Once Will and Ally made their way through the receiving line, he had excused himself to speak with a business associate he said he spotted across the room. He was graciously polite to her in front of those in the receiving line, but it had been obvious to her that he was still annoyed by their conversation back at the town house.

Ally pressed a gloved hand to her temple. Her head was pounding. The women around her were all talking at once. She felt as if she were drowning in the sea of white frocks and the music that wafted from the marble ballroom. It seemed that everyone wanted to meet the new Lady Bridle and those who already knew her wanted to be her closest friend. Someone had brought her a cup of punch.

Another, thinking she looked overheated, was fanning her with an ivory fan. Ally kept smiling, nodding, trying to answer with reasonable responses, but she wished she were anywhere but in public.

"Have you been to Viscount Bridle's country house?" A young woman with the pinched face of a ferret tapped her fan coyly. "It's quite fine."

"And which house would that be?" another questioned, puffing up with self-importance. "I've been to both of the viscount's country houses, Whitborne in Dorsetshire and Twyford Court near Canterbury."

Ally *was* overly warm now. She was so warm that she feared she was going to grow light-headed. She didn't want to stand here and talk of meaningless matters with these women; she just wanted to go home with her husband. Home, where she could settle this whole contretemps with Will before it got out of hand. "Excuse me, ladies," she said, giving a hasty curtsy and walking away before they gave her leave.

The women's voices faded as she glided off. They were probably talking about her, thinking her a rude Colonial, but Ally didn't care. She wanted to find Will and tell him she was ready to go home. As she entered the ballroom, she spotted him standing near the far wall. His back was to her, but she knew him immediately. They had been wed a short time, but she would recognize his silhouette anywhere—the broad shoulders displayed so finely within his well-cut coat, the long muscular legs, even the curve of the back of his head.

Ally's heart tripped. She loved him. Seeing him across the ballroom this way, getting this feeling in the pit of her stomach, she realized how much she loved him. This was not just some innocent young woman's infatuation, this was love, and she knew in her heart of hearts that this kind of love only came once in a lifetime. It was up to her to see that they settled this disagreement between them before it formed a chasm they could not breach.

Ally approached Will from behind, heard his laughter, even above a contredanse that was playing, his voice rich and masculine. She forced a smile for the benefit of his companion, took a breath to collect herself, and circled to join him.

Ally's gaze collided with Lucy's.

Lucy! What was Lucy doing talking to her husband? Why was Will laughing that way with her?

Ally immediately bristled. She knew full well that in polite society a woman could speak with a man she had previously been introduced to. There was no harm in Lucy inquiring about Ally's health, or his, for that matter. But the guilty look on Lucy's face told Ally she was up to no good and knew she was caught.

"Ally, dear," Lucy purred, her tone smug, "we were just speaking of you, weren't we, Lord Bridle?" She met Will's gaze with a flirting look Ally felt was utterly inappropriate.

Ally gave a curt nod, trying not to grind her teeth. "Lucy, good to see you. Lovely gown." She turned to Will without bothering to glance at Lucy's frock. "I'm not feeling well, my lord. I want to go home."

Will's eyes narrowed with what seemed like genuine concern. "Certainly, my dearest." He took her arm. "If you'll excuse us," he said to Lucy.

Lucy curtsied as they walked away.

Will sent a footman to get Ally's wrap and another to call for their coach. He said nothing to her as they waited in the entrance hall except to inquire if she needed to sit. As the coach pulled in front of the great porch, he walked her down the steps on his arm and opened the carriage door for her himself.

"Go home and sleep," he said as he helped her in. "I knew you were doing too much. There are entirely too many social obligations for a new bride and I will speak with Mama about it in the morning. This damned city will be the death of us all."

Ally turned in confusion. "You're not coming with me?"

"I can't possibly." He seemed surprised she would think he would attend her. "It would be terribly rude of me. Lord and Lady Commages were very kind to Mama when I was gone. To leave now would be an insult."

Ally's face fell. "Will . . . I—"

"Be a good puss now, and go home," he said. He gave her gloved hand a quick peck. "I will not be late. I promise."

Will kept his word and was in just after the clock struck midnight. By then, Ally had experienced a gamut of emotions. She had been hurt when he had sent her home alone. Then angry. He knew she wanted him to accompany her. Had he been punishing her for their argument?

As to catching him in intimate conversation with Lucy, she didn't know what to make of that. Just the thought made her blood boil . . . then it made her sad, then afraid. What if Will really *was* having regrets? Lucy said he had been seen about town without Ally, insinuating he had been with other women. Could Lucy have been trying to tell her something? Had she seen or heard something that had truth to it? Or was Lucy just being Lucy and covertly trying to ruin her marriage?

"You're still awake," Will said, closing the door behind him. "You shouldn't have waited up."

Ally clutched the bed linens to her chin, suddenly feeling lost. Everything was such a mess. Nothing was what she had thought it would be when she married Will. Her and her ridiculous wagers! How could she have done this to herself?

"If you want an annulment," she blurted suddenly, "just say so." She didn't know where that thought had come from, but she was glad she had said it.

He turned to her from where he was placing his hat above a chiffonier. "What did you say?"

She wiped her eyes, determined she would not cry. Granddaughters of pirates never cried. "I said that if you want an annulment, I'm sure it can be arranged."

He came to the side of the bed. "What are you talking about, Ally?" He pressed his cool hand to her forehead. "Are you ill? Should I call a physician?"

She lay back on the pillows behind her and closed her eyes. She could feel him studying her. "I'm sorry about tonight."

"It's all right. If you didn't feel well, there was no need for you to stay. I made your apologies to the host and hostess and they were quite understanding."

"Not that," she said softly. "I mean earlier. Making you angry." Suddenly the fight was all gone from her. She wanted him to hold her. Tell her everything was going to be all right.

He sighed and reached out to stroke her arm. "It would be my guess that it takes all married couples time to settle in. With us, everything happened so quickly. This is bound to take a little time—to find our footing."

It was not exactly an apology and he hadn't said a word about Lucy, but . . .

"And we've settled in so well here in our bed," he said, his tone teasing, "that there is bound to be unrest elsewhere." He slid his hand over her shoulder to caress her neck.

Against her will, Ally curled against him. "I don't want to argue," she said.

"I know." He drew her into his arms. "And I do not want an annulment."

"Oh, Will."

Ally didn't want to crumble at his touch. She wanted to stand her ground. She wanted to tell him now what she required of him as a husband. But he was so close, so warm, and he smelled so good.

Why did this keep happening? Why couldn't she be of stronger resolve?

His lips found hers. His hands slid beneath the bed linens to her waist.

She wanted to tell him that she loved him. She

knew this was probably too soon for him to say the same, but she wanted so badly to hear those words. She was probably completely mistaken about Lucy. Lucy probably waylaid him and he was only being polite.

"Ah, puss," he whispered, "I did miss you tonight. After you left, it was if the light had gone out in the ballroom. No jewel sparkles on the *ton* as brightly as you."

Ally kissed him back. Touched him. She unbuttoned his brocade waistcoat and tossed it aside. Boldly, she reached for the buttons of his breeches.

He laughed, his voice deep and already filled with desire for her. "My shoes," he said, as he crawled into bed beside her, still half dressed. "I have my shoes on, wife."

Ally urged him onto his back, pushing him into the feather tick. "Have no fear, husband," she whispered, tickling his earlobe with her tongue. "They'll not get in my way."

For the next week, it seemed that Ally and Will had reached a truce. Without further mention of the matter, he did not stay out too late at night and she tried not to be too demanding. He accompanied her to several luncheons, took her to a poetry reading, and attended a dinner party Mrs. Trumbell gave. One night he even came home, supped, and then retired early to the bedchamber with Ally.

Ally still made calls with her mother-in-law and received guests at their home each afternoon. She still wrote endless invitations, endless thank-you notes. But as long as she could be with Will, she thought she could manage the social obligations she had as his wife.

When Ally was not accompanying her mother-in-law, she spent her time pouring over several books she had purchased on exploring America. She read and began to take notes on places she always wanted to see, places she thought Will would want to go.

The same week, Ally received a letter of congratulations from her father and a bank draft for a large sum of money. A wedding gift. He wanted to know when she and her husband would be paying a visit to the Tidewater.

A little more than a week after the ball held by the Lord and Lady Commages, Will escorted Ally to their bedchamber after supper and a game of cards with his mother. She had carried a stack of books to the bed, thinking they could pour over them together. She was hoping they could spend the evening alone, perhaps making plans. The more she read, the more she wanted to go home to America. She didn't know if it was so much that she was homesick, or that she was beginning to realize this life in London was not for her. She didn't enjoy the luncheons, balls, and dinner parties. She didn't enjoy the hours it took to dress in the required fripperies, and the forced smiles and polite conversation. She had no desire, as her contemporaries, to go out on the *ton* to see and be seen. She realized now that she had never been like the other young women at Mrs. Trumbell's and probably never would be.

Perhaps a holiday was just what she needed.

"Look what I've found on the American West," Ally told Will as she lay across the bed on her stomach and reached for a book. "I find the Indians fascinating. We could go West to St. Louis by coach, but what would you think of going by horseback?" She waved him over. "Come see."

"Ally, I would like nothing more than to look with you, but I must go out for a short time."

She turned to see Will taking his hat. "Go out? Go out where?"

He buttoned his black and gray woolen coat over his waistcoat. "No need to worry yourself. I've a business matter to attend to, but I won't be late."

Ally rolled over and sat up. She had waited two days to show him this book. Last night there had been a ball they had had to attend at his mother's insistence, and the night before that, a friend of Will's had invited them to share a box at the theater with them.

She didn't want him to go. "Will—"

He glanced at the clock. It was nearly eight. "Ally, I really have to go. I have an engagement I cannot postpone, but I'll be back soon. I promise."

Before Ally could protest, he was gone.

For a moment Ally just sat on the edge of the bed and stared at the mahogany paneled door. Where was he going that was so important it could not wait? What business did he have that was more important than his wife?

A terrible thought struck her. Was he meeting another woman?

She couldn't believe he would do such a thing. But was she being naïve? Had there been more truth to Lucy's insinuations than she cared to consider?

Ally flopped back on the bed, on the verge of tears. What could she do? Will had given no explanation and it was obvious that he had no intentions of doing so later. She was helpless to do anything but to stay here and wait. It was the fate of women, she supposed.

Suddenly Ally sat up again. Helpless? Since when had she been helpless? What did she mean, telling herself she had no choice? Of course she had choices. As long as she drew breath, she had choices. She could lie here on her bed and cry, or she could get up and go find out what Will was up to. She could lie here and feel sorry for herself, or she could take matters into her own hands and do what she could to save her marriage.

Ally grabbed her cloak from a chair and hurried out the door. With any luck, Will would have taken the larger carriage and she could find a stable boy to harness the horses to the curricle. If she was lucky, she would be able to catch up with him in the faster vehicle.

The grooms were none too comfortable with their new mistress's unannounced presence in the stables, but Ally was firm, and in a few minutes the curricle was harnessed to two bays.

Ally knew it was not a good idea for a woman to be out at night, driving unescorted on London's streets, but if she was going to confront Will, she wanted no audience. She wanted no one from their household to have anything to gossip about at breakfast.

The question was, how did she get away without

a footman or an outrider? She didn't want to put any of the stable hands' positions at risk. She knew they would be held responsible in the morning, perhaps even lose their positions and be sent off without a reference, if they allowed her to leave unescorted. In the end, Ally went for the simple solution of feminine deceit.

A footman named Edwin led the horses and carriage into the short driveway that led to the street and assisted Ally up onto the bench seat. As she slid over to make room for him to drive, she covered her mouth with her hand. "Oh goodness," she declared, "in my haste, I do believe I have forgotten my bonnet. How silly of me." She chuckled for effect. "Edwin, would you be so kind as to go into the kitchen, find Fanny, and have her fetch it and bring it to me?"

The footman did not hesitate, of course, and took off at a trot to do his mistress's bidding.

The moment he disappeared into the darkness at the rear of the house, Ally glanced behind her. The other stable hands were busy talking as they swept up a stall, and gave no notice to her. She lifted the reins, clucked between her teeth, and the curricle rolled forward.

The moment she was out onto the street, she slapped the reins and the horses took off at a merry jaunt, leaving a perplexed Edwin, no doubt, in the middle of the stable yard holding a lady's bonnet in his hand.

By the time she was out on the street, Will was nowhere in sight, but she pressed on. She wasn't even sure where she would look for him, but she was determined now not to give up easily. There were many possibilities as to where Will was headed—the theater, a friend's home, White's. Her first guess was his men's club. After that, she didn't know where she might search. She'd cross that footbridge when she came to it.

Luck was with Ally. A short time later, she turned up a street and spotted her husband's coach in front of the brick building that housed White's Men's Club. She had no intention of going inside. She would not embarrass herself or Will that way, but she would wait all night for him if she had to.

Ally eased the curricle off the street and pulled the brake. It was cool this evening, but the sky was clear. She could smell the scent of the Thames and the faint odor of roasting mutton. In the distance, she heard drunken male laughter. While the street she was on was well lit, she felt uncomfortable. What if someone tried to accost her? Whom could she call to? There was a group of coachmen, including Will's own, Matthew, no doubt, but they were at the far end of the street.

Ally pulled her cloak tighter, wondering how much time had passed. Now she was getting impatient. Should she go to the door and inquire after her husband? Should she send in Matthew? Or should she return home and accept the role she had taken when she married Will to satisfy her ridiculous bet?

The door to the town house where Will and his friends gathered to read newspapers, play cards, and escape women, no doubt, opened and her husband appeared. His coachman hurried over, but to Ally's surprise, instead of opening the door for his lordship, he hailed a hackney that rolled down the street.

Why would Will take a ride for hire when he had his own closed coach? To move in secret, of course. Where was he going that he wanted no one to know?

Ally's stomach tightened, but then she set her jaw in determination. She had come this far; she'd not give up now. The hackney carrying Will lurched down the dingy street and she grabbed up her reins. Maintaining a safe distance, Ally followed the hired carriage down near the waterfront.

On a dark street, Will stepped down from the vehicle in front of a tavern. She watched as he paid the driver and then entered the establishment. As he walked through the door, bawdy laughter and twinkling candlelight spilled onto the street.

There was no way for Ally to deny her suspicions now. Will had to be up to no good. Why else would he have left his own carriage behind and come to a place like this, but to conduct illicit behavior? She would bet her perfect white teeth on it.

She took in the tavern. It appeared seedy to her, but as she watched the door, several well-clothed gentleman stumbled forth and into the night. Such places, she knew, were popular with even the finest men in London. It was considered adventurous for men of society to frequent common taverns.

Ally tied off the reins and jumped down from the curricle. She hoped above all hope that she was letting her imagination get away with her. As she walked along the street, she tried to tell herself that this was probably all just a misunderstanding.

Will had probably come to meet some gentleman for port.

She didn't care; she was gong to march inside and tell Will his behavior was not acceptable. She would not be wife to a man who did not have the time to spend an evening a week alone with her.

Ally didn't know just what she would say, but she was angry enough to know the words would come to her. The door to the tavern opened and a gentleman and a woman of questionable repute emerged.

"For you, miss," the man slurred, holding open the door for Ally.

Ally ducked inside. The single-room tavern was not as brightly lit as she had first thought. The air was smoky and the corners dark. There were rough tables clustered in groups, some surrounded with chairs, others stools. Heavens, was that the cluck of a loose chicken she heard? The place smelled of damp wool, strong ale, and unwashed bodies.

"Hey, missy, looking for me?" Someone tugged on Ally's cloak, but she jerked the hem from his hand and pressed on toward the back. She could not believe Will would frequent such a place. Of course she had been warned before she wed him that he was a rogue.

Then she caught sight of him. He was seated at a trestle table, his back to her as he spoke to someone. He had not even taken off his coat or hat.

The moment Ally stepped closer, she realized whom he was with.

Her stomach fell.

Her heart twisted.

It was Lucy.

Ally's first impulse was to turn and run. She

would go home to Park Lane, pack her things, and take the next ship home to America. She had been foolish to think she could ever make this marriage work. The wager had been wrong. The solution had been wrong, and she had no one but herself to blame.

Ally turned away. Neither had seen her. There was no need for her to cause a fuss. If there was one thing a lady never did, Mrs. Trumbell had taught her, it was cause a fuss.

Of course, ladies didn't wager away their virginity either, did they?

Ally spun back around on the heels of her slippers. "William Falcon," she called, purposely, using his surname rather than his title. She strode up to the battered table, not even bothering to make eye contact with Lucy. "May I speak with you?"

Will looked up in shock.

Caught. She could see it in his eyes. The regret. The embarrassment.

"Ally." Lucy rose from the bench she sat on. Her hair was pulled back hastily in a bit of ribbon and she wore a dark, hooded cloak that was large on her. One would barely have recognized her if they hadn't known her as well as Ally did.

"Ally, what are you doing here?" Will rose to his feet, his gaze boring down on her.

"I was going to ask you just the same thing, sir."

Will looked at Lucy, then at Ally. He reached for her arm. "You are not thinking what I think you're thinking, are you?"

Ally glared at Lucy, who seemed to be on the

verge of bursting into tears. Good. She deserved to cry, caught the way she was.

"We can discuss this here in public, husband, or out on the street." Ally folded her arms over her chest. "It is your choice, but we *will* discuss this now."

Will glanced at Lucy again.

"You do not need her permission," Ally snapped. "*I* am your wife."

"We will discuss this at home," Will said firmly.

"You can't tell her," Lucy protested shrilly. "You can't. You promised."

Will looked at Lucy, lowering his voice. "I said I would help you, but not at the risk of my marriage. Now don't worry. She'll be discreet." He patted her hand, which rested on the table. "I promise you."

Ally looked from Will to Lucy, and back at Will again. There was a tightness in the tone of his voice that made her think there was something wrong about this situation. His gentle, reassuring touch to Lucy's hand, the way he had looked at the young woman. Something was not as Ally thought it was.

"Shall we, ladies?" Will said, offering one arm to Ally, then the other to Lucy, as if they were at the finest ball and nothing at all was amiss.

Reluctantly admiring her husband's aplomb, Ally turned without a word and led the way out of the tavern, thankful for the cool air and the cloak of darkness outside. She turned to Will, hugging herself. There was a chill in the air now and the wind had picked up. In her haste, she had not worn a bonnet or gloves and now wished she had been more prudent.

"You have the money," Will said to Lucy. "Take it and go back to Mrs. Trumbell's before you are missed. Passage has been arranged to your aunt's in Rome for the day after tomorrow. We've no need to speak again. Good luck."

Lucy's lower lip trembled as she tightened her grip on her reticule.

What money? Ally wanted to ask. Why was he sending her away? More to the point, what had he done that made him feel responsible to pay her passage out of London?

Lucy was pregnant. Of course. Why else would a young lady so hastily take her leave of London?

Against Ally's will, tears came to her eyes. "Will—"

He turned to Ally. "Just a minute. Let me send her on her way." He flagged a hackney at the crossroad just past the tavern. He helped Lucy in and paid the driver, then turned back to Ally.

"I'm sorry you had to see this." He held out his hand, an intimate gesture that seemed out of place at the moment. "I meant to take care of the matter and not bring you into it in any way. Let's go home and discuss it over a brandy."

Ally's lower lip trembled. She jerked her arm from his reach and met his gaze, too angry to care if he saw her tears. Too hurt. "Is Lucy's baby yours?"

CHAPTER SEVEN

"Ally, we will get in the carriage and wait until we reach home to discuss this." Again, he reached for her; again she pulled away.

"It's a simple question, Will." The sounds of the noisy tavern and the call of a watchman faded as she waited for his response.

With a sigh, he grasped her elbow and ushered her toward the curricle. At her resistance, he simply picked her up and deposited her on the seat, then took his place beside her. "No," he said without preamble. "The baby is not mine. But it is a friend's. A scoundrel who refuses to do what is honorable." He met her gaze in the darkness, as if waiting for her to express disbelief or acceptance. Before Ally could form words, before she knew how she would answer, he went on.

"If you do not believe me, then you are right.

An end to our marriage would be in our best interests."

Ally felt as though she were tumbling through the darkness. An end to their marriage? He wanted an end to it? The words sounded so cold and . . . and final the way he said it, creating panic deep inside her chest.

But that was not precisely what he had said. Her father had always told her that half of all grievances could be settled if a person listened well. She forced herself to calm down, listen, and *hear* what he was saying.

"We're talking about trust," he continued. "Between man and wife. Between you and me . . . Ally and Will."

She wanted to believe him. Every fiber of her being wanted to believe he was being truthful.

"And if we do not have that trust then our marriage is doomed," he finished sadly.

Ally believed him. And suddenly she realized that she understood what had just happened. Will was not a rogue, but a gentleman in every sense of the word. "Lucy came to you for help, didn't she?" she said softly.

"Why me, I'm not sure. She said she felt she had nowhere else to go and I could not deny her my assistance."

"What about me? Her friends?"

Will removed his hat and ran his hand through his dark hair. "Could she have come to you without judgment? Be entirely honest with me. Could she have come to you or Anne or Elspeth and received kindness and understanding for that which cannot be changed now?"

Ally's gaze fell to the dirty street in front of the tavern. "No," she confessed, ashamed of herself. "Probably not. At least not at first."

"Ally, you should not have come here in the dark alone. Where is our footman?"

"Oh, please don't be angry with the stable hands." She pressed her lips together, feeling guilty. "I tricked poor Edwin and escaped."

He shook his head. "You could have been robbed. Harmed."

She grasped his hand. "Please tell me about Lucy." She was surprised by how upset she was for Lucy. How genuinely concerned she was despite their rival relationship. "What will she do?"

"She has an aunt in Rome who will care for her. We have already been in contact. Lucy needed funds and a discreet ticket out of London. In Rome, she can have the baby beyond prying eyes and wagging tongues." He wrapped his arm around her.

"I feel foolish," Ally murmured, clasping her hands contritely.

"You thought I had been with Lucy," he said, still seeming to be trying to understand. "Why? I thought what we had in our bedchamber was something special. Something between us we could never share with another. What made you think I would betray you in such a manner?"

Ally groaned. "I don't know what has been wrong with me. I don't know what I expected from this marriage. I don't know if I had time to expect anything. It was just that you've been gone so much, and there were so many rumors."

He took her hand in his. It felt good not to have the barrier of gloves between them.

"There are always rumors, Ally."

"I know, but Lucy said . . ." She exhaled and started again. "She insinuated—oh never mind. It doesn't matter. I was foolish, Will." She turned to gaze into his warm, dark eyes. "But I was so lonely."

He lifted a brow. "Lonely? You were invited to every parlor in London. I saw to it that you were included in every luncheon. Invited to every reading, every ball." He spoke honestly, and from the heart. She could see it in the lines of his face.

"Is that what you thought I wanted?"

"Isn't that what every woman wants?"

As Will spoke, her fear, her anger, her loneliness seemed to melt away. What she saw here was misunderstanding. Not at all surprising given the prevailing attitude of society toward marriage and their own hasty union. They barely knew each other . . . and yet she loved him. Dare she hope he felt the same?

Ally smoothed his arm beneath the crisp black wool of his coat. "That is what every woman wants, Will? Am I *every* woman?"

He gave a laugh that sent a trill through her heart.

"No, you are not, Ally."

"So why did you think I would want what other women want?"

He sighed, threading his fingers through hers. "You tried to tell me that, didn't you? I thought you were only asking me to escort you to your social engagements. I didn't understand that you wanted *me.*"

"I should have come right out and told you what I wanted. Only I suppose I didn't know." She smiled up at him. "I've never been married before, you know."

He smiled back. "Nor I." He gazed out thoughtfully into the darkness. "I didn't take the time to think about how I thought our life would be together. It was foolish to believe that I would not have to change my habits once we were wed. Most marriages are for convenience, as ours was in the beginning. Men and their wives are expected to go their separate ways in most cases."

"Is that what you wish? To be like all the others?" She searched his gaze. "Do you want to play cards with your friends? Acknowledge your wife only in the bedchamber?" Her voice threatened to crack over the last but she managed to control it.

He lifted her hand to his cheek. It was smooth-shaven. Warm.

"When you present the question that way," he said slowly, "I have to admit those things don't have the same attraction they once did. I was not as happy with such pleasures as I once was. But, it is what men of my class do, what we are raised to do."

"Let's go home," Ally said. "It's cold and I've forgotten my bonnet." She laughed, her shoulders and her heart feeling immensely lighter. "And it is warm in our bed."

"You think we can work this muddle out there?" he teased.

"I think so, my lord."

Will took up the reins and turned the open curricle around in the direction of Park Lane. A block from the tavern, he slowed to take the corner—

A man in a black cloak burst out of the darkness on Ally's side of the street. The horses reared and stepped back in their traces as the stranger grasped the harness and the carriage slammed back and then forward, coming to a sudden halt.

Another man appeared on the far side of the carriage and thrust a pistol in Will's face.

"Give up yer coin, or give up yer bloody life," he growled.

Ally stifled a scream. She was afraid, but more than anything else, she was angry. These two men were like many of the thieves in the alleys of London. They came out at night to prey upon the lost or the intoxicated. Well, she was neither.

"We want no trouble," Will said carefully with a sidelong glance at her. His knuckles were white on the reins, proof he was restraining himself because of her.

"The bloody hell, you'll have our coin," Ally said, rising to her feet.

"Ally, what are you doing?" Will threw up his arm to hold her back. "Sit down and be quiet."

"Ye 'eard him," the second thief cackled. "Sit and keep yer pretty mouth shut else ye might be goin' fer a little ride with me and my friend here."

Will pushed her back onto the carriage bench as he fumbled for his money purse.

"Don't do it, Will, don't give it to them."

"Hurry up, Jake," the thief holding the horses whispered harshly. "We ain't got all fricken night."

The one called Jake climbed up into the curricle. Ally stifled another cry of fear and leaned back as

Will stepped between them. Even from an arm's length away, she could smell Jake's foul, sour breath. The stench of his clothing made her gag.

Will gave the thief a shove with the heel of his hand. "I said I'd give you the purse. Take it and leave," he growled.

There was a flash of light in the darkness, and it registered in Ally's mind what the flash was even before it took form.

"He's got a knife," Ally said, forcing her voice to remain low and even.

With nothing to defend himself and Ally but his body and the element of surprise, Will threw himself against the thief.

Ally screamed as Will and Jake fell onto the street.

"Jesus, God a Mary," the thief holding the horses shouted. "Yer supposed to take the money, not get into a brawl with a swell."

He looked up at Ally, who was grabbing her skirts in her hands to jump down. Below her, Will and the thief were wrestling in the filth of the wet street.

"Stay right where ye are, there, missy," the thief hollered.

Ally leaped to the ground. The tail of her gown caught as she hit the ground. She yanked it hard and the silk ripped, setting her free.

Jake wrestled Will onto his back. It looked as if Will was stronger, but the thief had the advantage of the knife. They rolled in the street, first one on top, and then the other.

Ally didn't know what to do. There was no one around to call for help. Should she run somewhere? But she couldn't leave Will. She had to help him.

Will grunted in pain as the thief rolled him onto his back again. Ally looked for something to hit the ugly little man with. Seeing nothing, she ran toward them, hiked up her gown, and kicked the man as hard as she could in the side.

"Hey, hey, hey!" the thief holding the horses shouted. He let go of the harness, and the team lurched forward.

Ally kicked again.

Jake cried out in pain.

The curricle bounded down the street and into the darkness.

"Ally, get back!" Will shouted.

"Get off him!" Ally screamed. "Get off my husband or you will wish you had, you slimy scum!"

"Hey, what's goin' on down there?" a man shouted from the end of the street.

"Find the constable!" Ally called. "These men have attacked us and attempted to rob us." She kicked Jake again and this time he released his hold on Will. She stumbled back in time for Will to turn the criminal onto his back and press the knife from his hand.

"Good job ye done there, Jake," the other thief shouted as he took off down the street.

"Hey, where ye going, mate?" Jake groaned. "Ye can't just leave me here with this balmy wench."

Will kicked the knife away from them and grabbed Jake to yank him to his feet. Several men ran down the street toward them.

Will held tightly on to the thief's arms, pinning them behind his back. He was panting hard, his hat gone, his coat torn. His lip was split and bleeding, and even in the dark, Ally could see a place above his eyebrow beginning to swell.

"Are you all right, Ally?" Will panted.

"I'm fine." Her heart was racing, but she really was unharmed. She wasn't even afraid now.

Two burly men reached them. "Caught 'im finally, have ye?" one of the men said. "We've been after this bastard for weeks." He looked toward Ally and nodded his head. "Pardon my language, m'lady."

The two men took Jake from Will. "You two all right?"

"I think so," Will said, reaching for Ally. "Are you certain you're not injured?" He gazed into her eyes.

She smiled. "I'm fine, but you're bleeding." She searched for a handkerchief, but realizing she had none, she blotted the blood on his lips with the hem of her torn frock.

"If ye two think yer right enough," one of Jake's escorts said as he walked away, "I'll just send my boy up to the corner and find ye a hackney."

"We would appreciate that. As you saw, our horses ran off with our conveyance," Will said. "Should they be found, I am Viscount Bridle. There will be a reward for their return, of course."

"We'll find 'em." The man gave a wave. "And I'll give the constable yer name, should he need ye. That hackney will be ov'r directly."

In less than an hour Ally and Will were in their own bedchamber again. Their horses and curricle had been found. The other footpad was picked up only a few streets from where the robbery took place and both men had been taken to Newgate Prison.

Ally threw off her cloak and dropped onto the bed. "I think I must have a bath before I sleep. I can still smell that wretched man on my clothes."

Will removed his torn coat. "I cannot believe you did that, Ally. You could have been hurt. Killed, even."

She sat up, smiling.

"What do you find so amusing?"

She got up off the bed to go to him. "I had not known you were so talented at wrestling, Lord Bridle."

He cracked a smile as he lowered his hands to her hips. "I was merely defending my lady."

She giggled, studying him slyly. "Yes, you were defending my honor, but something tells me you were enjoying yourself more than most men would in that situation."

"A good robbery does get the heart pounding, the blood pulsing, doesn't it?"

She laughed with him. "You and I, my dear husband, are a disgrace to polite society."

He shook his head. "If Mama had seen the two of us—wrestling in the gutter, you kicking the man half to death—all of her illnesses would have manifested themselves all at once."

"I would have stopped kicking sooner if he had gotten off you sooner."

"Ah, Ally." Will wrapped his arms around her. "Have I told you how much I love you?"

Tears suddenly filled her eyes. At this moment, she was more afraid than she had been when the thieves attacked. "No," she whispered, "you have not."

"Then I regret my omission." He studied her solemnly. "Because I do love you, Ally. I love the woman who wagered away her virginity to allow an unattractive woman the waltz of her lifetime. I love the woman who listens to my mother babble." He brushed his nose to hers. "And most of all, I love the woman who leaps out of a carriage and comes to her husband's rescue—whom I hasten to add, was doing just fine on his own."

She smiled through her tears. Brushed her lips against his. "I think I have loved you since the day I tried to run you over in the park."

He laughed and hugged her against him. He was dirty, and wet, and smelly, and she didn't care.

"So now, the question is, what shall we do?"

She lifted her head from his chest to look up into his eyes. "Do?"

"It is obvious we cannot remain here in London." He smoothed her tangled hair. "Luncheons and balls are not what we are made of. No, it seems to me, especially after our experience tonight, that both of us possess adventurous spirits."

Ally wasn't sure where this conversation was leading, but she thought she was going to like it. "So what do you propose, Lord Bridle?"

"Well, Lady Bridle, I was thinking of an extended journey." He undid one button after the other down the back of her torn green silk frock. "I was thinking first a journey to the Tidewater to meet my father-in-law, the pirate."

She slapped him playfully. "I have told you. It

was my grandfather who was the pirate. My father is a respectable man of business."

Will slipped her gown off one shoulder and kissed the silken skin he had bared. "And then we shall go West in America. See some of this bounty we have read of. Meet a few Indians and then—"

"Then?" she breathed.

He peeled back her gown further, kissing her collarbone, the swell of her breast. "Then, perhaps a safari in Africa, a camel ride in Turkey, or another carriage ride in London."

She laughed as she leaned back, holding onto his shoulders. She was swimming in the sensations his mouth was creating.

He loved her! Will loved her!

He swept her into his arms and carried her toward the bed. "So would you care to make a wager?" he asked.

She hung onto his neck as he lowered her to the bed and climbed in next to her. "A wager?"

"What would you bet a life of adventure is what will make both of us happy."

She slid her fingers through his hair, bringing his mouth closer to hers. "Well, I would bet my virginity on that, my lord," she teased. "But since that is already yours . . . I'll offer my life. I will wager my life on you, Will."

"On us, darling," he answered huskily as his lips brushed hers.

There was no more need for words.

ONE NIGHT WITH LUCIFER

DEBBIE RALEIGH

CHAPTER ONE

Had anyone suggested to Miss Diana Howard that at the tender age of two-and-twenty she would be visiting London's most notorious courtesan to learn the art of seducing a gentleman, she would have laughed until her sides ached.

Or perhaps bloodied their nose, Diana ruefully conceded, shifting uneasily upon the silk and lacquer sofa.

Of course, until the past few weeks she would never have believed she would don gentlemen's clothing so that she could buy a horse at Tattersall's, go a round at Gentleman Jackson's Boxing Salon, enter a brothel, and race from London to Brighton. Such things would never have entered a polished lady's thoughts, even if she was of a radical nature.

The strong features, more handsome than pretty, hardened with annoyance.

It was all the fault of that devil, Lord Luceford, she seethed. Or Lucifer, as the *ton* appropriately branded him.

If not for his public mockery of the Athena Society for the Betterment of Women, she would never have been provoked to behave in such an outrageous fashion. She was quite content to prove the irrefutable truth that women were equal to gentlemen through the dignified means of intellectual debate. That was the reason she and her friends had produced the Athena pamphlets that outlined their well-conceived views and had distributed them throughout London.

She had hoped to spark the attention of women and those gentlemen with broad-enough minds to accept the truth. She was even prepared for the inevitable angry protests she was certain to stir up so that she could rebuff them with the cool logic she was famous for.

But rather than inducing a rational debate of the issues, her pamphlets had become a source of mocking amusement.

Diana's hands clenched in her lap as she recalled the infamous article written in the *Morning Post* only days after her pamphlets had been released.

It has come to the attention of this illustrious writer that a certain pamphlet issued by the Athena Society for the Betterment of Women has created a good deal of amusement among the gentlemen's clubs. During a recent evening of revelry at a club that shall remain nameless a certain Lord Lucifer proclaimed the Athena Society a haven for frustrated spinsters whose notions are as ill formed as they are ludicrous. As proof of his theory he proclaimed ten accomplishments a female could never achieve, thereby proving that women will never be capable of competing with a gentleman upon an equal footing. In addition, he managed to name these accomplishments in less than a minute while admittedly cast to the wind. In the humble opinion of this writer Lord Lucifer adequately dismissed the claims offered in the pamphlet. I will leave the ultimate decision of the matter to my readers by revealing the ten accomplishments. You may form your own view (although there can be no genuine doubt as to the general consensus) and in conclusion dare the Athena Society to disprove the obvious disparities between women and gentlemen.

1. *Spend an entire day without flapping their tongue*
2. *Buy a horse at Tattersall's without being fleeced*
3. *Knock down an opponent at Jackson's Salon*
4. *Spend an evening at a gaming hell*
5. *Enter a brothel*
6. *Ride from London to Brighton in under five hours*
7. *Stroll down St. James's Street*
8. *Tie a proper cravat*
9. *Seduce the Toast of the Season*
10. *Stand upon a field of honor at the break of dawn*

Although it had been nearly two months since the vile article had captured the amused attention of London, Diana could recall each and every mocking word.

How could she not?

The article had not only made her a source of amusement, but the society she had struggled so hard to build had lost its members with alarming swiftness. Suddenly no one wished to have their names linked with such a notorious ladies' club.

Indeed, only Emily Blum and Celia Snyder, her two dearest friends who had helped establish the society, remained publicly committed to her efforts. And the only two who had been willing to agree to her radical scheme to hoist Lord Lucifer upon his own petard.

He wished to challenge her claims of equality? Well, she would prove that a woman was more than capable of meeting his so-called impossible accomplishments. Then he could endure the mockery of his friends and perhaps realize that he had not only been wrong in his assumptions, but unnecessarily cruel.

With that thought in mind she had convinced her friends to set about the task of completing the accomplishments. There had also been the problem of ensuring that they possessed irrefutable proof that they had performed the tasks.

It had been difficult. Far more difficult than she had expected. Not only had she been forced to shear her thick chestnut curls to a short crop to pass as a young buck, but she had nearly had her jaw broken when she had stepped into Jackson's ring. Thankfully her opponent had been far too foxed to connect more than once.

In comparison, however, to her current challenge, the previous eight had been a stroll in the park, she ruefully acknowledged.

It had been bad enough to reluctantly conclude that it was Lord Lucifer himself who was the Toast of the Season, at least among the gentlemen. He was rich, titled, supposedly as handsome as the devil he had been named after, and fought over like a juicy bone thrown among a pack of dogs by society's hostesses. But to actually ponder seducing the gentleman . . .

It had taken an entire week of wrangling among the three friends before Celia had at last suggested that they draw cards to determine who would be forced to meet the unpleasant and scandalous challenge. Diana had been cowardly relieved at the notion. She had always possessed a rare luck with cards, which she had proven when she had walked away from the gambling hell with a considerable number of notes. It was almost certain that she would not be forced to make the ultimate sacrifice.

Her surge of relief had been short-lived, however. Turning over her card, she had stared at the two of clubs in shock. Just when she had needed her luck the most it had failed her.

For a moment her determination had wavered. Was proving Lord Lucifer wrong truly worth the price?

Then, viewing the expectant expressions upon the faces of her friends, she had grimly collected her rattled nerves. She had known when she had started the Athena Society that it would not be simple to alter the attitude of others. Prejudices against women were too deeply ingrained to be changed with a few pamphlets.

Was it not her duty to use this obvious opportunity to strike against those who doubted her message?

Decidedly uneasy, but convinced that her duty was clear, Diana had set about accomplishing her goal. First there had been a complete change of wardrobe. Her plain, sensible gowns might do very well for her quiet existence, but they were hardly designed to catch the attention of a renowned connoisseur of women. Her next step was to discover precisely how a woman set about seducing a gentleman.

Which, of course, was the reason she was currently seated in the drawing room of the most celebrated courtesan in London.

Drawing in a less-than-steady breath, she glanced about the ornate Chinese furnishings, which included several pictures not suitable for a proper maiden. She battled a ridiculous blush that threatened to rise to her cheeks. She had to put aside her natural modesty. Everything she believed in rested upon the success of seducing Lord Lucifer. She would not fail.

Her spate of nerves was firmly in check by the time the door was thrust open. She could even calmly assess the woman drifting over the oriental carpet to seat herself upon a lacquer chair.

At least five years older than herself, Sophia Van Kamp was at the height of her beauty. Golden-haired with sultry black eyes and lush curves, she had supposedly been wed to a foreign diplomat at the age of fifteen, although there were few who believed her clever tale. By the age of seventeen she was under the protection of a highly connected member of the House of Lords. Her reputation for possessing skill in the bedroom and prudent secrecy outside of it had swiftly led her to the top of her profession.

Which was the same reason Diana had chosen

her for her own purpose. For the right price she would learn the lessons of seduction without concern that her scandalous interest would be bandied about town.

"I hope you have been made comfortable?" the older woman asked, her husky tone only faintly hinting at the curiosity that must be consuming her.

"Yes, indeed." Diana forced a smile to her stiff lips. She was not about to confess that her stomach had been tied in such knots that she had been unable to do more than nibble at the delicacies that had been offered with tea. "I must compliment your cook on her lovely tarts."

"She does have a magic touch with pastries." The courtesan leaned back and narrowed her gaze in a speculative manner. "You must forgive me, Miss Howard, if I find myself somewhat at a loss for conversation. I do not often entertain ladies of Quality. In my experience most respectable women prefer to pretend the *demimonde* does not exist."

Diana's lips twisted. Of course women were not supposed to acknowledge the existence of the *demimonde*. It was just another means of keeping them submissive so gentlemen could indulge their pleasures without guilt.

"I fear I am quite unlike most ladies of Quality."

"So I have heard. You are, I believe, the founder of the Athena Society?"

Diana did not bother to hide her surprise. "You have heard of me?"

"But of course." Mrs. Van Kamp gave a low laugh. "Despite my profession I am not thoroughly without intelligence, nor the desire to keep abreast of what is occurring in society."

Feeling justly chastised, Diana smiled wryly. "I assure you that I never doubted your intelligence, I am merely surprised you would be interested in the Athena Society."

"Actually I found your pamphlet to be quite intriguing. As a woman who has made her way in the world I applaud your assertion that a female is capable of handling her own finances, and even acquiring the skills to pursue a career. Of course, in many other respects your claims of female independence are remarkably naive. No woman could be truly satisfied without a gentleman in her life. Not unless she possessed a rather peculiar nature."

There was a hint of question in her voice and Diana felt a sudden warmth flood her cheeks. Gads, she had never considered the woman might suspect she had come here for her own pleasures.

She met the dark gaze squarely. "I assure you that I have no peculiar tendencies and I am quite satisfied not to be under the domination of any gentleman."

The woman chuckled as she stroked a lazy hand over the rich fabric of her skirt.

"That is only because you are very young and very innocent. You will learn the truth between men and women. Only then will you realize that equality is a poor substitute for complete surrender."

"I did not come here today to discuss the views of the Athena Society," Diana retorted, not liking the patronizing expression on the older woman's countenance. Surrender, indeed.

"A pity. I believe we have much in common. And in truth it is rare that I encounter a woman with a daring spirit that is equal to my own." She shrugged. "Now why do we not come to the point of your visit?"

"Yes." Diana sat a bit straighter, her hands clenched in her lap. "Since you have heard of me, perhaps you have also heard of Lord Luceford's public challenges?"

"But of course." The lovely features surprisingly softened with a reminiscent pleasure. "Such a fascinating gentleman. I believe I shall always be a bit in love with him."

Well aware that Lord Luceford had kept this woman as a mistress for several months, Diana gave a shudder.

"Fascinating? I should rather think he is an arrogant, narrow-minded beast who lacks all respect for women."

"I presume you did not find his jest as amusing as the rest of London?"

"No, I did not," Diana retorted in tight tones. "Neither did the Athena Society, which is precisely why we have set about meeting his accomplishments."

The elegant nonchalance of Mrs. Van Kamp abruptly dropped as she leaned forward.

"What?"

"Lord Luceford believes he has given conclusive proof of the inferiority of women. We are determined to prove just how mistaken he is."

"You are attempting his challenges?"

"Not attempting," Diana crisply corrected. "We are accomplishing his challenges."

"Bloody hell." With a sudden motion the courtesan rose to her feet and moved to a side table to pour herself a large measure of brandy. She tossed the golden spirit down with a shake of her head. Diana realized that she was briefly glimpsing the woman who had determinedly pulled herself from the stews and made a success of her life. She could not help but feel a tiny prick of admiration regardless of the methods the woman had used. Turning about, the woman returned to her seat and regarded her with a glittering curiosity. "Now, I demand that you tell me all, and do not leave out a single detail."

Pushing aside her reservations, Diana revealed the efforts of the Athena Society over the past month. She was careful not to include details such as the fact that Emily had nearly overturned them on their race to Brighton, or that Celia still refused to discuss her visit to the brothel or how she had managed to slip away with the velvet hood that was given to the gentlemen to protect their identities. When she had finished, she sat back and watched Mrs. Van Kamp struggle to accept the truth of their daring deeds.

"My God, I do not know whether to admire you or slap some sense into you," she breathed at last, then a smile abruptly curved her lips. "I will say that I like your brass."

"Thank you."

Suddenly assuming a businesslike manner, she tapped her fingers on the lacquer arm of her chair. "Now, what is it you desire of me?"

Although Diana had rationally known that this moment would arrive, it did not make it any easier.

She drew in a slow, steadying breath, willing herself not to bolt in terror.

"My next challenge is to seduce the Toast of the Season."

A sharp, disbelieving silence filled the room. "Blessed heaven, you must be mad," the courtesan at last muttered.

"I have never been more sane."

"Fah." The woman waved an impatient hand. "You haven't the least notion what you are contemplating. Playing at politics is one thing. Such foolishness can be forgiven for the high spirits of youth. To become a fallen woman is a scandal that will never be forgiven nor forgotten. You will be forced from society and faced with shame each time you leave your home."

Diana shivered at the stark words. "I am well aware of the price I am about to pay for my beliefs."

The dark eyes narrowed. "And you are prepared to give up your reputation, your place in society, and any hope of a respectable marriage?"

"Yes."

The older woman studied Diana's set features for a long, unnerving moment before giving a shake of her head.

"You are mad."

"But you will help?"

"I should tie you up and deliver you back to your family before you ruin your life."

"I have no family and even if I did I would simply return and find another to help me."

"You are set upon this course?"

"Yes."

Sophia heaved a faint sigh, clearly sensing

Diana's grim determination. "What can I do to help?"

Diana wet her dry lips. "I need you to teach me how to seduce Lord Luceford."

The dark eyes widened, then without warning, the courtesan tilted back her head and laughed with rich enjoyment.

The home of Lord and Lady Alsworth was predictably filled to the attics with glittering guests. Lady Alsworth was not only a beautiful countess, she always managed to invite the sort of intriguing and unique individuals who were capable of tantalizing the most jaded members of the *ton*.

At precisely the stroke of midnight Lord Luceford strolled into the ballroom and surveyed the crowd with an expression of exquisite boredom.

All heads turned as Lady Alsworth eagerly pressed through the crowd to greet her notorious guest. Lucifer always created interest. Hardly surprising, of course. He was shockingly handsome with his silver blond hair and near black eyes. His features were crafted by the hand of an angel and his body chiseled to lean perfection. He also maintained an aloof disinterest that was destined to strike a challenge in the heart of every woman regardless of her age.

At last reaching his side, Lady Alsworth regarded him in exasperation.

"Lucifer . . . at last." She pouted with the skill of a woman who fully comprehends the power of her own beauty. "You horrid brute, where have you been?"

One of the few men impervious to the seductive charm of Lady Alsworth, his lordship waved a dismissive hand.

"One soiree or another. It is difficult to recall. They are all so depressingly similar."

A sly smile replaced her perfected pout. "I believe my modest gathering will hold some appeal even for a gentleman of your discerning demands."

Luceford slowly narrowed his gaze. Like the rest of the *ton* he found a certain amusement in Lady Alsworth's ability to gather the odd and unusual. He did not, however, care to be a part of her entertainment.

Well aware that all eyes were upon him, Luceford conjured a lazy smile. Nothing was ever allowed to ruffle his cool composure.

"Please do not tell me that you have a monkey serving champagne or a dog that jumps through hoops," he drawled. "Lady Sabatini offered such entertainment earlier this evening with disastrous results."

Momentarily distracted, the countess widened her eyes. "Do tell."

He gave a faint shrug. "There is very little to tell. It appears that dogs and monkeys possess a natural aversion to one another, much like Prinny and his wife, and within moments of entering the drawing room the dog was in pursuit of the monkey, who tossed his champagne upon a nearby duke, and climbed up the gown of Mrs. Wallingford, who fainted with all the drama of Kean. You can imagine the chaos that erupted among the guests."

Lady Alsworth gave a throaty laugh. "How utterly

delicious and precisely what you deserve for attending that hideous Lady Sabatini's soiree."

He carefully straightened the cuff of his black coat. "May I safely assume you have no animals you are about to spring upon me?"

"Certainly not. But I do have a guest I believe you will be intrigued to meet."

Luceford felt another flare of unease. Bloody hell. He would throttle the lovely countess if she sought to play one of her cruel games on him.

"An enticing widow, I hope," he said, a hint of danger in his tone.

"Not quite. Do you see the woman standing beside the far door?"

Hiding his impatience, Luceford cast a glance across the room. His lips twisted as he briefly glimpsed the maidens with their youthful features and anxious expressions.

"All I see is a clutch of debutantes. Have you noted that they always appear to hunt in packs? Like rabid dogs. Gads, it is enough to make a gentleman bolt in terror."

"Horrid man." Lady Alsworth batted him with her fan. "These are not just ordinary debutantes."

"Implying that they are somehow extraordinary?"

"Quite, quite extraordinary. Those three maidens are the founding members of the Athena Society for the Betterment of Women. The taller woman with her hair cropped in that ridiculous manner is the renowned Miss Howard."

Luceford felt a stab of shock as he returned his gaze to actually study the tall, striking maiden attired in a pure white ball gown.

This was the shrill, rabid leader of the Athena Society?

He had expected a dour-faced spinster, not this graceful vision with copper curls that flamed with vibrant life in the candlelight and boldly beautiful features. And that body . . . his blood stirred as she moved and the shimmering white satin outlined the curve of her hip.

Athena, indeed, he thought with a startling flare of lust.

"Good God."

"Rather clever of them do you not agree?" Lady Alsworth murmured. "Without their notorious society they would be as unremarkable as every other insipid debutante that floods into London. Now they are upon the lips of everyone, in no small part due to your own outrageous remarks."

Luceford grimaced as he recalled the ludicrous article in the *Morning Post*. Bloody hell. He had been cast to the wind when he had read that foolish pamphlet. Even worse, he had just received yet another pleading missive from his mother demanding money for her and her current lover. He had been in no reasonable state to debate anything, let alone the howlings of crazed spinsters.

Who the devil could have suspected his ramblings would be published in the paper? Or that he would be hailed as the unlikely defender of civilized society?

It had all been a great deal of nonsense.

Now, however, he regarded the beautiful Amazon with a peculiar fascination.

"I thought that the Athena Society shunned the Marriage Mart? Did they not liken it to Tattersall's, where helpless maidens were auctioned like common cattle?"

"No one is more surprised than myself that they accepted my invitation. Of course, I am delighted they did."

He raised a brow several shades darker than his silvery blond hair. "You are a disciple of the Athena Society?"

"No, but I am quite determined to maintain my reputation as society's unequaled hostess. I do believe a confrontation between Lucifer and the Athena Society is bound to be far more titillating than a dog chasing a monkey up Mrs. Wallingford's skirts."

Subduing a flare of anger at the woman's callous attempt to manipulate him into an embarrassing scene, Luceford raised a hand to cover a delicate yawn.

"I fear I must disappoint you, my dear. I have no intention of confronting Miss Howard. You better than anyone realize that I possess a violent distaste for debutantes."

A petulant frown abruptly marred the beauty of Lady Alsworth's countenance. "Surely you wish to at least be introduced?"

"I can think of nothing that would be a greater bore. You shall have to seek your entertainment elsewhere." He offered his hostess a mocking bow. "Now you must excuse me. I promised Grandmother I would meet her here."

With a languid elegance Luceford turned and began circling the crowded dance floor. Blast Lady Alsworth and her spiteful sense of humor. How dare she seek to amuse her guests with him?

With an effort he firmly dismissed the countess from his mind. Oddly, however, it was far more difficult to dismiss Miss Howard. As he neared the maiden standing like a goddess beside the door, he fully intended to sweep past her without so much as an acknowledgement of her presence. That would put a swift end to any gossip Lady Alsworth hoped to stir to life. He couldn't, however, completely resist a covert glance as he moved past her.

Gads, she should appear insipidly dull in that plain white gown. Instead the daring cut of the neckline provided a perfect frame for the tempting fullness of her breasts and allowed a clear view of the elegant line of her shoulders and long neck.

He felt a stirring of arousal at the knowledge that one sharp tug would rid her of the sheer material to reveal her magnificent form.

Disconcerted by the intensity of his reaction to this woman, he grimly set his gaze upon the dowagers settled in the far corner. He wanted to find his grandmother and leave. If he could be so sharply aroused by a woman who was obviously as batty as a Bedlamite, he was in dire need of a visit to his mistress.

He had already passed the bothersome minx when a low, husky voice brought him to a stiff halt.

"I did not think you a coward, my lord."

CHAPTER TWO

Diana watched in distinct trepidation as the large, indecently handsome gentleman slowly turned to regard her with glittering black eyes.

Her courage nearly failed as the dangerous power of him seemed to reach out and send a rash of prickles over her skin.

Dear heaven, she had expected a debauched libertine. One of those ridiculous fops who littered society and devoted themselves to indulging their pleasures.

Instead he lived up to his name. Lucifer. Handsome, compelling, and sinfully seductive.

A cold chill inched down her spine even as she chided her inner unease.

She had made her decision. It was time to discover if she truly possessed the courage of her convictions.

Stepping toward her, Lord Luceford swept a burning gaze over her rigid form. "Pardon me?"

Hoping that her voice would not reveal the ball of nerves lodged in the pit of her stomach, Diana conjured a cool smile.

"I said that I did not think you such a coward that you would not dare to acknowledge me."

A lethal anger shot through the dark eyes before a cold disdain hardened the beautiful countenance. Diana shivered. Mrs. Van Kamp had assured her that to gain the jaded lord's attention she must be provoking. She couldn't help but wonder if she had been a bit too successful. Then she gave an inward shrug. It was too late to change her battle strategy now.

"You are fortunate to be a female, Miss Howard. If you were a gentleman you would be meeting me at dawn upon the field of honor."

"The fact that I am a female should have no bearing on your decision to issue a challenge, my lord. Indeed, it has never done so before," she pointed out in dry tones. "I am accounted an excellent shot, although I prefer to use my wits rather than my dueling pistols to slay my opponents."

The dark eyes slowly narrowed as he studied her proud features. "I should rather think it is your shrill tongue that fells opponents rather than any supposed wits, Miss Howard."

She shrugged aside his deliberate insult. "You are welcome to your opinion. Unlike some I appreciate hearing others' viewpoints and attempt to keep my mind free of petty prejudices."

"So I am a coward and prejudiced?"

"You have made your opinion obnoxiously clear. You consider women of lesser value than men."

Surprisingly, a faint smile curved the sensuous lips. "You could not be more mistaken."

"Oh?"

"I may not desire a woman in my club or speaking in Parliament, but I do not believe them to be of lesser value." He deliberately moved to tower over her. Close enough that the heat and scent of him clouded her senses. "Indeed, I value them above all things."

"Providing they remain in their place?"

"Oh yes, there are certainly places that I would like them to remain. Would you care to know where?"

There was no mistaking how his gaze lowered to linger upon the curve of her breasts and Diana battled the urge to cover herself in embarrassment.

This was precisely what she desired, was it not?

"I believe I can guess, my lord," she managed to mutter.

"And what of you, Miss Howard?" he abruptly challenged.

"Me?"

"You clearly possess your own share of prejudices. Your pamphlet claims that a husband is no better than a slave owner. Hardly the words of a woman who respects men."

She felt a faint flare of surprise that he had even bothered to read her pamphlet. Most of her critics preferred to dismiss her out of hand.

"I was referring to the laws that give a husband full rights over his wife. Laws that give unfair power in the relationship."

"Then you do not hate men?"

"Certainly not." With great daring she managed what she hoped was a provocative smile. "They have their place."

The large body seemed to still as a disturbing heat simmered to life in his dark eyes.

"I see."

Unnerved by the predatory expression on the elegant countenance, Diana battled the urge to step away from the heat of his body.

"Tell me, my lord, why did you assume that the members of the Athena Society were frustrated spinsters?" she demanded, attempting to ignore the prickling awareness that lay thick in the air between them.

He shrugged. "In my experience young and beautiful women prefer luring gentlemen into their webs with their female charm rather than with logical arguments. Surely that gives them more power than a tedious society?"

"A very tenuous power that depends utterly upon the lady remaining young and beautiful. A rather difficult task for even the most determined woman."

"You need have no concern. Beauty such as yours far outlasts youth," he assured her in low tones.

"Even when I am a frustrated spinster?"

Astonishingly, he moved even closer, sending a bolt of alarm through Diana. She recalled visiting the tower, where she had witnessed a young, foolish boy baiting a lion in his steel cage. She suddenly realized she was doing much the same thing. Only there were no bars to protect her from the magnificent beast.

"Whether or not you become frustrated is entirely in your hands, Miss Howard," he said in husky tones.

Diana felt a sweat break out on the palms of her hands. She was ridiculously relieved that they were in a crowded ballroom. Surely he would not pounce when they were surrounded by hundreds of guests?

"I believe we are straying from the subject."

"Does it matter?"

"I suppose not. We each have our opinion and neither is likely to be easily swayed."

He deliberately lowered his gaze back to the pulse beating at the base of her neck. "Oh, I am not so certain."

"What?"

"Given the proper incentive I might be willing to consider your arguments."

She unconsciously licked her dry lips. "And what proper incentive would that be, my lord?"

He slowly lifted his gaze to regard her wide eyes with a smoldering intensity.

"I am certain a woman of your superior intellect could discover some means of seducing a mere gentleman to her way of thinking."

There could be no mistaking his meaning. Diana's breath caught as she struggled against a flare of panic laced with something perilously close to excitement. She had seemingly done the impossible. She had captured the elusive interest of Lucifer. She did not know whether to shout in triumph or faint in horror.

At the moment fainting in horror seemed by far the more preferable option.

"Presuming that I desire to make the effort to seduce you," she retorted, determinedly recalling her careful coaching by Mrs. Van Kamp. Provoke, tantalize, and retreat. She must always seem just out of reach to wet his appetite. She trembled at the precise nature of his appetite. "I will not keep you since you were clearly on your way to meet someone. Good night, my lord."

Turning about, Diana swept back toward the shadows, where her friends awaited her. She did not doubt every gaze in the room was upon her. The only gaze she was conscious of, however, was the searing, all-consuming gaze of Lucifer.

It was a relief to have the tiny, golden-haired Celia and the amply curved Emily surround her.

"Well? How did it go?" Emily demanded, impatiently brushing aside a tendril of brown hair that always managed to escape the sensible knot atop her head.

"I haven't the least notion," Diana confessed, pressing a hand to her quivering stomach. She was deeply relieved she had not eaten before traveling to the ball. She would hardly inflame Luceford's passions by casting up her accounts in the midst of the ballroom. "He is nothing at all like I expected."

Celia gave a delicate shiver. "Diana, I fear he is dangerous."

"I agree," Emily said, swiftly siding with her friend. "I think we should reconsider our plans."

The temptation was nearly overwhelming. Perhaps naively she had imagined a self indulgent lecher who could be easily manipulated. A fool whom she could control with his own passions.

But Lucifer. . . Gads, he was too intimidatingly

male, too powerful to be easily used. He was a man who controlled others.

And most disturbing of all was her dark, wholly unwelcome reaction to his compelling masculinity.

She gave a sharp shake of her head.

"No, it is too late," she retorted, unsure whom she was attempting to reassure. "We will finish this one way or another."

Like one of the great cats he had viewed in India, Luceford prowled through the crowded rooms of the town house. He was on the hunt. And as she had been for the past week, he found his prey annoyingly elusive.

His finely chiseled features hardened. He did not understand what compulsion led him to seek out Miss Howard. Granted she possessed a unique, statuesque beauty. And a keen intelligence that was as erotic as the soft curves of her delectable body. But there was no denying she possessed extreme, radical notions and even worse, she was an unwed lady of society. The most dangerous creature known to man.

He could only suppose it was the very fact that she was so unusual that captured his sated interest. What other woman had ever dared to call him a coward? Or challenge his very masculinity rather than batting her eyes and meekly consenting to his every opinion?

And of course, her calculated teasing proved beyond a doubt she was no innocent. Untutored debutantes inevitably revealed their inexperience by tossing themselves at a gentleman's feet. They did not realize that a man preferred to be the hunter rather than the hunted.

And Luceford was definitely on the hunt.

He might not fully comprehend his sharp, unexpected fascination with the minx, but he did know he had awakened every morning for the past week fully aroused and haunted by vivid dreams of Miss Howard in his bed. He intended to make those dreams a reality and put an end to his growing frustration.

Catching a brief glimpse of chestnut curls and a brilliant topaz gown, Luceford abruptly forged a direct path through the assembled guests. Blast it all. His prey was not going to elude him tonight.

She did not make his pursuit easy. He lost sight of her twice before he realized she was headed toward a small door that led to the gardens. Ignoring the numerous attempts to capture his attention, he thrust aside a large Russian diplomat and stepped through the door and into the darkness.

Using the faint sound of distant footsteps, Luceford left the wide terrace and headed down the steps to take a side path that was lit by flickering lanterns.

Ducking beneath the low arbor, he rounded a corner and at last came upon his quarry standing near a marble fountain.

"Fleeing yet again, Miss Howard?" he taunted softly.

She stiffened at the sound of his voice, and just for a moment Luceford wondered if she might truly flee into the night before she turned to face him.

His breath caught in his throat. Damn, but she was beautiful, he acknowledged. Not the sweet, dainty loveliness that was so fashionable. But a striking, shimmering beauty that was as evocative as the call of the Siren.

"My lord."

He strolled slowly forward, his fingers already itching to stroke the flawless white skin exposed by her daringly cut gown.

"And you accused me of cowardice."

"I fear I do not know what you mean."

He allowed a faint smile to touch his lips. "Despite having the poor taste to be born a man, I am not completely lacking in wits. It is quite obvious you are attempting to avoid me."

"That is absurd." Her chin inched upward. "Why would I wish to avoid you?"

"That, my dear, is what I am seeking to discover."

"I merely required a breath of fresh air. I do not comprehend why hostesses insist on torturing their guests with overcrowded, overheated rooms."

His smile widened at her smooth parry. She faced him squarely, without the giggling or blushing that so annoyed him.

"Your need for fresh air appears to be more closely connected with my appearance than with the vanity of hostesses," he pointed out.

"Is there something you desire from me?" she demanded, her eyes faintly widening as he stepped close enough to smell the faint hint of soap upon her skin.

"You, Miss Howard."

She sucked in a breath at his forward approach. "Pardon me?"

"Come, my dear, you are well aware that you have greatly intrigued me."

Her tongue peeked out to touch her full bottom lip and Luceford felt a surge of heat tighten his groin.

"That is absurd."

"Why?" He allowed his gaze to sweep over her half-exposed breasts. "You are beautiful, intelligent, and quite unique."

"You have hardly been an admirer of my unique tendencies."

"I will admit that I find your radical notions somewhat amusing."

Her lips tightened at his soft words. "They are not meant to be amusing."

His gaze narrowed as he studied the firmly carved features. "You know, there are many who believe you are merely attempting to attract the attentions of the jaded *ton* with your outrageous claims."

There was no doubting the genuine flare of anger that darkened the rich, hazel eyes.

"Fah. I do not care a fig what society believes."

"Then you are truly not in the hunt for a husband?"

"I would not have a husband if he came delivered upon my doorstep with a marriage license in his hand."

The fierce distaste in her voice should have pleased Luceford. After all, it only reassured him that he need have no fear of unpleasant complications. Instead he felt a pang of annoyance at her confident assertion that she had no need of a gentleman's guidance.

It was a direct, undeniable challenge.

"I almost believe you, Miss Howard," he murmured.

Perhaps sensing she had roused his predatory instincts, she regarded him with a hint of wariness. "My lord, perhaps you should return inside."

"In a moment. First there is something I wish to discover."

"What is that?"

"Whether those lips are as enticing as I have dreamed they would be." With a slow, deliberate motion he lowered his head, leaving her ample opportunity to deter his purpose. She stiffened, but did not pull away and with a surge of excitement Luceford pressed his lips to her own.

It was meant as a light caress. Just a taste to ensure that the desire he sensed between them was not a figment of his imagination. But even as he gently explored the satin softness of her lips his stomach tightened with need. He moaned as a burst of fiery pleasure flooded through him.

All thoughts of pulling away were forgotten as he felt her lips tentatively part in invitation. He sucked in a sharp breath, his hands reaching out to tug her close. He was a gentleman well versed in the art of seduction. He was intimately familiar with the sensation of lust. But even he was startled by the acute, pulsing need that burst to life with the simple kiss.

He wanted this woman. Wanted her with an

intensity that was unnerving for a gentleman who prided himself on always being in control of his passions. It was hot, consuming, and yet, underneath it all was an unfamiliar tenderness that gentled the impatient hands that traced the slender curve of her back.

Fully hard, Luceford reluctantly acknowledged he had taken matters far enough. As much as he might wish to lay her among the fragrant roses and press himself deep within her, he possessed enough sense to realize that this was hardly the setting for their first sexual encounter. When he made this woman his own it would be in the privacy of his bed with the entire night to make her cry out in fulfillment. Not an awkward coupling on the hard ground.

Pulling back, he dropped a light kiss upon her forehead. "Delectable."

"My lord," she breathed in satisfyingly unsteady tones.

"May I call on you tomorrow?"

"Call upon me?"

He gave a low laugh at her obvious bemusement. "You do not believe that after our kiss I intend to forget about you, do you, Miss Howard?"

He felt a fine tremor race through her body before she abruptly pulled away and turned toward the fountain.

"You must forgive my surprise, my lord. It was my understanding that you prefer beautiful courtesans to women of society."

He was briefly taken aback by her blunt reference

to his preference for ladies of the *demimonde*. It was hardly a suitable subject for any woman.

"It is true that I prefer my relationships uncomplicated," he said, a hint of frost replacing the husky passion. If she wished to discuss such indelicate matters then he would oblige her. It would help to make sure that she precisely understood the boundaries of their relationship. "With a courtesan there is no unpleasant jealously or absurd expectations. And of course, it saves one from the wrath of a cuckholded husband."

She slowly turned about, her eyes once again clear and disturbingly intelligent.

"A very tidy arrangement."

"It serves its purpose."

Just for a moment he thought her features tightened in anger at his offhanded reply, but then a sweet smile abruptly curved her lips.

"No doubt you are right," she drawled. "Perhaps the Athena Society should consider hiring gentlemen in a similar fashion. They could give countenance to a lady about town, keep her entertained, and be easily dismissed when they are no longer required or become too tedious to bear."

Luceford was deeply shocked in spite of himself. "Good God, you must be jesting?"

"Not at all." She gave an elegant shrug. "As you pointed out it seems to be a very convenient arrangement."

He gazed at her for a long moment, then he gave a sudden laugh.

Bloody hell.

She was by far the most provoking, outrageous female he had ever encountered.

Unfortunately that did not make him desire her any less.

"And they call me the devil," he said in low tones, catching her chin between his thumb and finger. "You, my dear, are a very dangerous woman."

CHAPTER THREE

Like a nervous butterfly Diana fluttered about the well-apportioned library. As a rule she always felt a deep sense of contentment in this lovely room.

It was here that she commanded full control of the inheritance she had received from her great-aunt. Here that she studied the great works of the ancient philosophers. And here that she wrote her impassioned speeches for the Athena Society.

It represented the security of her independence and helped to banish the lonely fears of a little girl without a family and unwanted by all except Mrs. Bailey.

Today, however, she felt trapped in the book-lined room.

She shivered, rubbing her hands over her arms left bare by the delicate bronze gown. Deep within her she could not deny a pulsing fear of Lucifer's impending arrival.

She had fully prepared herself to face society's censure at her outrageous daring, the loss of her virginity, and even Lucifer's fury when he realized that he had been used to meet his own challenges.

She hadn't, however, been prepared to face the shock of her own desire.

Diana pressed a hand to her unruly stomach, unwillingly recalling the sensations that had seared through her body. Dear heaven, he had merely kissed her, and yet her entire body had trembled with an odd pleasure that had clutched at her stomach and made her toes curl in her dainty slippers. She had wanted to lean closer to his hard male body and feel those elegant hands caress every line and curve.

She might be innocent, but she was not entirely stupid and she realized that such sensations were dangerous. Not only to her plans, but to her long-held belief that a woman of strength never allowed herself to be controlled by her passions, but only by her intellect.

She had naively supposed her greatest challenge would be intriguing Lucifer enough to pursue her. Now she had to accept that it might very well be her own response to his compelling masculinity.

Sucking in a deep breath, Diana felt a measure of relief when the door at last opened and a large, veteran soldier she had hired as a butler stepped into the room. As always a faint smile touched Diana's lips at the sight of the burly man with the forbidding eye patch. He provided ample security for three young maidens who lived on their own in London. Few would dare to spark his ready temper.

"Lord Luceford, miss."

"Please show him in, Rice. And have Mrs. Poston bring in tea."

"Very good."

Swift to obey commands, the servant backed out of the room. With brisk movements Diana hurried to the small sofa and picked up one of the numerous morning papers that had been stacked upon the low table to await her perusal. She hoped to give the image of a lady very much at her leisure rather than a nerve-wracked maiden who had been pacing the floor.

Keeping her head lowered even as she heard the sound of footsteps enter the library and cross to the center of the room, it was at last the prickles of awareness that forced her to lift her head and meet the glittering black gaze.

Gads, how was she supposed to concentrate when he stood there looking like an angel tossed to earth?

"Good afternoon, Miss Howard." He deliberately glanced at the large pile of newspapers. "I hope that I do not intrude at an inconvenient time?"

Diana set aside the paper with what she hoped was a casual smile. "Not at all. I was merely reviewing my investments."

"Investments?"

"Yes. I have recently entered the 'Change and of course, I do have several stocks in various businesses."

"I suppose I should not be surprised you handle

your own investments," he said in wry tones. "You seem determined to defy every accepted convention."

On firm ground with such remarks, Diana merely lifted her brows. "Would you depend upon another to make your investments?"

"Certainly not, but then I have been trained since I was in the nursery to handle the responsibilities of my inheritance."

Her smile never faltered despite his sheer arrogance. "Obviously I am a much quicker study."

He appeared momentarily taken aback by her bold attack before giving a low chuckle. "Obviously."

"Will you have a seat?"

Ignoring the solid mahogany chair she had indicated, Lucifer strolled toward the brocade sofa and settled next to her slender frame. Diana stiffened as the clean, warm scent of him enveloped her senses.

"You know, this house is not at all what I expected."

Disturbed by the rash of excitement that flooded her body, Diana forced herself not to shift from the hard male frame.

"You expected me to be dancing around a large cauldron?"

He flashed her an amused glance before studying the solid furnishings and enviable collection of leather-bound books.

"Not precisely. This is, however, rather disappointingly respectable for the Athena Society."

"The Athena Society happens to be very respectable." She could not prevent a hint of annoyance from entering her tone. "It is merely a collection of women who hold the view that we are as capable and worthy as gentlemen."

"A rather radical notion."

Diana bit her tongue. She could not afford a heated debate with this particular gentleman. The only way he would be convinced of the truth of her beliefs was to prove them to him beyond any doubt.

"If you say."

The dark gaze abruptly returned to inspect her determinedly placid expression with seeking intensity.

"How did this society come about? I can not imagine your parents encouraging such odd notions."

"I have no way of knowing if they would have or not. They died when I was just a baby." She gave a faint shrug. "My uncle had little interest in a mere girl beyond lecturing me on my lack of family duty for not being born a male. Thankfully when I was old enough he promptly shipped me off to Mrs. Bailey's School for Young Ladies."

The lean features abruptly softened. "I am sorry."

"Do not be," she said briskly, not wishing this man's pity. She had survived and succeeded despite her uncle's incessant strictures that females were a tool of the devil, who must be sternly restrained, and kept beneath the heavy hand of a male. "Mrs. Bailey was a great woman. Not only did she keep a school, she ran a home for unwed mothers and helped to patronize female artists and writers."

"She sounds quite remarkable," he murmured.

"She was the finest woman it has ever been my fortune to meet. My only regret is that she did not live long enough to be a part of my society."

He regarded her in an oddly knowing manner. "Clearly her ideas live on in you."

"That is my hope."

The entrance of the heavy-set housekeeper brought an end to the conversation. In silence they waited for Mrs. Poston to set the heavy tea tray upon the table, her broad face set in severe lines. The older woman made little effort to disguise her distaste for Diana's radical beliefs. It was only the fact that Diana paid a handsome wage and allowed her ample time off to visit her daughter that kept her from walking out of the eccentric household.

With a speaking glare at the gentleman settled negligently upon the sofa, Mrs. Poston gave a loud sniff and sailed from the room.

"I fear your housekeeper does not approve of you entertaining a gentleman on your own," Lucifer mused as Diana poured the tea and arranged two plates with the dainty pastries.

"Mrs. Poston disapproves of everything as a matter of principle," Diana retorted, handing him the refreshments. "Now, perhaps you will tell me the reason for your visit. I can not believe you possess any interest in the rather dull history of the Athena Society."

He set aside his cup and plate of untasted food and turned so he could lay his arm along the back of the sofa. Diana's breath caught as he allowed his fingers to lightly tease the bare skin of her neck.

"I thought that I was very clear last evening. My interest is in you, Miss Howard."

Diana clenched her hands in the folds of her skirts. She would not panic, she would not panic, she would not panic.

"I assumed that you had indulged a bit too heavily before arriving at the ball," she attempted to tease.

He leaned slowly forward, the determination upon his lean features making her heart falter.

"I do not need to be foxed to realize you are a most amazing creature."

"Hardly amazing," she protested weakly.

"Oh yes. So amazing I find myself quite unable to resist you."

Without warning his fair head dipped downward. Steeling herself for another disturbing kiss, Diana was unprepared as he instead continued downward to place his warm lips upon the bare curve of her breast.

Diana's mouth fell open as a shock of pleasure raced through her body. The lips barely stroked her soft skin, but every nerve stirred to life. Unconsciously her hands reached up to clutch at his shoulders, her cheeks growing warm as she realized her nipples had hardened and openly pressed against the soft fabric of her gown.

"Mmm . . . what is that scent?" he whispered against her skin, sending a rash of prickles through her.

Diana struggled to clear her foggy mind. "Jasmine."

"Jasmine. It haunted me the entire night. You, Miss Howard, have haunted me."

Overtly conscious of her body's strange reaction to his light caress, Diana sucked in a sharp breath as he once again shifted, his hand boldly lifting to cup the full curve of her breast.

"My lord."

With great reluctance Luceford lifted his head to encounter the shocked hazel gaze. He knew that he was pressing matters at a hasty pace. A most unusual occurrence for a gentleman who prided himself on the skill and patience of his seductions. But this woman had bewitched him. Everything about her excited and enticed his jaded senses. Her intelligence, her sharp wit, her fierce spirit. And perhaps most of all the unmistakable hint of vulnerability she so fiercely attempted to conceal.

"My name is Luceford," he said softly. "I wish to hear my name upon your lips."

"Luceford," she said, obediently obeying his command, but at the same moment he felt her hands tighten on his shoulders. Realizing that she intended to pull away, he deliberately moved his thumb to lightly stroke the tender thrust of her nipple. He was rewarded as her wide eyes darkened with an unmistakable response. "Oh."

"Oh, indeed," he agreed, his gaze sweeping over her flushed countenance. "How beautiful you are, my dear. So beautiful you quite steal my breath."

Her tongue peeked out to wet her lower lip. "Are you always so forward?"

"Only when I truly desire something."

"And you desire me?"

His blood quickened, an image of laying her back on the sofa and losing himself in her softness nearly overwhelming him.

"I thought I made my feelings quite obvious. Of course, if you would like further proof I would be happy to oblige."

Unable to resist, Luceford swooped downward to trace the smooth line of her shoulder with seeking lips.

"Jasmine and silk," he whispered, teasing the pebble hard nipple with his thumb.

"Luceford," she gasped.

"Does this please you?"

She shivered as he nipped gently at the curve of her neck.

"I do not think it appropriate behavior for my library," she retorted in strained tones.

Luceford chuckled. "And you are so very appropriate?"

"Perhaps not, but anyone might enter."

As much as he disliked admitting the truth, Luceford realized she was right. The fantasy of having her laid beneath him would have to wait.

"True enough." He pulled back, reluctantly removing his hand from her ripe fullness. "Such delicious pastimes demand privacy. Not to mention several hours of uninterrupted attention to detail. And I assure you that I never overlook the details."

The hazel eyes glittered with a hectic light. "And what makes you believe that I am interested in your attention to detail?"

"I am no schoolboy, my dear. You have been luring me into your web for the past week," he retorted, deliberately glancing at her obvious state of arousal. "Besides, there are some truths that can not be denied."

She appeared flustered by his teasing. "Yes, well,

I will not be seduced in my library in the middle of the afternoon."

A faint frown tugged at his brows at her unexpectedly coy manner. He had thought her above such foolishness.

"But you will be seduced?" he demanded.

Without warning she rose to her feet and moved to the center of the room.

"We shall see."

Luceford was in swift pursuit, grasping her elbow and turning her to face him.

"I would not take kindly to being teased," he said sternly. "I have been honest in my intentions. If you have reservations then you have only to tell me."

She stiffened as she met his narrowed gaze. "You are very blunt."

"I prefer to avoid complications whenever possible."

"So either I agree to be seduced or you will take your attentions elsewhere?"

Somehow when she said the words he did sound insufferably arrogant. Luceford briefly wavered then sternly chided his foolishness. He was merely attempting to be honest. Surely that was preferable to those gentlemen who wrapped their intentions in pretty words and promises only to walk away when they had achieved what they desired.

"I believe that there is a genuine spark of attraction between us. A spark that could bring us both a great deal of pleasure," he said slowly. "I do not, however, seek to seduce unwilling maidens. Even if they are the bold, unconventional leader of the Athena Society."

Her gaze abruptly dropped. "I know very little about you. Nothing except the fact that you possess a very annoying disapproval of my views."

His faint annoyance swiftly faded. Obviously she desired him, but her pride rebelled at the thought of submitting to a gentleman who had been so publicly critical of her society. Ah well, she would soon forget such nonsense.

"Do not fear, we shall soon know each other very well," he promised gently. "And perhaps I shall teach you that there are far more pleasurable means of expending your energy than fighting a hopeless battle."

Just for a moment her eyes glittered with a dangerous heat, almost as if she had been offended by his seductive promise. Then in a blink of an eye her expression had softened and she offered him a daring smile.

"Or perhaps, Luceford, I shall teach you not to underestimate the skills of a woman."

His hand unwittingly tightened on her elbow as his body clenched in anticipation.

Soon, he assured himself.

Very, very soon.

CHAPTER FOUR

Dressed appropriately in a gown of shimmering crimson silk, Diana settled her stomach with a healthy measure of brandy.

It had been the same all day, she silently brooded as she stood with her friends in the library. Ever since the note had arrived from Luceford, requiring a private dinner at his home.

The brief, initial flare of victory at having achieved the seemingly impossible task of seducing the elusive Lucifer had been sharply replaced with dread.

Dear Lord, this was it.

As Mrs. Van Kamp had warned, she was about to take an irrevocable step. After this evening she could never return to a life as a proper, respectable maiden. She would be without virtue and forever banned from society.

More than once her nerves had nearly failed her.

She had even gone so far as to write a terse note declining the scandalous invitation, only to toss it into the bin.

They were too close to success to turn away now, she had ruthlessly told herself. Besides, she had never cared for the opinion of society. They already considered her a source of mockery. A figure fit only for caricatures and acid commentaries in the papers. Being a fallen woman could hardly make matters worse.

Soon she would be able to prove to all of London that the Athena Society was fully capable of outwitting all of their critics.

Polishing off the last of the brandy, Diana set aside her glass and turned to confront her anxious friends.

"I do not like this, Diana," Celia was first to mutter, her hands clenched together.

Diana smiled ruefully. "I am not overly fond of the situation myself."

"There is no need to continue this madness. We will find some other means of proving our beliefs."

"No." Diana squared her shoulders. "We have come too far. After this evening we shall have only one further challenge and we will have vindicated ourselves."

Celia moved forward. "But what if Lord Luceford speaks of this to others? You will be ruined."

"You know I have no interest in society's strictures on young maidens. They only serve to keep us from seeking our destinies. Besides, we all knew the cost when we decided to attempt those accomplishments."

"But . . ." Celia halted, biting her lip.

"What?" Diana demanded, concerned by the glitter of unshed tears in her friend's eyes.

"What if he harms you?" she at last whispered.

Diana was genuinely surprised. Of all the things that she had fretted about she had never once considered the fear that Lucifer would be violent. He was far too self-possessed. Too certain of his own irresistible charm.

No, she did not believe he would harm her, she slowly acknowledged. The ball of unease in her stomach came from an entirely different source.

"Why should he do such a thing?" she demanded gently.

"I have heard that gentlemen can be unpredictable in their passions. Remember our maid Polly? She came home with that horrid black eye." Celia gave a sudden shiver. "And those gentlemen in the brothel . . ."

Feeling an intense pang of regret that she had ever allowed the sensitive maiden to enter the brothel, Diana gave her friend a swift, reassuring hug.

"I do not fear Luceford." She gave an unconscious grimace. "At least I do not believe he will become violent. He seems extraordinarily proud of his ability to please a woman."

"And you fear he will please you?" Emily abruptly stepped into the conversation, her expression far too knowing.

Diana heaved a sigh. Of course she feared her reaction to Lucifer, she silently acknowledged. She had only to think of his hands upon her body for her heart to race and a peculiar heat to burst into life deep within her. How could she possibly claim she was making a great sacrifice for her cause when she feared she might be betrayed by her own desires?

"He is very skilled," she murmured ruefully.

"Diana, do not go," Celia burst out. "I have a very bad feeling about this."

"Do not worry, Celia. It will soon be over and I will be home," Diana said, as much to soothe her own nerves as those of her anxious friend. "Everything will be well."

"Here." Emily abruptly moved forward to press a cold object into Diana's hand.

Glancing down in surprise, Diana regarded the small silver pistol with an ivory inlaid handle.

"A gun?" She could not prevent a faint smile. "Really, Emily, it will not be necessary. I have no need, after all, to defend my honor."

Emily reached out to touch her arm in a somber motion. "You can not be too careful."

Knowing that it would help to ease her companions' fears, Diana reluctantly slipped the pistol into the pocket of the heavy cape she had draped about her.

"Thank you."

The long-awaited knock at last sounded upon the door and Rice stepped into the room with a small bow.

"A carriage is here for you, Miss Howard."

"I shall be right there."

"Very good."

With deliberately crisp movements Diana tied a bonnet upon her short chestnut curls and lowered the heavy veil over her pale features.

At last prepared, she headed for the door, not

daring to consider her actions for fear she would lose what few wisps of courage she still possessed.

"Do not wait up for me. We shall speak in the morning."

Keeping her thoughts desperately centered upon the day she could claim victory and reveal the success of the Athena Society, Diana barely noted being led to the unmarked black carriage, or even the streets filled with the glittering *ton* as they dashed from one society event to another.

Shrouded in darkness, she waited for the carriage to come to a halt behind the large, predictably elegant town house. She did allow herself a rueful smile as she was led through the back garden to a servants' entrance, where a uniformed butler awaited her.

Such was the lot of a fallen woman, she told herself.

"If you would follow me?" the butler commanded in haughty tones, turning about to lead Diana through a warren of empty hallways, until they at last entered the front of the house and he pushed open a door. "In here."

For a moment Diana was frozen with panic. It was not too late. If she made a mad dash for the door, she could surely reach freedom before anyone could halt her.

Then she sternly gathered herself.

Courage, Diana. Battles were won by the daring.

Swallowing the lump in her throat, Diana stepped into the long, book-lined library. She was relieved that her knees did not buckle, not even when the tall, fair-haired devil smoothly crossed the room to join her.

"Diana," he murmured with a smile that was lethal, "forgive me for slipping you through the servants' entrance, but I assumed you would be anxious to avoid prying eyes."

"Yes."

He firmly shut the door before grasping her hands. The dark eyes widened with surprise.

"You are trembling."

Knowing there was no means of completely disguising her smoldering fears, Diana gave a faint shrug.

"You may be vastly experienced in this sort of intrigue, but I am not."

His expression thankfully cleared and he regarded her in a teasing fashion.

"Do not say the indomitable Miss Howard is shy?"

Scared out of her bloody wits, more like it, Diana inwardly acknowledged.

"Perhaps a bit."

"There is no need. Here, let me make you more comfortable." With a startling gentleness Lucifer untied the bonnet and lifted it from her curls. Then setting it aside, he performed the same service for her cloak and at last pulled her gloves from her hands so he could raise her bare fingers to his lips. A satisfied smile curved his mouth as he felt her fine shiver. "Why do we not have a seat?"

Diana did not protest as he steered her toward a small sofa and settled her upon the cushion. Or even when he settled close enough so that she could feel the heat of him sear through the thin fabric of her gown. Instead she desperately regarded the lovely rosewood furnishings and carved chimneypiece. Anything to take her thoughts off the large, powerful form encased in a black coat and breeches.

"This is a beautiful room."

He gave a smoky chuckle. "I must admit I took enormous effort in plotting how best to please you. My first thought was to have you shown to the main gallery so I could impress you with my exquisite taste in art. Then there was the temptation to reveal my chef's brilliant talent with a lavish supper. I even debated calling for my fencing instructor so you could marvel at my skill with a foil. In the end I concluded that the only certain means of turning the head of an intellectual radical was with my father's fine library."

His charm was almost tangible as he wove his potent seduction about her. Diana unconsciously wet her dry lips.

"It is very fine. Was he a scholar?"

"More of a collector." He reached out to grasp her hand, his thumb stroking the soft inner skin of her wrist. "There were few things that pleased him more than discovering a rare manuscript or first edition. I remember as a young boy being whisked through Europe as my father searched to increase his collection."

A shimmering heat raced through her arm, spreading throughout her tense form.

"How wonderful it must have been for you," she breathed.

Surprisingly his fingers abruptly tightened on her wrist. "No doubt it would have been if my mother had not devoted every waking moment to complaints about having been wrenched from her latest lover. Thankfully she discovered my father's young secretary an adequate replacement and we were allowed a measure of peace on the voyage home."

She abruptly turned to regard his tight features. His mother conducted her affairs beneath the nose of her own child? What sort of woman would do such a thing?

"I am sorry," she said with genuine sympathy.

"Do not be. It taught me a valuable lesson. I shall never make my father's mistake of allowing my emotions to play me for a fool." With an obvious effort he dismissed the unpleasant memories and raised her hand to place a kiss in the center of her palm. He carefully watched her eyes darken in response. "I shall content myself with delicious interludes such as this."

Diana found herself disturbed in spite of her best intentions. She wanted to consider this gentleman as an arrogant, insensitive lout. Not as a young boy wounded by his mother and taught from the cradle that women were untrustworthy.

"Are your parents still alive?"

"My father died when I was eighteen. My mother is very much alive."

His lips moved to stroke the pulse fluttering in her wrist. Diana caught her breath, resisting the urge to pull away from the melting touch.

"You are not close to her?"

"Thankfully Mother prefers to pretend she is still a young maiden rather than an aging widow with a grown son. It is only when she is in need of money to keep her and her current lover in luxury in Italy that she recalls my presence."

Diana gave a slow shake of her head, unable to accept the wretched selfishness of Lady Luceford.

"Not all women are so callous."

The dark eyes narrowed. "I have no desire to discuss my mother tonight."

He leaned slowly forward and Diana felt her heart skip a beat. It appeared the moment of doom had arrived. And she was not nearly prepared.

A wave of intense relief rushed through her as there was a discreet knock and the door was opened to reveal the butler pushing a wheeled cart.

"Dinner, my lord."

With a rueful smile Lucifer pulled back and waved an elegant hand toward the low table before them.

The servant briskly set the plates upon the table, adding two glasses and the silver without once glancing at Diana. She could only assume he was quite accustomed to his employer entertaining women in his home. Her stomach twisted.

"Thank you, Shore," Lucifer murmured as the servant finished his task. "That will be all for this evening."

With a bow Shore backed from the room, closing the door behind him.

Lucifer gracefully shifted to pluck one of the china plates off the table and began filling it from the various platters.

"Ah, let me discover what I can tempt you with," he said. "Duck in cherry sauce, poached salmon, lobster in butter, eggs with anchovies, and fresh asparagus." He pushed the plate into her reluctant hands before reaching for the bottle wrapped in a cold cloth. "And, of course, champagne."

Although relieved at the unexpected reprieve, Diana gazed at the mounds of food in dismay. Her stomach was far too queasy to be put to such a challenge.

"I can not possibly eat all of this," she protested.

Taking one of the glasses he had filled, Lucifer slowly pressed it to her lips until she sipped the golden bubbles.

"Tonight you are to indulge your senses, my sweet," he said softly, the dark eyes oddly tender and his hair gleaming like the purest silver in the candlelight. He was as handsome and seductively enticing as his namesake.

Diana gulped the champagne, allowing him to press a bit of the lobster between her lips. She shivered at the sheer intimacy of his slender fingers brushing her skin.

"If I indulge in such quantity then I shall never get to my feet again."

He smiled in a slow, wicked manner as he continued to feed her small bits of the delectable food.

"I can think of worse fates. I very much like the thought of you stranded upon my sofa."

"You would soon tire of my presence."

"No, not soon," he denied with a low intensity. For a moment he gazed deep into her wary eyes, then without warning, he leaned forward and kissed her with a heat that seared her to her very toes.

CHAPTER FIVE

Luceford groaned as he felt a fierce, clamoring need harden his groin.

When he had planned this evening he had every intention of savoring a slow and deliberate seduction. They had the entire evening to discover how best to please one another.

But he had realized the danger to his well-schemed plans the moment he had slipped the cloak from Diana's slender frame. The crimson gown had shimmered in the candlelight, the bodice cut low enough that he could almost see the rosy edge of her nipples. He had lain awake too many evenings imagining the feel of her shuddering beneath him.

Now he tasted of her sweetness, searching for a response that would indicate she was as eager as he was to drown in the heat of their desire.

Carefully parting her lips, he slipped his tongue

into the damp softness, urging a response. He wanted her trembling with the same ache that clenched deep within him. He wanted her pleading his name when he at last claimed her as his own.

Slowly pulling back, he gazed deep into her dazed eyes. "You taste of butter," he said softly.

The long lashes fluttered downward in enchanting confusion. "I am capable of feeding myself."

"Tonight I do not wish you to be the capable Miss Howard." He took the plate from her hand and set it on the table along with the glass of champagne. He was impatient to have her in his arms, in his bed. "I wish you to place yourself in my hands. I promise to take the greatest care."

Her tongue peeked out to touch the corner of her mouth. "Are you not going to eat?"

His hand rose to lightly trace the tempting line of her bodice. "I am not hungry. At least not for food," he said, his voice already thick. "I believe you have bewitched me, my dear. I can not eat, I can not sleep. I can think of nothing beyond possessing you."

"You must be easily bewitched," she said, her breath catching as his searching fingers slipped beneath the fabric to tease the tip of her nipple to sensitive life.

"Oh no, it is quite rare for me to be so consumed with desire. I am not wholly certain that I enjoy being so firmly entwined in your web."

"I could always leave if you wish," she breathed.

His gut twisted at the mere thought of being denied the pleasure he craved and with a swift motion he was on his feet. "It is far too late for that. I will not be satisfied until you are mine."

Reaching down, he scooped her slender body into his arms and lifted her off the sofa. She instinctively grasped his coat as he crossed the room and fumbled open the door.

"Luceford." Her eyes were wide with shock as he continued down the hall and began climbing the wide flight of stairs.

"I can wait no longer," he said simply, feeling almost drunk with the heady need flowing through his blood. He entered the large bedchamber lit only with a small candle and kicked the door shut behind him. Then with reverent care he lowered her onto the canopy bed. His heart gave an odd lurch at the sight of her proud form surrounded by the flowing crimson silk.

"How beautiful you are. Like Athena herself," he breathed, his hands impatiently tugging off his cravat and disposing of his coat and waistcoat. His shirt swiftly followed before he moved to slide onto the mattress beside her. He gazed deep into her wide eyes as he carefully sought the ribbons at her back and then lowered the gown to reveal the perfectly shaped breasts. He gave a low growl of satisfaction as his hands cupped the satin fullness. "My God, you are exquisite."

He dipped his head downward to tug the crown of her nipple into his mouth and suckled the already aroused nub, a surge of satisfaction racing through him as Diana gasped and arched herself upward. With practiced skill he moved to pleasure her other breast while his hand swept away the dress and stockings.

It was far more of a struggle to remove his own clothing, but at last free of all constraints he gathered her into his arms and pulled her close.

"Touch me, Diana," he murmured as he nuzzled the line of her jaw. "I wish to feel your hands upon me."

At first tentatively, then with growing boldness her hands smoothed over his chest, tracing the lines of muscle as if fascinated by their texture. Luceford felt his shaft grow rigid beneath her gentle ministrations and he groaned with a soul-aching need.

Not even the most experienced courtesan had brought him to this point of exquisite torment and he struggled to wait until she was ready before plunging into her.

Pushing her onto her back he smoothed a hand over her stomach, watching her lips part as she struggled to breathe.

"Tell me what you want," he urged softly, his hand lightly tracing its way down to the small patch of chestnut darkness.

She gave a strangled moan, her hands grasping the sheet upon the bed. "I . . . can not."

He gave a low chuckle, fascinated by the play of emotions over her strong features. He wondered if any of her previous lovers had ever taken the effort to bring her to the pinnacle of her own satisfaction.

"There is no need to be shy," he assured her, gently parting her to discover the silken heat. She gave a sharp cry as he found the small center of her pleasure.

"Luceford." She instinctively clenched her legs together in shock at his intimate exploration.

"No, Diana, open yourself to me, I want to feel your sweetness," he coaxed, waiting patiently for her muscles to slowly relax so he could stroke her gently. "Ah yes."

"Oh." She panted, her hips rising in silent invitation.

Luceford was swift to press his advantage, moving his hand downward so he could sink his finger deep within her. She shuddered in response and he gritted his teeth as he nearly embarrassed himself by losing all control. Bloody hell, but she was magnificent with her pale limbs spread beneath him and a flush of desire upon her face.

"Do you like that?" he rasped, slowly stroking his finger in the velvet softness.

"I . . . yes," she moaned, her hips beginning to move in the rhythm he was establishing.

"You are so tight, so sweet." He gave a deep growl in his throat, realizing that he could wait no longer. "Gads, I wished to make this last the entire night, but I can not. I have to be inside you."

Covering her lips in a demanding kiss, he shifted over her, pulling her legs wide so he could settle between them. Pressing himself upward he positioned the tip of his shaft within her. He felt her stiffen beneath him and he raised his head to regard her with a searching gaze.

"Are you prepared for me?" he asked gently.

There was a moment of silence before she gave a sharp nod. "Yes."

"You are certain?" he demanded. "I want no regrets."

"Please, Luceford," she whispered, wrapping her arms around his back.

It was all the encouragement he needed and scattering urgent kisses over the curve of her breasts he at last caught a nipple between the edge of his teeth. As her breath rasped loudly in the silence, he surged into her tight passage.

For a moment Luceford was lost in the nearly unbearable pleasure that shuddered through his body. She was so blessedly tight, almost as if . . . abruptly realizing that Diana had grown rigid beneath him, he glanced down in shock.

Dear God.

"Are you a virgin?"

Biting her lower lip, she gave a slow nod. "Yes."

"Damn. Why did you not warn me?" he demanded, his voice harsh with the effort to contain his pulsing desire.

"Does it matter?"

Sweat beaded on his forehead as he closed his eyes. "Obviously not now. I could not halt if I wished to." She shifted beneath him and he gave a choked groan. "Wait, Diana."

"Are we not done?" she demanded in strained tones.

His angry disbelief suddenly faded beneath a wave of wry amusement. He did not know why this proud beauty had chosen him to offer her innocence, but he did know he intended to ensure that this first encounter would be an experience she would carry with her for the rest of her days. She had given him a rare gift and he would treasure it with all the gratitude it deserved.

"No, we are far from done," he promised, pulling out of her so he could trail his lips over her breasts and down the slender curve of her waist. He edged lower, his hand stroking the soft skin of her inner thigh.

"What are you doing?" she demanded as he shifted himself between her legs and sought her sweet innocence with his tongue. She gave a soft scream of shock. "Luceford."

"It is all right, my dear," he murmured, using every skill he had learned to reignite the fires of her passion.

"No." Her head twisted against the mattress.

Sensing she was once again building toward her release he carefully slipped a finger into her. He smiled as her muscles instinctively clenched in need.

"That is it. Do not be frightened."

"Oh, dear heaven," she whispered in broken tones.

"Yes, Diana, just concentrate on what you are feeling."

Continuing to stroke her with his finger, he raised himself to cover her once again. He found her lips, fiercely pleased when she returned his kiss with a hunger that matched his own. Still he continued to tease and tantalize her until she gave an impatient moan and wrapped her legs about his hips. His lips trailed over her cheek, finding the sensitive skin of her throat. Only when he was certain that she was on the brink of fulfillment did he position himself at her entrance and slowly press into her passage.

She was still tight, but there was no protest as he slid ever deeper into her. Propping himself on his elbow, he set a steady, deliberate pace, watching her face as a sweet bewilderment was gradually overtaken with a bewitching pleasure. He increased his tempo as her lips parted and her fingers dug into his back. Suddenly her hips were lifting to meet him and Luceford felt the building pressure of his own release.

Lowering his head, he pressed his lips to her forehead, their bodies surging together with a searing heat.

"Luceford," she cried out softly.

"Yes, my sweet, that is it. Dear heaven."

He gave a hoarse shout as she convulsed about him, toppling him over the edge with a burst of sweet agony. With a last shred of sense he managed to pull out as his seed spilled onto the sheet.

Shaken by the explosive pleasure that had wracked his body, Luceford rolled onto his side and drew her shivering body into his arms. Then covering them with the sheet, he settled her head upon his shoulder.

"Now, my dear, I believe you owe me an explanation," he said softly.

She heaved a faint sigh. "Can we discuss this later? I am so tired."

He moved to tilt her chin upward, but her lashes were already drifting to rest upon her cheeks. He realized the sudden lassitude was no doubt due to the shock of her first intimate encounter as well as the tension she had no doubt endured since making her decision to offer him her innocence. Why?

His hand moved to softly stroke the chestnut curls that held a hint of fire in their depths. She had seemed so confident, so sure of herself. He could never have guessed that she was a virgin.

So why him? Why now?

They were questions only this exasperating, unpredictable, utterly breathtaking woman could answer. Trailing his fingers over her cheek, he gently outlined the lips that had called out his name with gasping delight.

How perfect she had felt lying beneath him. Strong and supple as she had matched him thrust for thrust. He might have set out to seduce her, but in the end they had ridden the storm of sensations together. Equal in a manner that he had never before experienced.

Settling more comfortably on the pillows, he studied the pale features until the candle at last sputtered and burnt out. Only then did he fall into a deep, contented sleep, with none of his usual desire to have his companion returned to her own establishment.

It was hours later when he was awakened by the feel of a soft body snuggled close to his own. He smiled in the shadows as his hands began to stroke over her back and over the curve of her hips. With a small sigh Diana rolled onto her back, the moonlight bathing her in a halo of silver.

Propping himself on his elbow, Luceford circled a dusky nipple, teasing it to a point before bending his head to take it into his mouth. He heard Diana's sleepy sigh, then her fingers were threading into his hair as she was as swiftly caught in the web of magic as himself.

With less time than he imagined possible, he was once again rigid with need. Her hands guided him

to her other breast and as his fingers slid downward
she readily parted her legs for his caress.

Any thought for a more practiced, more skilled
performance was shattered. He slipped his finger
within her, eagerly stroking her toward her goal.

Her breath rasped in the silence as he tugged at
her nipple, his fingers continuing their persuasive
rhythm. Her hands moved to his shoulders as she
began to arch in trembling pleasure.

With an abrupt motion he rolled on top of her,
finding her parted lips as he sank deep into her
ready heat.

"Diana," he muttered, his thoughts already
becoming a hazy blur as he pulled out and plunged
back into her body.

It seemed as if there was something he wanted
to say. Something important.

But even as the thought fluttered through his
mind, Diana had lowered her hands to grasp his
hips, her soft pants like the sweetest music to his
ears.

At the moment nothing was as important as the
wild passion between them, he acknowledged. He
felt her shatter in delight and with a low shout he
plunged into paradise.

Luceford awoke with a sense of contentment that
he could not recall ever having experienced
before. It was more than the physical satisfaction
of a night spent with a woman in his arms, he
drowsily acknowledged. It was a deeper pleasure
that spread through his entire body.

Stirring upon the bed, he vaguely considered the

day ahead, wondering if Diana would be better pleased to remain in the house or if she would enjoy a drive into the country, where they could share a private luncheon. Whichever she desired he knew he would be happy. As long as he was in her company.

He stretched out his arm, wanting her close to his wakening body, but he discovered nothing but rumpled sheets. With a frown he wrenched open his heavy lids, startled to find he was on his own in the wide bed.

Damn.

Had she already gone down to breakfast?

Or had she left his home altogether?

Luceford struggled against the clinging webs of sleep. Why the devil would she simply disappear? After their incredible night of passion, she surely realized that he would wish to be with her? Gads, he was already stirring with need at the mere thought of her. It would take weeks, perhaps months, before he was sated.

Then a sudden smile curved his lips.

Of course, he told himself. She was no doubt embarrassed. Although he had never before made love to a virgin, he realized that women often felt shy after their first sexual encounter. And the erotic abandon with which she had given herself to him on the second occasion might very well have shocked her sensibilities.

She was no doubt at home sorting through her confusion of emotions. He would have to go fetch her and reassure her that her response had not only been perfectly natural, but highly pleasurable. Perhaps he would even suggest that they leave town so they could spend time together without fear of London's gossipmongers.

Pushing himself to a sitting position, he was on the point of slipping from the bed when he noticed the scrap of paper lying upon the pillow. Certain it was from Diana, he eagerly reached to retrieve it and held it in the sunshine slanting through the slit in the curtains.

> *Dear Lord Luceford,*
>   *The Athena Society is pleased to inform you that they have now completed nine of your ten impossible accomplishments for women. We sincerely thank you for your contribution to our efforts.*

It took a long moment for Luceford to comprehend the baffling words scrawled across the page. Then a searing fury rushed through him.

She had used him.

The entire evening had been no more than a calculated, shameless plot to punish him for his impetuous words spoken months ago.

He trembled with an anger he had never before experienced. He had been made a fool of. All for the sake of a ridiculous clutch of women who wanted to pretend they were men.

He slowly crushed the note as he recalled the practiced seduction, the manner in which she had so carefully lured him into her devious scheme. Then he thought of the feel of her lying beneath him.

No.

She might wish to pretend that she had sacrificed

her virginity for the grand advancement of the Athena Society, but he knew the truth.

He had watched her stunned wonderment as she had shuddered beneath him, heard her cry out in unbearable pleasure. She had wanted him. Wanted him as a woman wants a man. Not out of some misplaced sense of duty.

Yes, Miss Diana Howard had been as much a slave to her desire as he, and by God, he was going to make her admit the truth.

Luceford reached for the bell to summon his valet. He had a great deal to accomplish in the next few days.

Miss Howard was about to discover she had chosen the wrong gentleman to play her games upon.

CHAPTER SIX

No one had been more surprised than Diana when she had received the message from Lady Banfield requesting her presence in Devonshire. Although the older matron was well known for her eccentric belief in education for young ladies and her dislike of London society, Diana had never suspected she was such a free-thinking woman.

Still, there was no mistaking the contents of the brief but concise letter. Not only was Lady Banfield interested in learning more about her efforts, but she had also implied that if Diana met with her approval she would be willing to add her name and considerable prestige to the Athena Society.

It would be a triumph past all imagining to have such a lady on the membership roster, Diana had acknowledged. She would add the air of respectability they so desperately needed, but better yet, where Lady Banfield led, other social matrons would be swift to follow.

It had taken only a moment for Diana to make her decision. She would leave the society in the hands of her friends and travel to Devonshire. She could not possibly ignore such a wonderful opportunity, she had told herself. And the eagerness with which she had packed her bags had nothing at all to do with her desire to flee London.

Unfortunately the long, tedious trip left her with considerable time to ponder her impetuous retreat.

She might have fooled Celia and Emily, but she could not fool herself.

Her ready willingness to accept Lady Banfield's invitation had far more to do with her need to be away from Lucifer than with her hope that she could convince the older woman to join the Athena Society. Absurd really since he had not made the slightest push to seek her out or contact her in the past fortnight.

That, however, did not keep her from flinching each time there was a knock on the door or glancing over her shoulder each time she walked down the street. And as for her nights . . . she shuddered at the thought of her vivid, deeply disturbing dreams.

Dear heaven, she simply wanted to forget her night in Lucifer's arms. She wanted to banish the memories of her shocking response and the fever of delight that had raced through her body. She wanted to pretend that she had merely done her duty and nothing at all had changed in her life.

With a sigh Diana glanced out the window at the

fog-shrouded countryside. At least there would be
no fear of bumping into Lucifer in this remote
location. Perhaps she could also manage to elimi-
nate the ghosts that haunted her nights.

After what seemed to be an eternity, they at last
turned onto a tree-lined drive and swept to a halt
before a large weathered manor house that over-
looked a high cliff. There was a quiet beauty to
the setting, but she could not deny a faint chill at
the eerie solitude.

Shaking off her vague sense of premonition
Diana allowed herself to be handed out of the
carriage by the waiting groom. She climbed the
wide steps, rather surprised when the door was
opened by a round-faced housekeeper rather than
the butler.

"Welcome, Miss Howard," the woman said in
cheery tones. "I trust you had a comfortable
journey?"

"Yes, indeed. Thank you."

"If you will follow me?"

With the chink of keys that hung at her waist the
housekeeper turned and led Diana up a flight of
stairs. She had only a brief glimpse of paneled walls
and striking paintings from the hands of a master.

"Is Lady Banfield at home?" she demanded as
she hurried to keep pace.

The housekeeper did not respond as she reached
the landing and moved to push one of the numerous doors open.

"Please wait in here, Miss Howard."

Diana entered the spacious drawing room,
pleased by the delicate satinwood furnishings and
rose damask walls. It looked elegant, yet wholly

feminine. Just what she would expect from a respectable matron.

Assuming the housekeeper had gone in search of Lady Banfield, Diana moved to gaze out one of the arched windows. She gave a small grimace at the nearby cliffs and the faint sound of waves pounding onto the sharp rocks. Birds wheeled overhead, their shrill cry echoing through the lingering fog.

She was once again struck by the sheer loneliness of the estate. A vast difference from the bustle and noise of London.

Slowly removing her bonnet and gloves, she set them on a table and was smoothing the folds of her sensible gray gown when the door was slowly pushed open.

With great anticipation Diana awaited the woman who could alter the fate of the Athena Society.

There was a moment's hesitation, then a tall, unmistakably masculine form stepped into the room. Diana's smile faltered as a fierce, painful flood of disbelief nearly sent her to her knees.

Dear heavens. It couldn't be.

No one's luck was so ghastly.

She clutched at the back of the rose brocade sofa as Lord Luceford strolled toward her, appearing large and utterly dangerous in the buff coat and buckskins.

"Welcome to Fairfield Park, my love," he drawled, his fair hair glinting in the pale light and his dark eyes smoldering with a wicked fire.

"Luceford." She swallowed heavily, unable to

deny a growing ball of fear in the pit of her stomach. "What are you doing here?"

His smile was without humor as he at last halted far too close to her stiff body.

"You are an intelligent woman, Diana. You surely realized that I was not yet finished with you?"

Her heart skipped a beat, but pride refused to allow her to reveal her sharp unease.

"I haven't the least notion what you mean."

"Then I shall make it very clear." He reached up to lightly toy with a chestnut curl that lay upon her temple. Diana shivered and his smile widened with satisfaction. "I do not appreciate being used in your childish games."

Diana had known deep inside that this moment would arrive. Even as she had tried to reassure herself with the passing days and his seeming lack of interest in pursuing her. In her heart she had realized that eventually she would be forced to pay for her wound to his pride.

"There is nothing childish about the Athena Society," she attempted to bluster.

His nose flared with distaste. "It is nothing more than a handful of ill-educated maidens who are terrified to be women." He paused, his gaze deliberately lowering to her mouth. "Although you were a woman for one night, were you not, Diana? A pity you were too cowardly to admit the truth."

A terrifying flutter of excitement raced through her and Diana desperately battled to smother the sensations. No. Not again. Not ever.

"And what truth would that be?" she demanded in tight tones.

"That you gave yourself to me because you

desired me. Not for any righteous need to meet those absurd challenges."

Her hands clutched the back of the sofa, her face flaming with humiliation in spite of her best intentions.

"I suppose your pride is wounded at the thought that a woman may not find you as irresistible as you believe?"

Her feeble thrust was met with a husky chuckle as his fingers drifted from her temple over her heated cheeks.

"This has nothing to do with my pride. Do you think I did not feel you shudder with pleasure while I was deep within you? That I did not watch your face as you experienced your first release? I still have the marks of your passion upon my back."

Diana desperately wished to crawl beneath the patterned carpet. Dear Lord, it was bad enough to have her dreams consumed with the memories of her violent response to his touch. Must he toss her humiliating weakness into her face?

"This is hardly the time or the place to discuss such intimate matters, my lord," she protested in low tones. "Lady Banfield might arrive at any moment."

Those distracting fingers dropped to trail the line of her jaw. "I fear my aunt will not be arriving anytime soon."

Diana froze in horror. "Your aunt?"

"You did not realize that Lady Banfield is my mother's eldest sister?" he taunted.

"No."

"A lovely lady, nothing at all like my mother." The dark eyes slowly narrowed. "Indeed, she is so attached to her children that she recently closed down this house so she could remain with her daughter in Brussels.''

"But I received a letter from her requesting that I visit her here.''

"A small deception on my part, I fear.''

Her stomach twisted with dread. "You wrote the letter?''

"Yes.''

"But . . . why?''

The fingers abruptly grasped her chin. "Because there is something unfinished between us.''

She licked her dry lips, silently acknowledging that she had been a fool to disregard her initial wariness. Every instinct had warned her that Lord Luceford was not a gentleman to be toyed with. She should have fled the moment she had caught sight of that wickedly handsome countenance.

"You intend to punish me?''

"Punish is such a harsh word,'' he chided. "I only demand that you fulfill your promise to me.''

"I made you no promise.''

"Of course you did, my love. With every coy glance, with every calculated retreat, with every smile you stirred the embers of my desire. It was a deliberate seduction that promised fulfillment.''

An unexpected twinge of shame at her charade raced through her. Ridiculous, of course. This man was no innocent schoolboy. He was a hardened rake who had no doubt broken countless hearts.

"As I recall I did fulfill your desire,'' she forced herself to mutter.

"One brief night?'' he mocked. "Ah no, Diana. My desire is far from fulfilled. I still want you.''

Sudden panic had her sharply pulling from his grasp.

"This is absurd. I am leaving at once."

He folded his arms over his broad chest. "And how do you propose to leave? The few servants who are here are in my employ and under strict instructions to ensure that you do not leave the grounds."

"I will walk to London if need be."

"Very dramatic, but hardly sensible. Besides, I would only fetch you back."

Diana attempted to ignore the chill trickling down her spine. He was merely attempting to frighten her, she sternly told herself.

"You can not keep me here against my will."

"Of course I can. Although it will not be against your will for long. You can cowardly deny your lust from the safety of your own home, but we both know the truth. You desire me with the same fire that I desire you."

For a moment Diana was mesmerized by the dark seduction in his voice, but even as a prickle of awareness crawled over her skin she was giving a sharp shake of her head.

"No."

"Yes," he assured her with smooth confidence, running a bold gaze over her trembling body. "And in the end you will come to my bed with satisfying eagerness."

She forced herself to take a deep breath, refusing to allow him to see the panic clamoring to take control.

"I believe you must be a bit daft, or so obsessed

with your own arrogance that you have lost all sense."

The elegant features hardened, but the lethal smile remained intact as he reached out to tug on a slender rope.

"We shall see." They regarded one another in brittle silence until the door was pushed open and the familiar form of Lucifer's butler stepped into the room. Diana abruptly realized why she had been greeted at the door by the housekeeper. The devious gentleman had obviously realized she would have easily recognized the servant. The knowledge that he had taken such care with the smallest details made her heart grow cold. "Shore, please show Miss Howard to her room."

"Very good, my lord."

Not about to be dismissed without an answer to her overriding question, Diana tilted her chin to a defiant angle.

"May I at least be told how long you intend to hold me prisoner here, sir?"

Indifferent to the presence of the discreet servant, Lucifer prowled toward her, framing her face with his powerful hands.

"I thought that was quite obvious, my love. You will remain my guest until I tire of you."

CHAPTER SEVEN

With great care Diana drew back the bow and aimed her arrow at the distant target. As she had been taught, she sternly sought to rid herself of the distractions that surrounded her.

Not an easy task.

The afternoon sunlight was warm and inviting as it tumbled onto the vast parkland. Not far from where they stood, the relentless surge of the waves crashed into the rocks. And just to her side Luceford lounged against a tree, the dark gaze nearly tangible as it rested upon her determined profile.

In spite of herself Diana shivered. Not out of fear. After a week in Devonshire she had long since concluded that Luceford had not lured her to Fairfield Park to physically punish her for her charade. Since her arrival he had treated her with all the consideration of a valued guest. There had been no angry recriminations. No attempts to browbeat her into an apology. And most surprising of all no attempts to force her into his bed.

Instead he had been at his most charming. He had kept her entertained from morning to night; he had pretended an intense interest in every word she spoke and attended to her slightest need. And always that disturbing gaze carefully watched and weighed her every expression.

Laying awake in her bed at night, Diana had at long last come to the conclusion Luceford was playing a deep and devious game with her. His pride had been wounded by her deceit. It was not enough that she be held a virtual prisoner in the remote estate. Or that she regret her use of him in her scheme.

He wanted her to abandon herself to the wild passion that had so briefly burned through her body. He wanted her consumed with desire.

Only then would his pride be satisfied.

Unfortunately, having discovered his dark reasoning did nothing to ease her concern.

It was one thing to calmly assure herself that she need only maintain a cool composure until he tired of his game. It was quite another to ignore the shivers of pleasure that raced through her whenever he was near. Or deny the fierce ache that haunted her dreams.

She did desire him. She desired him with a force that shocked her to her very bones.

More than once she hovered on the edge of panic, determined to flee from his disturbing presence. Only the knowledge that her flight would be as revealing as succumbing to her need kept her grimly in place.

Drawing in a deep breath, Diana briefly closed her eyes and cleared her mind of all thoughts. Only when she was certain that she was firmly focused on the task at hand did she at last open her eyes and allow the arrow to fly.

With a graceful arch it soared through the air and landed directly in the center of the target. A smile curved her lips at the knowledge she had bested Luceford yet again.

With an abrupt motion her companion pushed himself from the tree and regarded her shot with a narrowed gaze.

"Impossible," he muttered.

"You did not expect to be beaten by a mere woman?" she demanded with unabashed satisfaction.

His hands upon his hips, he slowly turned to regard her. Her breath caught as the sun glinted off his fair hair and crisply outlined the wicked beauty of his features.

Gads, he should be locked away for the safety of gullible maidens everywhere, she thought wryly.

"I did not expect to be beaten by anyone," he informed her with a deliberately arrogant tone. "I happen to be a very skilled archer. It was no more than a lucky shot."

"A rematch then?"

"I would love nothing better; unfortunately the angle of the sun is no longer in the correct position."

She lifted her brows at his absurd excuse. "The angle of the sun?"

He smoothly moved forward to take her bow and led her toward the small grotto where a table and chairs had been set. The lovely aroma of freshly baked scones and tea greeted them as they entered the shadows.

"A true marksman is aware of all the elements when in competition," he informed her as he settled her in one of the chairs and then took a seat beside her.

"I am relieved that we do not depend upon your skill to provide us with game for our table, my lord. We would no doubt starve awaiting the sun to be at the proper angle."

His lips twitched as he leaned back in his chair and stretched out his legs. He was once again dressed in a casual fashion, but there was nothing casual in the manner the fawn breeches clung to the powerful line of his legs, nor the smooth flow of muscles beneath the buff coat. Diana had discovered her gaze lingering upon that decidedly masculine body more than once during the afternoon. A dangerous pastime, when she could still remember every sinewy line and chiseled curve with perfect detail.

"What else did you learn at that school of yours beyond archery?"

Diana shrugged, becoming accustomed to his probing questions. It was impossible to determine if he was genuinely interested or if it was merely a means of lowering her stiff guard.

"I learned to shoot a pistol and ride both sidesaddle and bareback."

"Imminently suitable accomplishments for young debutantes," he murmured dryly.

She gave a faint sniff. "We read Greek, Latin, Italian, and French. We studied mathematics, geography, and literature, including the classics as well as the less known poets and philosophers. We were also encouraged to express our own thoughts through writing and art."

"Were there no frivolous pastimes?"

"We had a dancing instructor and we often went on walks or traveled to view the various sights. In the evenings we occasionally played at cards or chess."

"And what about young suitors?" he demanded softly. "Surely you indulged in an occasional flirtation?"

Diana grimaced as she recalled Mrs. Bailey's determined effort to keep eligible gentlemen strictly forbidden from her students. To her mind they were no more than a dangerous distraction that lured maidens from more important matters.

"The only gentlemen about were either in their dotage or local farmers who were terrified of Mrs. Bailey. Besides, we were encouraged to devote our time to pursuing knowledge not behaving like witless debutantes."

He steepled his fingers beneath his chin as he studied her with a piercing intelligence.

"I find that difficult to believe."

She instinctively stiffened. Trust a man to assume a woman had nothing better to do with her time than learn the art of flirtation.

"You find it difficult to believe that a lady could be more interested in improving her mind than in landing a husband?"

"Obviously you learned your well-honed skills of seduction from someone. I am curious if such a useful talent was taught along with your other varied studies or if you developed your education by other methods."

Caught off guard by the silky question, Diana felt her cheeks flame with heat before regaining command of herself.

"I am a scholar," she at last managed to retort. "When I have a question or wish to learn, I go to an acknowledged expert in the field of my study."

"An expert in the field of flirtation?"

"Mrs. Van Kamp."

A smothering silence filled the grotto before Luceford slowly leaned forward, his features taut with disbelief.

"You visited a courtesan to discover how to seduce me?"

When said like that it did sound rather outrageous, but Diana forced herself to meet his glittering gaze.

"Yes."

"Bloody hell." He gave a sharp shake of his head. "Do you have no sense of shame?"

"You were the one who forced me to such drastic measures," she said in defensive tones. "You had made a mockery of everything I believed in. The only means of retrieving our honor was to meet your challenges."

His hand landed upon the table, making Diana jump.

"Only a woman could manage to blame a gentleman for her outlandish behavior."

She refused to be intimidated. It was all very well for him to condemn her desperate attempt to defend her honor, but when it came to his own he was swift to react.

"And yet when you were the one to be made a fool of you went to great lengths for retaliation," she pointed out in tart tones. "Or do you not consider kidnapping to be outlandish behavior?"

His gaze narrowed as her shaft slid home and with a graceful motion he sat back in his chair.

"Why me?"

Diana lowered her head as she made a show of smoothing the folds of her stout gray gown.

"You specifically stated the Toast of the Season and you, of course, are considered London's most eligible bachelor. Besides, we have been very careful to make sure that we have proof of all the challenges. We did not want you claiming there was no proof of the seduction."

From the corner of her eye she watched his hands clench the arms of the chair. It was obvious he was still furious at having been duped.

"Did you consider the notion there might be far more proof than you ever desired?" he demanded with a lethal softness.

Her head abruptly lifted in confusion. "What?"

"Not even you can be that naive, Diana. What if you are carrying my child?"

Diana felt as if a very large, very angry mule had just kicked her in the stomach. It was not that she hadn't considered the notion. She was not a complete idiot. But after discussing her fears with the experienced courtesan she had set her concern aside.

"Mrs. Van Kamp assured me that it was vastly unlikely with only one encounter."

"Unlikely, perhaps, but not impossible. Two

entirely different matters. Besides, if you will recall it was more than once."

She did recall. She recalled all too well. A sharp, hungry ache clenched within her as the memory of awakening to the persuasive stroke of Luceford's fingers rushed through her. Even now her skin prickled with awareness and a heat bloomed deep within her.

"It is still an unlikely event," she retorted, not allowing herself to dwell on the possibility for even a moment. There was something indescribably dangerous about allowing the image of a fair-haired, dark-eyed baby to even form in her thoughts. "Especially since it will never happen again."

Distracted by the strange sensations tingling through her body, Diana paid little heed to her words. It was not until the elegant features hardened that she realized what she had said.

"You are not the only one who never backs away from a challenge," he said, slowly rising to his feet.

Diana's heart lurched as he leaned forward and scooped her from her chair. With the same powerful ease he turned and headed to the back of the grotto, where he settled on a padded bench, keeping her firmly cradled in his lap.

"What are you doing?" she squeaked.

"Making us more comfortable."

"More comfortable for whom?"

"Relax, my dear," he soothed, his grip loosening so one hand could lightly trace the curve of her waist while the other lifted to cup her cheek. "I have no intention of doing anything that does not please you."

That was precisely the trouble, Diana acknowledged. Everything about him pleased her. The feel of his hard body as she rested upon his lap, the fingers that inched ever closer to her oddly heavy breast and the searing heat of his hand against her face.

There was no explanation for the poignant desire that he stirred within her. It was as mystical as why the stars hung in the heavens or why the sun rose each morning. She only knew the longer she was in his company the harder it was to disguise her growing need.

"The only means of pleasing me is for you to return me to London," she forced herself to mutter.

"I do not believe you." With a deliberate motion he shifted his hand to cup her breast. Her lips parted as he captured her nipple and gently rolled it between his finger and thumb. A pang of pleasure arrowed straight to the pit of her stomach. "I feel you tremble at my touch."

Lost in the dark promise of his eyes she struggled to breathe.

"Luceford."

"Why will you not admit the truth?" he coaxed, his fingers continuing to weave their magic. "Tell me that you desire me."

Danger hung thick in the air.

Diana knew she only had to admit the truth for Luceford to lay her back among the cushions. He would easily rid her of the heavy gown and cover her with his warmth. He would caress her to madness before entering her and . . .

"No," she breathed, banishing the treacherous images that threatened her very sanity.

"What a stubborn minx you are," he muttered, his head lowering to capture her lips in a kiss edged with frustration. It was a frustration that shimmered through Diana. She was a woman of logic, but passion threatened to cloud all sense. With a low groan Luceford lifted his head to regard her flushed countenance. "Bloody hell, you taste good. I do not think I could ever tire of kissing you."

"Luceford." Diana placed her hands against his chest, knowing she was swiftly plunging toward disaster.

His fingers tangled in her chestnut curls. "Did you know your eyes darken to the color of emeralds when you are aroused?"

"I wish to return to the house," she whispered, knowing she was standing on the edge of a precipice.

"In a moment," he murmured, his gaze lowering to her lips.

"No." With an awkward motion she tumbled off his lap, nearly landing on her nose before she scrambled to her feet and regarded him with barely concealed panic. She had experienced this building excitement before. She knew that within moments she would be lost to reason. Her only options were flight or surrender. Flight seemed by far the wisest course of action. "I wish to return now."

Leaning back on the cushions, he regarded her shivering form with a smoldering darkness.

"Very well, Diana, run away if you will," he mocked. "You can not escape me forever."

Perhaps not forever, she silently acknowledged, but she had escaped for the moment.

It was enough.

Turning on her heel, she fled the grotto.

CHAPTER EIGHT

Shoving his fingers through his hair, Luceford shifted on the cushions. His body was hard and aching with unfulfilled desire.

Not an unusual occurrence lately, he ruefully acknowledged.

He had spent a great deal of time over the past week battling the need to sink into the jasmine softness of Diana.

Damnation.

He should carry her to his bed and be done with it.

He did not doubt that he could seduce Diana if he put his mind to it. A few moments ago he could easily have pressed her into the cushions and swiftly ended any protest she might have made. He was not so green that he could not sense her rising desire.

But a part of him realized that it was not enough to simply bed Diana. Oh, his body might be momentarily satisfied, but it was not enough.

He wanted her to say the words.

He wanted her to admit that she desired him.

Only him.

CHAPTER EIGHT

The warmth and scent of the kitchen wrapped about Diana like a comforting blanket.

As a young girl she had often sought refuge in the kitchen of her uncle's oppressive household. It was the one place his grim displeasure did not permeate. And the one place she was treated with a measure of welcome. The old cook rarely noticed her presence as she sat in a dark corner and even on occasion offered her a treat that Diana would treasure as the greatest gift.

It was little wonder when she had arisen that morning she had sought out this place. After a fortnight in the company of Lucifer she was sadly in need of a measure of peace.

Absently regarding the dough she was kneading, Diana heaved a sigh.

Peace.

She was beginning to fear that was a feeling she would never experience again.

It was not bad enough that her body trembled whenever Luceford was near or that her nights were spent haunted by dreams that would shame a courtesan. But during the past fortnight she had discovered that she actually enjoyed being in the company of her captor.

She enjoyed his swift intelligence and how he did not attempt to patronize her when they shared a conversation. She enjoyed his amusing stories, which never cruelly belittled others but were often about his own foibles. She enjoyed his powerful presence, which made her feel as if she were protected from the world when she was with him. And how he sensed when she wished to become immersed in one of the numerous books that could be discovered in the library.

The sheer danger of the situation had struck her last evening as she had been seated by the fire reading a fascinating fourteenth century manuscript. Glancing up, her gaze had sought out Luceford's large form seated on the sofa, reading the paper. A warm, startling flare of contentment had rushed through her. It was a sensation she had never before experienced, not even in the company of Celia and Emily. And then his head had suddenly lifted and her heart had come to a halt.

For a long, silent moment they had regarded one another. Diana's mouth had gone dry and she could not think of one clever word to utter. It was as if a spell of enchantment had been woven through the room. An enchantment that stole her breath and scattered her thoughts.

It was at last Luceford who had brought an end to the strange sorcery. Tossing aside the paper, he had risen to his feet with an uncharacteristically jerky motion. Then with only the barest nod of his head he had walked from the room, shutting the door behind him with a loud snap.

Diana had sucked in a sharp breath, uncertain about what had just occurred.

Just for that moment London had seemed far away. There had been no one in the world but the two of them.

The knowledge had sent her scuttling to her bed, determined to banish the unwelcome sensation.

Dear Lord, she must be losing her wits, she had told herself as she had tossed and turned upon the mattress. She could not desire to be with Luceford.

It was impossible.

Absurd.

Dangerous.

So rather than dressing and making her way to the breakfast room to join Luceford this morning, she had instead made a cowardly retreat to the kitchen. Thankfully, Mrs. Philips did not appear to find anything particularly curious in her request to learn the secret of her delectable bread. With a resigned shrug at the vagrancies of the Quality, she had promptly shoved the mound of dough toward Diana and watched with a critical eye as she hesitantly pushed her hand into the floury surface.

With a loud click of her tongue the woman bustled forward and eyed her with disapproval.

"No. No. You must push forward and roll it back. You must be firm." Abruptly pulled out of her thoughts, Diana made a concerted effort to follow the crisp directions. She was rewarded by a satisfied nod. "That is better. Forward and roll back. Forward and back. Now stand aside and let me feel." Diana was hustled out of the way as the cook briskly tested the dough, then covered it with a cloth. "Perfect. Perhaps I shall make a cook of you yet."

Diana smiled ruefully as she whisked the apron from her plain gown and wiped her hands free of flour.

"I do not believe I shall ever acquire your talent, but I always enjoy learning new skills," she said, watching the efficient manner in which the woman set about peeling the apricots lying on the counter. Although a small, slender woman with iron gray hair, she moved with the swift ease of a woman half her age. "Who knows when I might be called upon to bake a loaf of bread?"

The woman flashed her a strangely knowing smile. "You sound just like his lordship. Always poking his nose into everything and demanding explanations. Never seen a lad with such an inquiring mind."

Diana bit her lip in vexation. She had come to the kitchen to forget about Luceford for a time. To find a measure of peace. But even when he was not near she was consumed by her thoughts of him.

"Have you been with the Luceford family long?" The question tumbled out before she could halt the words and she gave an inward sigh. The temptation to discover more of the unfathomable gentleman was too great to resist.

"I have been a cook at Luceford Estate for near on twenty-five years."

Diana had already guessed that the woman was not Luceford's cook in London.

"So you knew Lady Luceford?"

"Aye, a heartless jade that one. Never a care for her husband or son. Danced about playing her games upon every poor gentleman that happened by. It is said more than one poor sod put a gun to his head when she tossed him aside for another. Never did see the fascination myself. She might have been pretty enough, but you only had to look into her eyes to see she was a vain, thoughtless creature."

Diana felt a pang of sympathy for Luceford. How horrid to be raised by a mother who cared for no one but herself. And to endure the endless scandal that must have followed him. It was little wonder he had reacted with such force when he thought she had made a fool of him. The only surprise was the gentle kindness he had shown her since her arrival.

"It must have been very difficult for Lord Luceford," she murmured.

"Poor lad." Mrs. Philips gave a sad shake of her head. "He had to watch his father wither to an old man before his time. It was many a night I prayed the trollop would run off with one of her besotten fools and never return."

Diana unconsciously grimaced. She knew all too well the damage supposed guardians could wreak upon hapless children.

"Unfortunately children are often in the care of those who are too selfish or too callous to give them the love that they need."

The older woman shot her a speculative glance. "True enough."

Belatedly realizing that she had revealed more than she had intended, Diana gave herself an inward shake. Gads, she had stooped to gossiping about Luceford with the servants. She was truly losing her wits.

"Thank you for teaching me to make bread," she said, turning to head for the door. She had hidden away long enough.

"Miss Howard."

Reluctantly pausing at the door, Diana turned to regard the cook. "Yes?"

"The master can be a hard man, but it is only because he is afraid of being seen as weak. A wise woman would be patient until he can learn the truth for himself."

Diana frowned. Surely the woman did not think there was more between her and Luceford than a battle of wills?

"I fear I am neither wise nor patient, Mrs. Philips. Lord Luceford and I were born adversaries. Nothing more."

A mysterious smile curved the cook's mouth. " 'Tis the differences between a man and woman that make the world such an interesting place."

A quiver shot through Diana as she whirled about and hurried from the room. She did not want to consider the differences between men and women.

Not now when her treacherous body hummed with an ever-present desire.

Intent on escape, Diana paid little heed to her direction. It was not until she stepped into the library that she realized she had thoughtlessly sought out the one location where she would be certain to encounter Luceford.

Not surprisingly, she had barely stepped through the door when the fair-haired devil rose from behind the desk and crossed toward her.

"There you are, Diana." He regarded her with a hooded gaze. "I have been searching for you."

With a sense of resignation Diana felt the fine tremor of awareness race through her. It did not seem to matter how often she was in this gentleman's company. Her reaction was always swift and intense when he was near.

"Mrs. Philips was kindly demonstrating the proper technique for making bread."

His brows lifted in mild surprise. "You are interested in the culinary arts?"

She could hardly admit she would have mucked out the stables if it kept her out of his company, so instead she offered him a cool smile.

"I am interested in many things."

"Yes." The dark eyes burned a restless path over her features. "I do not believe I have ever encountered a woman with such a curious mind."

A faint frown pleated her brow. She sensed a tension with Luceford that was at distinct odds with his determined air of casual ease.

"No doubt because women are sternly discouraged from revealing any interest in anything beyond the current fashions and *on-dits.*"

His lips twisted as she raised her familiar arguments.

"Come now, Diana, there are many society ladies who are quite well educated. Especially about the latest politics."

"Yet they have no voice in those politics."

"You have obviously not been in the company of Lady Devonshire," he retorted dryly.

"And what of those females who are interested in things that are unseemly for women, such as mathematics or the sciences? Or even philosophy?" she demanded, thankful to slip into her familiar role of the outspoken radical. It was far preferable to that of an uncertain, vulnerable maiden. "Can you imagine the frustration of traveling down a path only to have it come to an end, and you must stay there no matter how desperately you wish to proceed?"

"Obviously there will always be those who do not wait for a path to be constructed." He paused as an indefinable emotion flickered over the handsome features. "You are a very courageous woman, Diana."

She was unprepared for the compliment and a sudden warmth filled her heart as her gaze dropped in confusion. Somehow this gentleman always managed to keep her off balance.

"My uncle insisted that I was an obstinate conspirator to the devil who would be punished for my evil beliefs. Indeed, on the few occasions I returned to his home I was forced to sleep in the attics so that I did not contaminate his household."

She heard his breath rasp loudly through

clenched teeth. She lifted her gaze, surprised by the stark anger etched onto his features.

"He made you sleep in the attics?"

"He feared I might influence his staff."

"The man should have been horsewhipped," he stated in flat tones.

Diana gave a faint shrug, uncertain why he appeared so angry. Surely he realized that her unusual views were often met with disgust and at times shrill condemnation?

"He was no worse than many others. Change is not easy to accept. Especially to those in power."

His gaze abruptly narrowed. "I suppose you include me in the same cast as your uncle?"

She shifted uneasily, realizing that she would never compare this gentleman with her uncle. He possessed none of the cold desire to bring pain to others or the narrow-minded refusal to contemplate the world from another point of view.

Indeed, he was one of the few people she had ever encountered with the questing intelligence to contemplate a logical argument without allowing prejudices to cloud his judgment.

Still, she could not entirely forget that he had been as anxious as the rest of London to dismiss her as a screeching lunatic.

"You did manage to thoroughly humiliate the Athena Society," she said in stiff tones.

"Bloody hell." His brows snapped together. "I was half foxed and in no state to be held accountable for my ramblings. I had no notion they would be printed in the paper."

"You would not have said the words if you did not believe them."

Without warning he turned about to pace across the length of the room. Then, reaching the heavy chimneypiece, he slowly turned back to regard her with an unreadable expression.

"I will admit that I possess little patience for women determined to embroil themselves in scandal."

For no reason at all Diana felt a sharp pain lance through her heart. And something perilously close to disappointment. She determinedly hid her weakness behind a mask of annoyance.

"And you think it scandalous for a woman to struggle against the narrow expectations society has allotted her?"

He paused before giving a sharp shake of his head. "When such a struggle harms others."

Suddenly Diana felt weary. What did she care about this gentleman's opinion of her? Soon she would return to London and never see him again.

"It is obvious that we shall never agree on this subject. Excuse me."

On the point of leaving, she was halted as Luceford suddenly stepped forward.

"Diana."

She watched warily as he moved to stand close in front of her.

"Yes?"

"I regret that my unfortunate challenges caused you pain," he said in low tones. "It was certainly never my intention."

She stilled at his unexpected words. "Do you mean that?"

"Yes." He grimaced in a rueful fashion. "As I told you I was far from sober. I had also received a letter from my mother demanding yet more money for her young and demanding lover. I was in no humor to ponder the plight of women.''

It was not the most elegant apology she had ever received. But for a man with the devil's own pride Diana realized that it was far more sincere than any flowery speech.

Her annoyance faded, allowing that unnamed, disturbing warmth to swirl through her body.

"I suppose I owe you an apology as well," she forced herself to admit.

"Indeed?"

Her hands clenched together in front of her. "I was very angry with you. So angry that I did not consider your feelings when I decided to seduce you."

He regarded her for a long, silent moment before he reached out to touch her cheek in a tender motion.

"Do you regret our night together?"

Her breath caught as she became lost in the midnight temptation of his gaze. The same magical bewitchment that shimmered in the air last evening sparkled to life.

She felt bewildered, giddy, and utterly happy.

She felt . . . in love.

Her hand rose to her lips to halt the shock cry of dismay.

Dear Lord, no.

Of all the horrible consequences she had considered before carefully plotting her revenge, this had never, ever been one of them.

She had wagered her soul to Lucifer and lost.

It was abruptly all more than she could bear.

"Yes," she breathed in broken tones. "I regret it with all my heart."

Realizing she had stunned him with the force of her words, Diana was swift to take advantage.

Opening the door, she slipped into the hall and bolted for the safety of her chambers.

CHAPTER NINE

Seated in the library with nothing but the glow of one candle, Luceford diligently applied himself to the task of emptying his second glass of brandy.

It was not that he was intentionally attempting to become foxed, he told himself. There was just something satisfying in the warm glow that was beginning to settle about the knot of ice lodged in the pit of his stomach.

A knot of ice that had formed when Diana had turned and walked away from him that afternoon.

Damnation.

The minx was going to drive him to Bedlam.

He gulped the brandy in an angry motion.

How dare she look him in the eye and claim to regret their night together?

Did she think him so naive that he didn't realize when a woman was responding to his touch? That he hadn't felt her convulse about him as she had claimed her pleasure?

Gads, she had gone up in flames in his arms.

And she would do so again if he swept her into his arms and carried her to his bed.

An appealing notion, he conceded as his body hardened with swift anticipation. Far more appealing than continuing his plot to force her to admit her desire of her own free will. Blast, they could be there for the next twenty years awaiting her to speak the truth.

What did it matter if she said the words or not? Once he had her beneath him she would be ready enough to prove her heated response.

But even as his blood quickened at the mere thought of seeking Diana as she lay in her bed, he stretched out his legs and refilled his glass from the brandy at his side.

He might desire Diana with a hunger that was near painful, but something even more disturbing had occurred over the past few weeks. Without even realizing what was happening he had discovered a deep, grudging respect for the proud woman.

Who else would have braved society's censure with such self-confidence? Or risked everything to meet his absurd challenges?

Gads, she had dared to visit his ex-mistress to learn how best to seduce him.

He had tried to tell himself that she went beyond the pale. She was an irresponsible, overly bold jade who courted scandal as willingly as his mother. But the words refused to ring true.

Diana was not a woman who wallowed in her own selfish needs. She did not seek notoriety for her own vanity. Nor did she use others with a ruthless calculation.

She was quite simply a woman who held her beliefs and her honor as highly as any man. And was willing to battle to prove them.

Luceford gave a shake of his head.

He had brought her to Devonshire to punish her for her audacity. To make her regret using him in such a fashion. But tonight he was forced to acknowledge that his lust for revenge had died long ago.

The obvious solution was simply to return to London, he told himself. There was certainly nothing to keep him in Devonshire.

The thought, however, did not bring the relief that it should have.

As the brandy flowed through his body he reluctantly conceded that he was content to be in this house alone with Diana. She was an intelligent companion, a skilled competitor at any game from cards to archery and capable of pursuing her own interests when he was occupied.

There were none of the usual demands for his constant attention or petulant scenes because he was not escorting her from one party to another.

The entire household was filled with a satisfying peace that he had never before experienced.

And of course there were the delicious sensations that prickled through his body when she walked into a room.

There was certainly something to be said for good old-fashioned lust.

He gave a shake of his head. He had intended

for Diana to be the prisoner here. Now he could not help but fear he was the captive.

The faint sound of footsteps upon the terrace was a welcome distraction from his disturbing thoughts. Rising to his feet, Luceford crossed to the open French windows and stepped onto the terrace. At the far end, shrouded in darkness, he could just make out the slender form of Diana.

Without allowing himself to ponder the danger of being with Diana in the enticing moonlight, he moved silently to join her. She had avoided his company the entire day and he was hungry to be in her presence.

Coming to a halt at her side, he regarded the taut line of her profile and the manner in which her fingers clutched the stone railing. Then slowly he allowed his gaze to lower, realizing that she was attired in nothing more than a thin lawn night rail.

A stunning heat flared through him, before he sternly managed to regain control of his senses. This was no time for such wicked sensations, he warned himself. He feared that Diana was not simply out here to enjoy the fine night air.

"It is rather late for a stroll, my dear," he said in cautious tones.

Clearly having sensed his approach, she did not even bother to turn her head to face him.

"I could not sleep."

He felt a twinge of unease. Since arriving in Devonshire, Diana had maintained a calm, pleasant demeanor. Her pride had demanded that she act as though she were a willing guest rather than having been duped by his clever ruse. There had been no tears, no recriminations, no foolish attempts to escape. He had admired her courage to face her predicament with dignified grace.

There was something in her voice tonight, however, that spoke of the strain just below her air of composure.

"Is something troubling you?"

"I must return to London," she said in low tones.

Although he had been expecting the words, Luceford stiffened.

"Surely there is no haste? You admitted yourself that you care nothing for the Season."

"The Athena Society is my responsibility. I can not simply abandon it, especially not now."

A sharp, wholly unexpected bolt of anger shot through him. Damnation. They were standing together in the magic of darkness, with the scent of roses and the salted air settled about them. Surely most women would have her thoughts turned to the lure of romance, not some bloody woman's club?

"Is that all you can think of?" he demanded with more force than he intended. "That damnable society?"

She at last turned to regard him with a faint frown. "That society has given me purpose in my life. More importantly it has taught me that I can achieve whatever I desire. That is something of a miracle for a young girl who was taught she was without worth."

Luceford fully understood the struggle to grasp onto a means of finding self-worth. He had endured his own battles. But the restless irritation of knowing this woman was wed heart and soul to her cause did not dissipate.

"And you intend to become a lonely spinster as you write your pamphlets and battle those who will never alter their opinions?"

A stubborn expression settled upon her countenance. "What would you have me do? Toss myself into the Marriage Mart and once again be forced to endure the grim rules of some gentleman?"

"Not all gentlemen are cast in the same mold as your uncle," he said in exasperation. "Besides you would no doubt have any poor sod who wed you firmly beneath your heel."

"I have no desire to take such a risk."

"And what of children?" The question tumbled out without him knowing where the words came from. "Do you not wish to hold your own child in your arms?"

A startling hint of vulnerability darkened her eyes.

"Of course I do." Her hands gripped the railing until her knuckles gleamed white. "I may be eccentric but I am not without a few finer feelings. There is nothing I would desire more than to have a child."

Luceford sucked in a sharp breath at the image of Diana heavy with child. His child.

"But you are too cowardly to fulfill your desire?"

Her features tightened at his blunt challenge. "I could ask the same of you. Do you intend to grow old and alone?"

He paused a long moment before he gave a shrug. "I have rarely given thought to the future," he at last admitted. After his father's death he had made it a strict rule to concentrate only on the present. The past was best forgotten and the future would take care of itself. "It has always been enough to enjoy the pleasures of each day. I will, however, admit that recently I have begun to realize that it is past time that I begin to consider my nursery."

She appeared unimpressed by his confession. "Do you not have matters rather backwards?"

"Backwards?"

"It is generally accepted that you first consider a wife and then your nursery. Otherwise it seems as if you are choosing the most convenient broodmare."

He gave a choked cough at her accusation. "Good God. You are nothing if not blunt, Diana. I assure you I shall not consider my wife a brood-mare. She will be treated with the greatest respect."

"As long as she keeps her place?"

Luceford heaved a frustrated sigh. He did not wish to argue with the maddening woman. Not tonight.

"I have no certain place that I would demand she keep. I do, however, expect her to be an honorable woman, as well as honest and trustworthy. Such traits are important in a marriage."

With a jerky motion she removed her hands from the railing and wrapped her arms about her waist.

"A paragon of virtues, you mean," she retorted, an edge that might have been bitterness in her low words. "Well, you should have little difficulty discovering such a maiden. The London drawing rooms are overflowing with demur, well-trained misses."

Luceford stilled as he gazed down at her shadowed countenance, his annoyance abruptly fleeing as he was struck by a sudden suspicion.

"You sound very disapproving, my love," he said gently.

Perhaps realizing she had revealed more than she intended to, Diana gave an uneasy shrug.

"Not at all. I wish you very happy."

He stepped closer, breathing deeply of the warm scent of jasmine.

"I do not believe you."

"I beg your pardon?"

"You are jealous."

Her tongue peeked out to wet her lower lip. "What?"

Warm satisfaction melted the knot of ice deep within him. Her wary expression revealed the truth.

"You do not wish to think of me with another woman."

"That is absurd."

"No, it is the truth."

Her breath quickened as he took another step closer. "And how could you presume to know what I am thinking?"

"Because it is precisely what I am thinking," he confessed, reaching out to trail his fingers along the scooped neckline of the night rail. He felt her tremble at his touch, her lips parting. "To even imagine you in the arms of another man is enough to make me feel quite violent. You belong to me, my proud, spirited goddess."

"Luceford, you must stop this at once," she breathed, but she made no attempt to pull away.

The air shimmered with heat. A heat that clouded his thoughts with its sweet promise.

"Do you know how often you haunt my dreams? I close my eyes and I can see you lying beneath me. I can almost hear your soft moans as I enter you."

"No. Please."

"What are you frightened of, Diana?" he demanded, his hand moving to cup the softness of her breast. Her nipple hardened to an inviting pebble as his thumb brushed over it.

Her breath quickened even as she struggled to battle the fierce pull between them.

"I am not frightened. I simply do not wish you to touch me."

He smiled wryly, his gaze lowering to the unmistakable signs of her arousal.

"Your lips may be capable of telling lies, but your body is not."

Her eyes slipped closed as he teased the tender nipple, her expressive features revealing the gathering storm of need within her.

"I believe I shall return to bed," she whispered.

Luceford growled deep in this throat. Gads, he had wanted this woman too much for too long. Perhaps all his life. He needed her in his arms and in his bed. He needed to know that she was his.

She belonged to him.

Only him.

"An excellent notion," he muttered.

Lost to all reason, Luceford reached down to sweep Diana off her feet. He cradled her in his arms as he entered the house and strode straight toward the stairs.

Her eyes widened in shock, but she made no protest. Not even when he entered his chamber and laid her gently upon the bed. Shrugging off his brocade robe he climbed onto the mattress and framed her face with his hands.

"I want you, Diana."

She searched his tense expression with darkened eyes.

"To punish me?"

"Do I appear to be consumed with thoughts of punishment?" he growled, grasping her hand and lowering it to the rigid hardness of his shaft. His breath caught and he nearly came undone as her fingers tentatively encircled his swollen member. Bloody hell, he had never felt anything so good. With an effort he battled the urge to stroke himself against her soft hand. He wanted to be deep within her when he found his satisfaction. More importantly he wanted to hear her sweet cries as she climaxed with delight. Nothing was more important to him at this moment than knowing he could bring her pleasure. "I want you, it is as simple and straightforward as that. But what of you?"

"What?"

Her expression was dazed as he slipped his hand down the curve of her waist, discreetly pulling the soft lawn fabric upward to reveal the inviting line of her thighs.

"Do you want me, Diana?"

There was a moment of silence and Luceford stiffened, wondering if he could actually expire from frustration. He had never needed to make love to a woman so badly in his life. Not even during the earliest days of his stirring masculinity. Then just as he was preparing to withstand the agony of having Diana walk away from him, she gave a tremulous smile and gently touched his cheek.

"Yes."

"No tricks? No deceit?" he demanded, unable to bear the thought of being used once again.

"No tricks," she whispered, her eyes glowing with a sudden fire.

"Diana."

With a groan he lowered his mouth and captured her lips in a kiss of utter possession. She was his, he thought with a flare of satisfaction. This glorious, bewitching goddess belonged to him. And he would treasure her with every breath, every touch.

Trembling with the force of his desire, Luceford carefully shifted to untangle the ribbons of her night rail, then slipping the garment from her slender frame, he gazed at her in breathless wonder.

"Dear Lord, I will never have enough of you, Diana. Never."

Her arms lifted to encircle his neck and Luceford readily covered her with his large body.

It was like coming home, he thought with startling clarity. Not to the tumultuous, unpredictable atmosphere of his childhood. But to the warm, welcoming place he had only dreamed existed.

This was where he belonged.

Breathing a soft sigh, he lowered his head and lost himself in the magic shimmering between them.

CHAPTER TEN

Luceford stood on Mount Olympus, regarding the world below him. At his side Diana stood attired in a flowing white toga, her hand on his arm. A fierce pride filled him as he regarded his very own Athena.

How strong, how vividly alive she appeared. Strong enough to face life's troubles with the dignity he so admired. And yet there was a hint of softness about her that stirred a protective instinct that he did not even know he possessed.

Pulling her close to his side his heart melted as she slowly turned to smile into his watchful eyes. He felt bathed in the golden glow of love.

The distant sound of barking dogs intruded into his pleasant dream and with a rueful groan Luceford turned onto his side. He felt lazily satisfied and not at all ready to face the light of morning.

What if Diana once again regretted giving in to

her desire? Even though she had offered herself with a dazzling eagerness, he suspected that there had been a part of her that she had held distant from him. Almost as if she feared to surrender herself completely.

Luceford impatiently smothered his dark thoughts. She only needed time, he reassured himself. He had to somehow convince her that she could trust in him. Like himself, she had been hurt on too may occasions to readily place her faith in another.

He would woo her slowly, he told himself sternly. And despite the undoubted pleasure he experienced in her arms, he would be careful to assure her that there was far more between them than mere lust.

Smiling slowly at the thought of wooing Diana, Luceford opened his eyes to regard the woman lying beside him.

"Bloody hell." Jerking himself upward, he studied the ominously empty bed with angry disbelief.

Blast the unruly minx.

How dare she abandon him? Was she attempting to drive him batty?

No.

Not again.

He had allowed her to flee in panic on the last occasion.

This time she would not be given the luxury of hiding behind her practiced image of indifference. She would be forced to face the bond between them whether she wished to or not.

She would realize that they belonged together.

Climbing from the bed, he dismissed the notion

of ringing for his valet and instead dressed himself with swift, angry motions. In less than half an hour he was downstairs, storming through the rooms in search of his unmanageable mistress.

He had reached the back parlor when he stumbled across Shore.

"Damnation. Have you seen Miss Howard this morning?"

Finishing his inspection of the recently filled decanters, the butler turned to regard his thunderous employer with faint surprise.

"I believe she decided to take a ride before breakfast."

Luceford's hands clenched at his side. "A ride?"

"Yes, sir."

"Did she take anything with her?"

The servant blinked at the edge of danger threaded through his voice.

"I am uncertain," he confessed. "She received a letter in the morning post, then a few moments later she requested that a mount be saddled. I did not actually see her leave the house."

An ominous premonition clenched at Luceford's stomach. Although they had ridden often together during the past few weeks, Diana had never taken off on her own. The fact that she had chosen to do so this morning did not bode well.

"Where is this letter?"

"I delivered it to her in the breakfast room."

With a muttered curse Luceford turned on his heel and marched to the breakfast room. It took a long moment to discover the sheet of paper lying underneath the table. Bending downward, he retrieved it and swiftly read the brief note.

Diana,

We shall soon complete the accomplishments. The duel is set for next Wednesday.

Emily

Luceford felt his heart freeze in horror.

Duel?

Dear heavens, it had to be a mistake.

Not even maddening, utterly outrageous Diana would be so foolish, he attempted to reassure himself.

But the words would not ring true.

He was intimately familiar with the lengths she would go to meet his challenges. Including sacrificing her virginity. Why would she hesitate to risk her bloody neck in a duel?

He crushed the letter in his hand.

Damn her stubborn soul.

He had not found her just to lose her to some idiotic bid for female equality. He would take a bullet himself before he would allow that to happen.

The image of the proud woman standing on a field with a pistol pointed at her heart sent an icy, nearly unbearable pain through his heart.

He had to halt her.

Barely restraining the urge to run like a madman from the house, Luceford forced himself to take a calming breath. Diana could not have had much of a head start. He would hunt her down long before she reached London.

Feeling somewhat more in command of himself and the situation, he calmly made his way back to the anxious butler.

"Shore, see that my carriage is prepared. I shall be leaving within the hour."

Not even years of training could prevent the servant from lifting his brows in surprise. Luceford was not a man prone to impetuous flights of fancy. He preferred a well-planned schedule that allowed his staff a pleasant sense of organization. Unfortunately there had been nothing well planned or predictable about his life since a beautiful radical had turned his life topsy-turvy.

"Within the hour?"

"Within the hour," Luceford repeated grimly. "And tell my groom we will be traveling swiftly. I have a renegade goddess to capture."

Diana shifted restlessly on the leather cushions. Although the carriage she had rented in the local village appeared steady enough, it was far too bulky to travel at more than a snail's pace and bounced over the bumpy road with enough force to rattle her teeth. Even worse, there was a peculiar odor that clung to the interior that made her shudder with distaste. She was quite certain that she did not wish to know the precise nature of the ghastly scent. She had few choices if she wished to reach London before Emily did anything ridiculous.

She gave a sharp shake of her head as she recalled the unexpected letter.

It had never occurred to her that her friends would take matters into their own hands while she was gone. They had always depended on her guidance, even in the most mundane decisions.

Which only made matters worse, she acknowledged with a twinge of shame.

It was because of her that Celia had nightmares about her evening in the brothel. Because of her that Emily had nearly killed them all in their race to Brighton. And because of her that they were treated with amused disdain throughout London.

For so long Diana had convinced herself that she possessed the virtue of a true martyr. The battle she fought was for all women, was it not? Surely any means justified the end?

She did not question what she demanded of her loyal friends. Or whether she could achieve her goals with more maturity rather than striking out like an angry child.

Now she could only look back with a sense of shame. She had allowed her past bitterness to cloud her judgment. Had she approached matters in a more rational manner she would have realized that she was using her friends for her own selfish purposes. She had to make amends to them.

First, of course, she had to put a halt to this absurd duel. If anything were to happen to Emily . . . dear Lord, she would never forgive herself.

Squeezing her eyes shut, Diana inwardly willed the carriage to a faster pace. She simply had to get to London.

Her eyes were still shut when the sound of a carriage approaching from behind echoed through the air.

Her heart dropped as she instinctively sensed that it was Lucifer upon her heels.

Blast.

She had deliberately slipped away to avoid this

inevitable confrontation. Not that she feared he would truly hold her in Devonshire against her will. They both knew she could have slipped away at any time. But she simply was in no state to continue their game.

After last evening she could no longer deny the emotions that had been steadily growing within her. When she had given herself to him it had not been out of uncontrollable lust. Or a brief desire for satisfaction.

She had quite simply fallen in love with Luceford.

A love she knew all too well was doomed to break her heart.

Why did he not simply allow her to disappear, she wondered with a sigh? He had clearly achieved what he wanted. She had willingly proved that she desired him. His pride had been restored. It was best for both of them to end this with as little fuss as possible.

"Halt the carriage," Luceford's familiar voice commanded.

For a moment they continued down the path and Diana dared to hope the hired groom would ignore the arrogant order. Then without warning the carriage lurched to a stop, nearly throwing Diana from her grimy seat.

" 'Ere now, what the devil is about?" her groom demanded in gruff tones. "Hold on. There is a young lady inside. I shall have the magistrate see to you if she is harmed."

"That young lady is in my care. I would not be pleased to discover you have been a party to her rash flight from my home," Luceford warned in dark tones.

Diana grimaced as she realized the inevitable. Her hired groom was no match for Luceford under the best of circumstances, let alone when he was in a thundering fury. It was clearly up to her to be rid of him so she could continue on her way to London.

"No, sir. I mean . . . I did not realize," the servant predictably stuttered in defeat.

Squaring her shoulders, Diana was prepared for the door to be wrenched open and Luceford to glare into the dim interior with a glittering gaze. She was not prepared, however, when he smoothly reached inside and plucked her from the seat.

"Luceford," she squeaked in shock, cradled next to his chest as he firmly strode to his carriage blocking the road. "What are you doing?"

"Taking you back to where you belong."

His expression was implacable as he climbed into the well-padded and thankfully clean carriage. Dumping her onto the seat, he firmly closed the door and placed himself across from her.

Straightening her skirts, Diana sternly battled her instinctive glow of happiness at the sight of him.

What did it matter if he was so handsome he stole her breath? Or that he had followed after her despite the fact he had already achieved what he wanted?

This was no time to indulge in foolish fits of fancy.

"I must return to London," she said sternly.

His hands clenched upon his legs as if resisting the urge to shake her.

"The devil take it, Diana. You are not going to

risk your life for the Athena Society. I will not allow it."

It took a moment for Diana to realize that he must have discovered the letter from Emily and that he had mistakenly assumed that she was the one who would be standing upon the field of honor.

A tiny thrill at his obvious concern raced through her.

"But, Luceford . . ."

"No." He leaned forward, his eyes as black and hard as ebony. "If this means so much to you I will make a public apology. Bloody hell, I will have it published in every paper and shout it on every street corner."

She regarded him in disbelief. "A public apology?"

"I will admit that I was a pompous fool. I will tell everyone in London that the Athena Society is an institution with the finest, most intelligent, most courageous woman I have ever known."

Diana felt as if her head were spinning. None of this made the least amount of sense.

"But why?"

"Because it is the truth." With an oddly hesitant manner he reached out to grasp her hand. Diana felt her stomach quiver in reaction. "And because I love you."

It took a long, painful moment for her to actually accept that she had heard the low words correctly. Then her head was shaking in an instinctive denial.

"You can not love me," she rasped.

He smiled wryly, the heat and scent of him wrapping about her. "I fear my heart does not agree."

"But I am scandalous and outspoken and not at all demur. You said . . ."

"I said a lot of damn nonsense," he growled, his thumb absently running a path over her clenched knuckles. "I told you to forget the past, but I had not yet done so myself. Deep inside I compared every woman to my mother. I expected to be betrayed."

"Which I did," she pointed out sadly.

"That is what I told myself," he softly agreed. "It made it far easier to reconcile myself to the notion of kidnapping you. I did not wish to face the truth."

Diana desperately searched his countenance for a hint of what was in his heart. Could it be possible that he did truly love her?

"What truth?"

"That I wanted to be with you," he said simply. "You had bewitched me, my sweet. As surely as Athena herself."

Her fears melted as she met the soft tenderness of his gaze. Despite her horrid behavior and scandalous reputation he had been touched with the same magical sensations as herself.

"Luceford."

A hint of uncertainty flickered across his strong features. "Do you believe you can ever learn to trust me?"

A slow smile curved her lips. "I have trusted you since I became your lover. I would have never given myself to you had it been otherwise."

"Not even for the good of the Athena Society?"

She grimaced, realizing it was past time for honesty between them. For too long they had hidden behind lies and deceit.

"It was safer to pretend that I was merely doing my duty than admit that I desired you."

He lifted her hand to kiss her fingers with a smile of satisfaction.

"It seems we are well matched. Overly stubborn and wounded by our pasts. We must heal one another. Be my wife, Diana."

A ready heat threatened to cloud her mind, but with an effort Diana forced herself to maintain a bit of common sense. A difficult task when all she wished to do was throw herself into his arms and remain there the rest of her days.

"You must know that I can not change," she warned him in anxious tones. "I will never be a comfortable, biddable wife."

His eyes glinted with amusement. "You mean that you intend to remain a maddening, scandalous, independent radical?"

Her expression became wry. "That was not how I intended to describe myself, but yes."

The carriage filled with his warm laughter. "All I have ever desired is a woman of honor and you have proven you are willing to go to frightening lengths to defend your honor."

Honor.

Diana's eyes widened as she realized she had completely forgotten her dear friend. Good heavens, this man managed to muddle her thoughts without even trying. A talent she would do well to remember for the future.

"Idiot," she muttered, cursing herself for her

momentary distraction. Emily's very life hung in the balance.

"What is it?" Luceford demanded.

"I must get to London. The duel is set for the day after tomorrow."

Without warning his brows snapped together and he hauled her out of her seat to land in his lap.

"No. I forbid it, Diana. I am willing to support your beliefs and allow you a great deal of freedom, but you will not risk your life in some bloody duel. I will lock you in a dungeon if need be."

Not nearly as annoyed at being manhandled in such a fashion as she should have been, Diana reached up to touch his grimly set jaw.

"Luceford, I am not going to London to fight a duel. I am going to halt it."

He regarded her warily. "You wish to halt it?"

She heaved a faint sigh. "I have realized I have behaved rather rashly."

"You could say that," he agreed dryly.

"I was so determined to meet your challenges that I gave little thought to the dangers I was exposing my friends to."

His arms tightened about her. "Not to mention yourself."

"Now I realize that my pride is not so important as the well-being of those I care about."

He gave a blink of surprise. "Are you giving up the Athena Society?"

"Certainly not," she denied, knowing that she could not turn her back on all she hoped to achieve. It was as much a part of her as her love for this gentleman. "But we shall devote ourselves to convincing others by our unwavering logic and the dignity of our behavior. Besides, I believe that we shall soon have any number of converts."

"When you reveal you have met the challenges?

"No, when I reveal that Lord Luceford has become our newest member," she pertly retorted.

His eyes widened, then, without warning, he tilted back his head to laugh with rich delight.

"Well where else would Lord Luceford be but at the side of Lady Luceford?"

"Lady Luceford," Diana repeated with a sense of wonder.

For so long she had resigned herself to the thought of being alone. After the grim disapproval of her uncle she had convinced herself that she far preferred a life of independence to placing herself at the mercy of a man.

Now she felt nothing but joy at the thought of placing her heart and her life in the care of Lucifer. She possessed utter faith he would keep both safe.

"It has a rather nice sound."

"Yes, indeed."

With a swift motion Luceford leaned sideways to open the window.

"To London, Rushmore."

"Very good, sir."

Closing the window, he pulled the curtain over the glass and settled her more comfortably. She regarded him with a faint smile.

"I can not possibly remain upon your lap the entire journey, Luceford."

"You can and you will," he said, a wicked glow entering his dark eyes. "You have run from me for the last time, my elusive goddess. From now on I intend to keep you firmly within my grasp."

''Where I belong,'' she said softly.

''Yes.''

With a faint sigh Diana rested her head upon his sturdy chest.

She might have lost the wager to seduce Lucifer, but she had gained what she had never dared hope possible.

A gentleman who could teach her the true joy of being a woman.

Celebrate Romance With
Meryl Sawyer